"What we had was over a long time ago. I don't believe in reliving the past."

"How about changing the future?" Mason asked.

Bliss's heart stopped for a crazy minute, and in her mind's silly eye, she saw herself walking down an aisle in a white dress, swearing to love him for the rest of her life, becoming his wife and bearing his children. Mason's babies. A part of her heart shredded when she remembered he already had a child, one who had nothing to do with her.

Her heart twisted at the thought of children. *Someday,* she silently told herself. *Oh, sure, and when is that going to happen? Remember, Bliss, you've got a long way to go. You're twenty-seven years old and still a virgin....*

Dear Reader,

The blissful days of summer may be drawing to a close, but love is just beginning to unfold for six special couples at Special Edition!

This month's THAT'S MY BABY! title is brought to you by reader-favorite Nikki Benjamin. *The Surprise Baby* is a heartfelt marriage of convenience story featuring an aloof CEO whose rigid rules about intimacy—and fatherhood—take a nosedive when an impulsive night of wedded bliss results in a surprise bundle of joy. You won't want to miss this tale about the wondrous power of love.

Fasten your seat belts! In these reunion romances, a trio of lovelorn ladies embark on the rocky road to true love. *The Wedding Ring Promise*, by bestselling author Susan Mallery, features a feisty heroine embarking on the adventure of a lifetime with the gorgeous rebel from her youth. Next, a willful spitfire succumbs to the charms of the tough-talkin' cowboy from her past in *A Family Kind of Guy* by Lisa Jackson—book one in her new FOREVER FAMILY miniseries. And in *Temporary Daddy*, by Jennifer Mikels, an orphaned baby draws an unlikely couple back together—for good!

Also don't miss *Warrior's Woman* by Laurie Paige—a seductive story about the healing force of a tender touch; and forbidden love was never more enticing than when a pair of star-crossed lovers fulfill their true destiny in *Meant To Be Married* by Ruth Wind.

I hope you enjoy each and every story to come!

Sincerely,

Karen Taylor Richman,
Senior Editor

Please address questions and book requests to:
Silhouette Reader Service
U.S.: 3010 Walden Ave., P.O. Box 1325, Buffalo, NY 14269
Canadian: P.O. Box 609, Fort Erie, Ont. L2A 5X3

LISA JACKSON

A FAMILY KIND OF GUY

Silhouette®

SPECIAL ▽ EDITION®

Published by Silhouette Books
America's Publisher of Contemporary Romance

The books in the FOREVER FAMILY miniseries are
dedicated to my family, those who are living and those
who have passed on. I was lucky enough to have lived an
enchanted childhood thanks to my parents, grandparents,
aunts, uncles, cousins and sister. My adulthood has been
blessed with two incredible sons, a fabulous niece, three
great nephews and a host of new members.
Thank you all.

 SILHOUETTE BOOKS

ISBN 0-373-24191-7

A FAMILY KIND OF GUY

Copyright © 1998 by Susan Crose

LISA JACKSON

has been writing romance novels for over ten years. With forty Silhouette novels to her credit, she divides her time between writing on the computer, researching her next novel, keeping in touch with her college-age sons and playing tennis. Many of the fictitious small towns in her books resemble Molalla, Oregon, a small logging community, where she and her sister, Silhouette author Natalie Bishop, grew up.

Forever Family
Family Tree

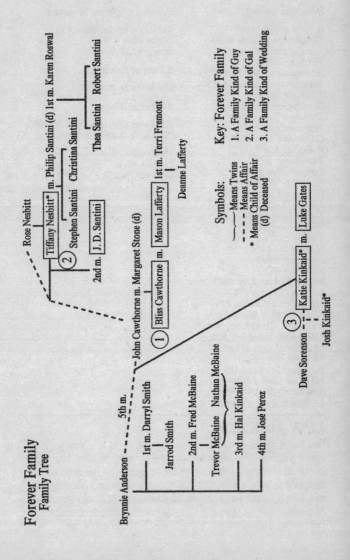

Brynnie Anderson

5th m. — John Cawthorne m. Margaret Stone (d)

1st m. Darryl Smith
- Jarrod Smith

2nd m. Fred McBaine
- Trevor McBaine — Nathan McBaine

3rd m. Hal Kinkaid

4th m. José Perez

Rose Nesbitt — Tiffany Nesbitt* m. Philip Santini (d) 1st m. Karen Roswal
- Stephen Santini
- Christina Santini
- Thea Santini — Robert Santini

(2) J. D. Santini

(1) Bliss Cawthorne m. Mason Lafferty 1st m. Terri Fremont
- Deanne Lafferty

Dave Sorenson — Katie Kinkaid* m. Luke Gates

(3) Josh Kinkaid*

Symbols:
—— Means Twins
- - - Means Affair
* Means Child of Affair
(d) Deceased

Key: Forever Family
1. A Family Kind of Guy
2. A Family Kind of Gal
3. A Family Kind of Wedding

Prologue

Bittersweet, Oregon
Ten years past

She was the most beautiful woman he'd ever set eyes upon and she was mad. Mad as hell. At him. He had the sting of her slap to remind him. "Just listen—"

"You listen, Mason, okay? I love you and I don't want to. That's the bottom line."

Blue eyes snapped furiously above cheeks that were flushed in anger. One fist clutched the reins of her intended mount's bridle, the other hand looked as if it itched to slap him again.

"You don't."

Thin lips compressed and she hooked a thumb at her chest. "Don't tell me what to feel, okay? Or what to say or do. Got it?"

"Yes, princess."

She stiffened. "And don't ever, *ever*, call me that again." She stepped forward a bit, dragging the pinto's head with her. "And get this straight, okay? You can't tell me what to do, Lafferty," she said in a voice that reminded him he was but a hired hand and she was, in fact, "the princess"—the daughter of his millionaire boss. "Don't even try." She placed one small, booted foot in the stirrup and hoisted herself into the saddle, then yanked on the reins. "A-di-os." The horse whirled before Mason had time to grab hold of the reins.

"Bliss, come on. Don't be a fool."

"Too late for that, don't you think?" she asked with more than a trace of irony. The anger drained from her face and was replaced by sadness. "Way, way too late."

The sky was dark, threatening, the air hot and cloying as a storm brewed over the hills. Clouds moved in the barest of breezes, and Mason wished that he could shake some sense into her.

"Wait a minute, Bliss." Again he reached for the bridle, but she was quick. Too quick. She slapped Lucifer on his rump.

"Just stay away from me!" Leaning forward, she pressed her knees into the pinto's sides. "Hi-ya!"

"No—"

Ears flattened to his head, the colt bolted forward at a dead gallop. His hooves flung mud and dirt. Aptly named Lucifer, the demon tore across the paddock and through the open gate to the grassy fields beyond.

Mason's back teeth ground together. He was torn. Bliss Cawthorne was a stubborn, prideful creature who deserved to get caught in a downpour, but then again, the storm might be worse than just a summer shower.

I love you. Words he'd longed to hear but which scared

the stuffing out of him. There was no future for them; there never would be.

You can't tell me what to do, Lafferty, so don't even try! Just stay away from me!

As if he could. Hadn't he spent the past weeks trying to do just that?

Thunder rumbled over the surrounding hills and he silently cursed himself up one side and down the other. He shouldn't have let her go. Should have physically restrained her, but short of hog-tying her, there'd been no way to keep her at the house.

You could have told her you loved her, too, and right this minute you might finally be in bed with her, feeling her hands on your body, kissing those pouting lips and making love to her.

Hell. He didn't love her and wouldn't lie, so he'd been between the proverbial rock and a hard place.

Eyes narrowing against the first spattering of rain, he rubbed his jaw where she'd slapped him as he'd argued with her. The skin stretched over his cheek still stung, but he'd been turned on by the fury in her eyes. "Dammit all." He kicked at a rock and sent it careening into the fence post, but his gaze was fixed on Bliss again, now far in the distance astride Lucifer.

Just the sway of her rump as the horse loped gave him an arousal that ached against his fly. What the devil was wrong with him? The boss's daughter was off-limits. *Way* off-limits. No one who worked on the ranch knew it better than he, yet he'd found excuse after flimsy excuse to be next to her, or close enough that he could watch her.

The smell of her skin aroused him, the way she angled her chin and wrinkled her nose caught him off guard and was sexy as all get-out. But why?

Sure, she was pretty with her pale blond hair and cornflower-blue eyes. Her cheekbones were high, her jawline strong, her eyebrows arched, but, come on, Lafferty, there were lots of pretty women in the world. Yet, this woman— no, make that *girl*, she wasn't quite eighteen yet—was different and appealed to him on another level, a level that scared the living tar right out of him.

She was like no other.

For a fleeting second, he thought of Terri Fremont, the girl he'd dated before Bliss had come to visit her father this summer. At twenty-one, Terri still looked like a pixie. Petite with freckles, short brown hair and huge brown eyes, she'd chased Mason down mercilessly and vowed to love him despite the fact that he had, at the time, been dating several women.

A little prick of guilt jabbed at his brain because he knew in the deepest parts of his soul that he'd never cared for Terri the way she'd cared for him. He'd tried to explain it to her, over and over again, but she had refused to listen, assuring him instead that he would "learn to love her" as much as she loved him.

She was wrong and he'd been forced to break it off with her. They had no future. He had dreams and they didn't include a wife. He glanced at Bliss's form again, just as horse and rider disappeared into the dark shadow of pine trees that skirted the base of the hills. Maybe a woman like Bliss would eventually change his mind. But not now.

The rain began in earnest. Thick, fat drops shimmered from the dark, foreboding sky. In the next field, the horses, sensing the change in the atmosphere, lifted their heads, noses to the wind, nostrils quivering in anticipation. This storm would be a bad one. And Bliss Cawthorne, headstrong fool, was out in the middle of it.

He had no choice but to follow her and haul her back to the ranch.

Just stay away from me.

"No way, lady," he growled, as if she could hear him. He squared his hat on his head and whistled sharply to Black Jack, a rawboned ebony gelding blessed with the speed of Pegasus and the temperament of an angel.

"You and me, partner," he said as he hitched Black Jack to the fence, ran to the stables for a bridle and threw it over the gelding's head. He buckled the leather straps with deft fingers and climbed onto the beast without a saddle. "Let's go," he said, digging in his heels as Black Jack took off.

Lightning sizzled above the hills.

Great. "Come on."

The horse's strides lengthened and they were through the open gate, flying over the bent grass and wildflowers mashed by the rain. Thunder rumbled ominously through the dark heavens.

He should never have let her go and he silently swore at himself as the wind pressed hard against his face and the downpour flattened his hair. There were too many things he shouldn't have done to count them all.

He'd had no right to touch her. No reason other than lust to kiss her. No sane excuse for taking off her clothes and... "Oh, hell." This wasn't the time to think about how yielding she'd been, or how, out of some vague sense of duty he hadn't, when offered the chance, made love to her.

"Come on, you miserable piece of horseflesh!" His knees prodded his mount as rain drenched his shoulders. Maybe he should have made love to her and been done with it, but he'd realized, almost too late, that Bliss Cawthorne wasn't the kind of woman to love and leave. Nope, she was the type of female who crawled into a man's blood and settled there—the kind of woman who spelled trouble with a capital *T*.

He gave Black Jack his head and the game horse flattened his ears, stretched out his neck and sprinted through the fields, his legs eating the sodden ground in quick, even strides. Wind tore at Mason's face and hands and he smiled grimly to himself. Bliss Cawthorne, princess and only daughter of John, was in for one hell of a surprise when he caught up to her.

"Son of a bitch," he muttered, swiping at the water on his face. He glanced at the spot in the trees where she'd vanished, then cursed himself for being a fool. Bliss wasn't his kind of woman; but then no one was. He'd make sure of it.

Bliss ignored the rain. She dug her knees into Lucifer's sides and urged him ever upward along the old cattle trail. The colt, incited by the storm, streaked forward, his hooves digging into the soft mud, his sides heaving with the effort. Bliss felt free and unfettered, as if she didn't have a care in the world. Her hair, bound in a ponytail, streamed out behind her.

The rain fell more steadily, in thick, heavy drops, sheeting in the distance. Still she didn't stop. If she got a little wet, so what? Her anger was slowly dissipating, but the thought of Mason with his arrogant high-handedness telling her what to do after...after... Oh, Lord, she'd nearly made love to him just last night; practically begged him to take away her virginity when he, poised above her, muscles straining, sweat dampening his brow, had rolled away.

"Bastard," she muttered. "Come on, come on," she urged. The pinto, wide-eyed, with nostrils quivering at the smell of the storm, began to lather. Grasshoppers scattered. A startled pheasant flew away in a rush of glistening feathers. Bliss yanked out the rubber band restraining her hair as she leaned over Lucifer's shoulder, encouraging him to speed even faster along the path—upward, through thickets of spruce and oak toward the cliffs that guarded the river. "Run, you devil."

The horse responded, his legs a flash, the wind causing tears to run from her eyes and fly off her cheeks with the rain. Trees were a blur.

The crest was close, just through this last copse of trees. As the saplings gave way, she pulled back on the reins and looked over the valley, this southern part of Oregon her father often called his home. Lucifer, tossing his head, slowed to a mincing walk.

"Thata boy." She was winded and breathless, her heart drumming, exhilaration replacing anger. Who cared about Mason Lafferty, anyway? If she had any brains at all she would forget him.

Telling herself that she'd get over the creep, she urged Lucifer to the crest near the edge of the ridge. From that vantage point she could see for miles, over the tops of the surrounding hills, past wineries and ranches and toward the town of Bittersweet.

Lucifer was spooked and blowing hard; the storm was getting to him. She'd only stay for a few minutes, then double back. By then she wouldn't have to face Mason again. At that thought her heart wrenched and she silently called herself a dozen kinds of fool.

She'd get over him. She had to. When she got back to Seattle—

A sizzling streak of lightning forked from the sky, singeing the air.

Lucifer reared.

"Whoa—" Bliss slipped in the saddle.

Thunder cracked, reverberating through the hills.

"It's okay—"

With a panicked shriek, Lucifer stumbled.

Bliss, already unbalanced, tumbled forward. "Hey, wait—" The reins slipped from her fingers. "Damn."

Crack! Thunder crashed, snapping through the forest and reverberating against the outcropping of stone.

Lucifer shied.

The saddle seemed to shift.

She started to fall, grabbed for the pommel and missed. The rain-washed world spun crazily. She scrabbled for the reins. "Whoa—oh, God."

With a wild, terrified whinny, the horse stumbled again. Bliss pitched forward. Wet strands of his mane slid through her fingers.

"Stop! Please—Lucifer!" The ground rushed up at her.

Thud! Pain shot through her shoulder, jarring her bones. Her head smacked against the ground. Lights exploded behind her eyes. Her boot, still caught in the stirrup, twisted, wrenching her leg.

A shaft of lightning struck, sizzling and sparking. Crack! An old oak tree split down the middle. Fire and sparks spit upward to the heavens.

Half the tree fell. The ground shook. Bliss screamed as she tried to free herself from the horse and saddle. Lucifer, spooked, bolted.

"No—no—oh, God!" she cried. Frantically she struggled to wiggle out of the boot or yank it from the stirrup as the frightened horse dragged her along the trail near the edge of the ravine.

Hot, blinding pain seared up her leg as she tried to grab at something, anything that she could find with fingers that were bleeding and torn. Still the horse ran forward, bolting at a fever pitch along the jagged edge of canyon that dropped hundreds of feet to the riverbed below.

"Stop! Lucifer, for God's sake..."

A blast—a loud, eerie whistle—pierced the sodden air

just as some of the rocks beneath them gave way. Through horrified eyes she saw the river, winding silvery and snake-like what seemed a million miles below.

For a second, day turned to night. Another piercing blare of the whistle. Lucifer shuddered to a stop. Bliss's head slid over the edge of the canyon. Hair fell in front of her eyes. She was going to die.

She blinked, rolled over and clutched the rimrocks. Through a heavy curtain of raw pain she saw the vision of a rain-soaked cowboy atop a black stallion. Mason's face, white with fear, came into view.

"For the love of God!" He jumped down from Black Jack and rushed forward as one of Lucifer's hooves slipped over the edge.

"No!" Mason caught hold of her booted ankle. Her thigh wrenched and popped, burning with new, searing pain. Blackness threatened her vision.

Lucifer found his footing and reared, trying to shake himself free of the dead weight still attached to his saddle.

"Hang on!" Mason ordered. His grip was slick. Her weight pulled her ever downward as her fingers found no purchase on the rough stone.

"Mason!"

"I've got you."

Steel-shod hooves glimmered as lightning flashed.

One hoof struck Mason in the temple. Crunch. He toppled, his fingers refusing to give up their grip.

The second hoof hit him in the side and Bliss began to slide over the edge even farther. Something deep inside her tore. His fingers relaxed, and the boot was slipping from her foot. She knew in that instant that she was about to die.

"I love you," she tried to say, but the words caught in

her throat. She heard noises. Voices. Panicked voices. Her father? Mason? She couldn't tell as she reached upward, hoping to find his hand but grabbing only air as she began to slide downward.

Chapter One

Now

Bliss snapped off the radio as she wove her convertible through the slick streets of downtown Seattle. Traffic was snarled, horns blared and she couldn't stand to listen to Waylon Jennings talk about cowboys—a breed of man she knew more than a little about.

Hadn't her father started out as a range rider? Not to mention Mason. Not for the first time she wondered what had happened to him. He'd married, of course, and had a child—her heart bled at the thought. In her schoolgirl fantasies she'd imagined she'd be the mother of Mason's child; and in that dreamworld, her mother was still alive—an adoring grandmother—and her father and Mason had reconciled because of the baby.

But of course that would never happen. Her mother had

already died and now her father was battling for his own life. As for Mason...well, he'd just turned out to be her first love. Nothing more.

Stepping on the gas as the light turned green, she shoved all thoughts of Mason from her mind. Her Mustang convertible surged forward toward the freeway entrance. She didn't have the time or patience to reminisce about a love affair gone sour.

Her windshield wipers slapped rain off the glass as she maneuvered through the traffic. In the distance lightning flashed, and again she thought of that long-ago storm and how its fury had changed the course of her life forever.

She'd never seen Mason after that day.

"Don't think about it," she warned herself as she headed toward the hospital where her father had been a patient for nearly a week, ever since he'd returned to Seattle to sign papers on some property he'd sold. "It's over. It's been over for a long, long time."

Within minutes she'd exited the freeway and was winding through the wet side streets surrounding the hospital. She nabbed a parking spot not too far from the main entrance of Seattle General and braced herself. Her father, irascible and determined, would demand to be released. And would probably insist upon returning to his ranch in Oregon, though he still owned property here. She, as strong-willed as he, would insist that he abide by his doctor's orders.

"Give me strength," she muttered under her breath as she locked her car and sidestepped puddles as the wind tugged at the hem of her raincoat and rain pelted her hair.

Inside the hospital, she ignored the sense of doom that threatened to settle in her heart. Barely three months before, in this very facility, Margaret Cawthorne had lost her battle with cancer. Bliss had been at her side.

But it wouldn't happen again! Not this time. Her father was too strong to let some little heart attack get him. She punched the elevator call button and shook the rain from her hair.

On the third floor, she headed straight for her father's room and found him lying under a thin blanket, his face pensive, turned toward the window. His television was on, the volume low, tuned in to some golf tournament in progress. Flowers, cards, boxes of candy and balloons were crammed onto every inch of counter space.

John Cawthorne looked thinner and more frail than she'd ever seen him. Hooked up to a heart monitor and an IV he was nothing like the man she'd grown up with, the tough-talking, badgering cowboy-turned-real-estate-mogul. At the sound of her footsteps, he glanced her way and a half grin teased the corners of a mouth surrounded by silver beard stubble.

"I wondered if you were gonna stop by," he said, pressing a button on a panel of the bed in order to raise his head. The electric motor hummed and he winced a little as his stitches pulled.

"I wouldn't miss a chance to see you cooped up, now, would I?" she teased.

His blue eyes twinkled. "I hate it."

"I know."

"I'm not kiddin'."

"I know," she repeated, walking to the windows and adjusting the blinds. "Don't tell me—you want out of the prison and expect me to help you escape."

He chuckled, then stopped abruptly, as if the pain was too much. "Look, I'm about to go stir-crazy around here, but the doc, he thinks I need to stay another couple of days."

"I'm on his side. Don't even argue with me about it."

She leaned over and kissed his forehead. "So tell me—and I want the truth—how're you feeling?"

"Like I was dragged through a knothole one way, then pushed back through the other."

"I thought so. You're better off here, Dad."

"But I've got things I gotta do."

"Oh, quit whining," she said with a grin. "Whatever it is, believe me, it'll keep."

As quick as a cat pouncing, he grabbed hold of her hand and wouldn't let go. "No, honey, this time, I'm afraid it won't."

"Oh, Dad—"

His lips compressed thoughtfully for a second. "There's something I've got to tell you, Bliss. Something I should've told you about a long time ago."

For the first time since entering the gleaming room, Bliss felt a premonition of despair. An unidentifiable urgency etched the contours of her father's face and his gaze was steady and hard as it held hers. "Oh, God," she whispered, suddenly weak in the knees. Tears, unbidden, formed in her eyes. "The doctor found something else—"

"No, no," he was quick to assure her. "I'm gonna be all right, just gotta take care of myself."

"Then what?" Her shoulders sagged in relief.

He hesitated, muttered an oath under his breath, then said, "I'm gonna get married again."

"What?" She stiffened. Surely she hadn't heard correctly. "Married? You're joking." He had to be.

"Never been more serious in my life." His expression told her that he wasn't pulling her leg.

She steadied herself on the rail of his bed, clutching hard enough that her knuckles showed white.

"Now, wait a minute—"

"I've waited too long as it is."

She was missing something here. Something important. "But Mom—"

"Is gone."

"Oh, Lord." She swallowed back the urge to argue with him and told herself she'd better hear him out. Maybe he was hallucinating from the drugs, maybe he'd grown attached to one of the nurses attending him and had developed a silly, dependent crush on her, or maybe—could it be?—he had a lover. No way.

"Sit down." He waved her into a chair.

Gratefully, she sank into a chair wedged between the bed and the window. "I think you'd better start at the beginning," she suggested, though she knew she wasn't going to like what she was about to hear. "Who—who is this...this woman?"

"Someone I love very much." His smile was weak, but the set of his jaw was as hard as granite, and while the sportscaster on the television spoke in hushed tones as a golfer approached his tee shot, Bliss felt a welling desperation.

"I—I don't understand."

"I know. Trouble is, neither do I, and I've had a lot of time to think about it." His lips, dry and chapped, curled in over his teeth in a second's indecision, and with his free hand he tugged on the crisp white sheet covering his body.

"Is she someone you just met?"

"No." The words seemed to ricochet off the stark hospital walls and echo dully in Bliss's heart. "I've known Brynnie for years."

"Brynnie?" The name was familiar, but Bliss couldn't place it. "But Mom just passed away—"

"That's the hard part." His gaze found hers and she saw the secret lingering in the blue depths—the truth that he'd been in love with another woman for years.

Bliss's heart twisted painfully. "No." Though she had known her parents' marriage had been far from perfect, Bliss had told herself they had loved each other in their own special—if unconventional—way. After all, they had celebrated their thirtieth wedding anniversary just this past year. There hadn't been tension or arguments in the house; just a general sense of apathy and drifting apart as they'd aged. "Who is she?" Bliss asked, cringing inside and feeling suddenly cold as death. "Who is this Brynnie?"

A twinkle lighted her father's faded blue eyes and his lips turned up in a semblance of a smile. Even the skin on his face, paler than his usual tan, seemed to grow a little rosy. Bliss thought she might be sick. He looked like a love-struck teenager. Shifting in the bed, he pulled on the IV again and winced when the tape tugged on the back of his hand. "Brynnie Perez... Well, her name's changed a few times over the years. She's been married more than once, but..." He stared at his daughter and reached forward, taking her hand in his again. The cool plastic tubing of his IV brushed her arm. He hesitated, as if unsure of his next words.

"What, Dad?"

His gaze slid away for a second and he squared his shoulders. "This isn't easy for me to admit, Blissie, but I've loved Brynnie most of my life—well since I met her twenty-six—no, twenty-seven years ago."

"You what?" Bliss whispered, feeling as if a thunderbolt had shot through her. "Most of your life?" *And all of mine!*

"Adult life."

"But—" All the underpinnings of Bliss's life were suddenly shifting, causing her to lose her sense of balance, her security, her knowledge of who she was. "Wait a minute. I don't believe—"

"It's true, Bliss."

"No—" Had John Cawthorne been living a lie for years? Bliss's stomach tightened into a hard knot. It was one thing to think that this infatuation had been recent, but to admit to years—*years*—of loving someone other than his wife. This was too much to take. *Way* too much.

Her father's bony fingers tightened over hers. "I've loved her forever. Still do."

"But Mom…"

A sadness stole over his thin features—the same sadness she'd witnessed a dozen times before but had never understood. "Your mom and I, we cared about each other, but it was a different feeling…hard to explain. She was a good woman, that's for sure. A real good woman."

"Of course, she was." Bliss felt a jab of indignity for the proud woman who had borne her father's name for most of her life. "Mom…Mom was the greatest." Tears threatened her eyes and she had to swallow hard.

"No doubt about it."

"But you loved someone else." Despair flooded her insides and she stared at the fragrant white blooms of a gardenia someone had sent him. "Oh, Dad, how could you?"

"I just fell in love, honey. I know, I know, I shouldn't have, but…well, there it is. Your mother, she knew about Brynnie, but we thought it would be best for you if we stuck it out together and gave you some kind of normal family—"

"Normal family? You call this normal? Living a lie?" The room seemed to spin for an instant and there was a loud rush in her ears, like the sound of the ocean pounding the shore.

"People do it all the time."

"Do they?" She pulled her hand out from his grip. Repulsed and stunned, she shrank into a corner of the chair. She loved and hated him in one second, even though she herself knew about love gone wrong. Isn't that what had happened with Mason? Hadn't he been involved with two women? Oh, Lord, she felt like she might throw up. She stared at her father and tried to understand. "So why tell me now?"

"I said I was gonna get married. Soon."

Her laugh was brittle and forced. "Don't tell me you expect me to come to the wedding?" When he didn't answer she rolled her eyes and felt the hot moisture that had collected beneath her eyelids. "Oh, Dad...please don't even ask. I...I can't believe this is happening."

He glanced away, ran his tongue around his teeth and seemed to weigh his next words carefully. "Listen, honey, there's more."

"More?" she whispered, feeling a sense of doom sneak through her insides. What "more" could there possibly be? She didn't want to hazard a guess.

He sniffed, ran a hand under his nose and sighed. "It's not just me and Brynnie."

Bliss bit her lip.

He hesitated, searching for the right words. "There's a girl—well, a woman now—"

"I—I don't know if I want to hear this," Bliss interrupted, rubbing her hands together to ease the intense cold that had permeated her bones.

"You have to, honey. Because, you see, you have a half sister."

"Wh-what?" The white tiles of the hospital floor seemed to buckle beneath her chair.

"Well, more than one, actually."

"More than one?" *This was too absurd to be true.* And yet she knew as she looked at him that he wasn't lying. "Wait a minute, Dad. Something's wrong, here. Very wrong." She tried not to glare at her father who was still recuperating, but, damn it, she could barely make sense of his words. "You're trying to tell me that I have a sister—no, make that two?"

When he nodded she said, "But how?" Her mind was spinning in furious, complicated and very ugly circles. Everything she'd believed in, all that she'd trusted in her life, had been a lie—a dirty, dark and shameful lie. "Why?" she asked, trying to sound rational when her entire world was turned upside down. "This…this Brynnie is their mother?"

"She's Katie's mother," John said slowly and scratched the side of his cheek. "My other daughter—"

"Does she have a name, too?" Bliss couldn't hide the sarcasm in her words.

"Tiffany. She's older than you by a few years. The result of an affair I had before I met your mom."

"Oh, Dad," Bliss whispered, the tears she'd been fighting beginning to slide from the corners of her eyes. How could she have been so wrong about this man she'd loved all her life? The man who'd taught her how to ride bareback and lasso a wayward calf and swim in a river where the current was strong and swift? "You—you didn't marry her?"

"I was ridin' rodeo at the time. It wouldn't have worked. Matter of fact, she wasn't interested. I offered, she said 'No, thanks,' told me that she was givin' the baby up for adoption. Seems as if she lied about that, though. I found out a few years back."

"Oh, Lord."

"As I said, I didn't know it, but she kept the girl. Tiffany's almost thirty-two now, and…well, it's time she and I met. Especially now that she's moved back to Bittersweet. Living in the same town, it doesn't make much sense not to acknowledge that we're father and daughter."

"Are you sure? Maybe she's not interested in meeting you." Bliss, who had always prided herself on her strength, felt suddenly weary. She was usually a woman who moved easily in business circles, handled herself well at sophisticated and elegant social events, could adjust her style so that she felt as at home in a Seattle high-rise overlooking Puget Sound as she was in a low-slung ranch house that hadn't seen fresh paint in twenty years. But this—this complete alteration of what she'd grown up believing to be right and true—was more than she could deal with. Nothing in her life had been this mortifying, except maybe her faith in Mason Lafferty all those years ago.

"It's not so bad," her father insisted. But then he had no choice but to believe his own words, did he? If what he was saying was the God's honest truth, then he had to trust that the situation would someway, somehow, work out. His graying brows drew together as if he were confused by the puzzle that was his life.

"Not so bad?" she repeated. "Well, it's damned unbelievable." Bliss, raised as an only child had not one, but two half-sisters—grown women she'd never heard of before, never had known existed.

Clearing his throat and squaring his shoulders beneath the thin cotton of his hospital gown, her father mustered up as much bravado as he could. "So now I'm gonna change things. Brynnie and I are gonna get married as soon as the docs tell me I can move back to Bittersweet." He fingered the edge of his sheet. "I'd like you to come with me, Blissie. Meet Brynnie and your sisters."

"Meet them?" Boy, her father had really lost it. "Dad, it's not just that simple. I mean...do *they* want to meet *me?*"

"Brynnie does."

"And the others?"

"Don't know."

Could she do it? Go back to Bittersweet, a town that held all kinds of bad memories? She felt a familiar ache in her heart—one she'd tried to bury for ten years—and that old, dark pain seared through her. She rubbed her thigh where she still sometimes felt a jab of pain from the accident so many years before. She could only hope that Mason was roasting in his own private hell. "I don't think so, Dad," she heard herself saying. "My life's here, in Seattle."

"What have you got other than an apartment and a job?"

"Oscar." She hitched her chin up an inch.

"That mutt of a dog can move with you. You can sublet your apartment and work from Oregon, what with fax machines and computer links and all. I know you spent one summer working out of a cabin in the San Juan Islands and another in Victoria. So don't give me any guff about having to be near the office. I'll have the phone company put in more telephone lines to the house for your modem and whatever else you need. The way I understand it—" he eyed her as if expecting her to mount a protest "—or at least what you've always led me to believe, is that you're pretty much independent anyway."

That much was true. She worked with two other architects restoring old buildings in Seattle, but she was between projects right now and had planned to take a vacation to Mexico or the Caribbean or somewhere in the sun. So why not Bittersweet? A dozen reasons why. Mason Lafferty was at the top of the list. If he still lived there. She hadn't heard from him in a decade and had never asked her father about him, though she had, over the years, gleaned a little about his life from people who had run across him. Not that it mattered. He'd betrayed her. Pure and simple.

Like your father betrayed your mother.

Well, she, for one, wasn't about to dwell on the mistakes of her past. Not now. Not ever.

As for the half sisters she'd never known existed, what would be the point of meeting them now? True, she'd been raised as an only child and had always wished for siblings—brothers or sisters—but now that she was faced with her father's infidelity, she wasn't sure she could accept her sisters. Oh, what was she thinking? Sisters? *Half* sisters? Two of them? What would she say to them? What *could* she say?

"This is way too sudden for me, Dad."

"And I'm runnin' out of time." He scowled and clicked off the television. "Who knows when the Grim Reaper's gonna knock on my door?"

"Don't talk like that!"

"I've already had one heart attack. I think it's time to live my life the way I want to." He rubbed his jaw, scratching the silver bristles covering his chin. "Besides, you'll like Brynnie, if you only give her a chance."

Bliss wasn't so sure. Brynnie, was, after all, her father's mistress and even though Bliss had known that her parents had drifted apart over the years, she couldn't just accept this other woman as part of her family. Bile climbed steadily up her throat, but she forced it back down.

"Your mother and I... Well, we were never right for each other. We were from different worlds. I was at home in the saddle with a plug of tobacco, and she wanted to see the damned ballet."

"I remember." Margaret Cawthorne was from old San Francisco money. John had been a cowboy with a keen mind who had bought land during the recession and made a fortune. He'd split his time between Seattle where he owned property and Bittersweet, Oregon, where his ranch was located.

A cloud passed behind his eyes, as if he still felt some kind of regret.

"But you stayed married."

"Believed in the institution. And there was you to consider."

"You made a mockery of the institution, Dad. And of me." Bliss stood, folded her arms over her chest, leaned against the cool wall and stared out the window to the parking lot three stories below. Rain drizzled from oppressive gray clouds, streaking down the panes. She could scarcely breathe. Her parents hadn't loved each other? Her father had been and still was involved with another woman? How could she not have known or guessed? She swallowed against a suddenly thick throat. Everything she believed in seemed to be falling apart, and more rapidly by the moment.

"I always thought opposites attracted," Bliss said lamely. Heat stole up the back of her neck when she thought of her one experience with a man as opposite from her once-prim city-girl ways as could be. Mason Lafferty, the randy tough-as-rawhide ranch hand who had worked for her father the summer she was almost eighteen, had managed to steal her naive heart before her father had stepped in.

"I suppose there's some truth to the saying, but not as opposite as we were. In the beginning, I guess we didn't realize how different we were and then...well, I found Brynnie...." He had the good grace to look sheepish and Bliss felt the bleak ache in her heart thud painfully. He'd cheated on her mother with this woman he intended to marry. He'd fathered a child with her. "Brynnie's had her share of troubles, you know. Been married a few times and has some older boys that give her headaches you wouldn't believe."

From the half-open door Bliss heard the reassuring beep of heart monitors and the quiet conversation of the nurses busying around their station from which the corridors fanned toward the private rooms on the outside walls of the building. A medications cart rattled by and the elevator call button chimed. Sighing, Bliss looked down at her father, her only living parent.

"Come down to the wedding, Bliss," John said, his leathery skin stretched tight over his cheekbones. "It's important to me. Damn it, honey, I know it will be hard for you, but you're tough, like your ma. The way I see it, I've lost too much time already and I think we should start over. Be a family."

"You and Brynnie and her children and me," she clarified.

"And Tiffany."

"Right." She shook her head and blinked back her tears. "Dad, do you know how absurd this all sounds? It's not that I don't want to, but I need some time to catch up. I walked into this room an hour ago and didn't know anything. Now, you expect me to accept everything you're telling me and be a part of a family I knew nothing about. I don't know if I can."

"Try. For me."

She wanted to agree to anything, to promise this man who had nearly met his Maker that she'd try her best to make him happy, but she didn't want to lie. "I'll give it a shot," she said, wondering why she would even think of returning to Bittersweet, the place where, as far as she knew, not only her half sisters lived, but where she'd lost her heart years ago to a cowboy who had used her and thrown her away.

As if reading her thoughts, her father fingered the edge of his sheet and announced, "Lafferty's back in Bittersweet." His mouth tightened at the corners and Bliss's heart lost a beat. "Lookin' for property, the way I hear it."

"Is he?"

"His ex-wife and kid are there, too."

Wonderful, she thought grimly. "Doesn't matter."

His eyes narrowed a fraction. "Just thought you'd want to know."

"Why?"

"Well, you and he—"

"That was a long time ago, remember? He got married."

"And divorced."

She'd expected as much. Mason wasn't the kind of man who could commit to one woman for very long. She'd found that out. The hard way. "I couldn't care less," she lied, and cringed inside.

"Good. You'll have enough to deal with."

"If I come."

"I'm countin' on it, Blissie," her father said with an encouraging smile. "It's time for me to start over and I can't do it without you."

A huge lump filled her throat. *Half sisters.*

She'd have to meet them sometime, she decided without much enthusiasm, but that didn't mean that she had to like them.

Chapter Two

"Bliss Cawthorne's coming back to town."

Mason froze, his pen in his hand as he sat at his desk. "What?"

"You heard me." Jarrod Smith snagged his hat from the hall tree as he walked to the door of Mason's office. "Just thought you'd like to know."

"You're full of good news, aren't you?" Mason said, leaning back in his desk chair until the old springs creaked in protest. His stupid pulse had jumped at the mention of Bliss's name, but he calmed himself. So she was returning to Bittersweet. So what? He didn't doubt that she cursed the day she'd ever set eyes on him. He didn't blame her.

She was, as she always had been, forbidden.

Jarrod grinned like a Cheshire cat. "Supposedly it'll be a short visit, just coming back for her old man's wedding."

"To your mother." Mason had already heard the news that had swept like wildfire through dry grass along the streets of Bittersweet. In the taverns, churches and coffee shops, the topic of John Cawthorne's marriage had been hashed and rehashed. Not that Mason cared so much about what Cawthorne did these days, except when it came to the ranch, the damned ranch. Behind the old man's back he'd made a deal with Brynnie to buy out part of it. His conscience twinged a bit; he had a ten-year-old deal with the old man, too. One he no longer intended to honor.

"Yep." Jarrod squared his hat on his head and paused at the door. "This *is* a small town."

"Too small." Nervously, Mason clicked the pen.

"But you couldn't stay away."

Mason grimaced and glanced at the picture propped on the edge of his desk. In the snapshot a pixie of a girl with dark hair and amber eyes smiled up at him. Freckles dusted her nose, teeth too large for her mouth were a little crooked in a smile as big as the world. Dee Dee. Well, really, Deanna Renée, but he'd always called her by her nickname. "I've got my reasons for coming back," he admitted.

"Don't we all?"

"I suppose," Mason allowed. He and Jarrod had been friends for years, ever since high school. Jarrod had been everything from a log-truck driver, to a detective with a police department in Arizona somewhere, but he'd been back in Bittersweet for a couple of years running his own private-investigation business. Mason had hired him to track down his younger sister, Patty. So far, no luck; just a few leads that always seemed to peter out.

Jarrod's smile was slow as it stretched across his jaw. "So what're you gonna do about Bliss?"

Bliss Cawthorne. "Not much." His stomach clenched as he remembered her eyes, as blue as a mountain lake, and lips that could curve into a smile that was innocent and sexy as hell all at once. She'd nearly died. Because of him. Because he'd been weak.

Jarrod pretended interest in his knuckles. "You and she had a thing once."

If you only knew. "A long time ago." *But it feels like yesterday.*

"Old feelings die hard."

"Do they?"

"She's not married. Never been." Jarrod twisted the knob and shouldered open the door. "It's almost as if she's been waiting for you."

Mason nearly laughed as he folded his arms over his chest. "My guess is that she'd just as soon spit on me as talk to me."

"Still blaming yourself for that accident?"

Mason shrugged, as if he didn't give a damn, but the muscles in his shoulders tightened like cords of a thick rope that had been wet and left to shrink in the sun.

"Hell, Lafferty, it wasn't your fault."

Mason didn't answer.

Jarrod shook his head. "I probably shouldn't have said anything, but you were bound to find out sooner or later. I was just letting you know that she'll be back. She's still a good-lookin' woman—or so her old man brags—and still gonna inherit a pile of money, so if you're not interested, I'm sure a lot of other men around these parts would be."

Jealousy, his old enemy, seeped into Mason's blood. "Including you?"

"Maybe," Jarrod admitted with that lazy smile still fastened on his face. "You know it's nice to keep it in the family, and now she'll be my what? Stepsister?"

"If the wedding of the century ever comes off." He knew that Smith was needling him, and yet he couldn't take anything, when it came to Bliss, lightly. Even after ten years.

"See ya around."

"Right."

Jarrod left the door open when he left. Mason watched as his friend, wearing jeans, cowboy boots with worn heels, and a faded denim jacket, sauntered out of the exterior office, stopping long enough to say a few words to Mason's secretary, Edie, to make her blush.

Jarrod Smith had a knack for breaking women's hearts. Though he owed the man his life, Mason didn't like the idea of Jarrod being anywhere near Bliss Cawthorne. She deserved better than to be another of Smith's conquests.

Oh, right, because you were so good to her.

Frowning, he picked up his coffee cup and scowled as the weak, cold brew hit the back of his throat.

Bliss Cawthorne.

The princess.

The one woman he could never quite wedge from his mind, even though he'd married another.

In his mind's eye, he saw her again at the edge of the cliff, slipping from his grasp. He heard the sound of his own terrified scream, felt that same horrifying certainty that she would be dead in an instant.

But her old man had shown up just in time.

Thank God.

John Cawthorne had arrived on horseback, his foreman with him.

"What's going on here?" Cawthorne had shouted, then reached around Mason and grabbed hold of Bliss's leg just as his own grip had given way.

"Hang on, Blissie— For the love of God, man, pull! Pull!"

Mason's ebbing strength had revitalized. Though pain

jolted through his arm, he caught hold of her free leg and yanked. The two men dragged her back to the ledge where she'd lain, eyes closed, blood streaming from the cuts on her head.

"Ride like hell to the truck, call the police and get a helicopter for her," John had commanded the foreman. Rain dripped from the brim of his hat, mud oozed around his boots. His face was etched in fear and his eyes, two smoldering blue coals, burned through Mason with a hatred so intense it nearly smelled. "You miserable son of a bitch, you nearly killed her." He bent down on one knee and touched his daughter tenderly on the cheek. "Hang on, honey. Just hang the hell on."

The minutes stretched on.

Mason was in and out of consciousness and barely heard the helicopter or the shouts from the pilots. Nor did he feel the whoosh of air as the rotor blades turned above him and bent the wet grass skirting the ledge.

All he knew was that when he awoke, battered and broken, the helicopter had taken Bliss away and left him alone with John Cawthorne and the older man's festering hatred. A half-smoked cigarette bobbed from the corner of Cawthorne's mouth.

"Now, you lowlife son of a bitch, you listen to me," Cawthorne commanded in a voice barely above a whisper. His face was flushed with rage, his hands clenched into hard, gnarled fists. "You stay away from my daughter."

Mason didn't answer. He couldn't. Pain screamed up his left arm where the horse had kicked him and his chest felt so heavy he could scarcely breathe. Rain, in cold, pounding sheets, poured from the sky, peppering his face and mud-caked body as he lay, face up, at the edge of the ravine.

"Bliss is half-dead, Lafferty, all because of you. You nearly cost me my best stallion as well as my daughter's

life. If I had the balls I'd leave you here for the buzzards."
The cords of his neck, above his grimy slicker, were taut
as bowstrings. "It would serve you right." He wiped his
face with a muddy hand, leaving streaks of brown on his
unshaven jaw as he glared up at the heavens. "But you're
lucky. Instead of letting you die like you deserve, I'll cut
you a deal. Twenty-five thousand dollars over and above
your medical bills if you walk away."

Mason blinked, tried to speak, but couldn't say a word.
His arm wouldn't move and his breath came in short, shallow gasps that burned like hell and seemed to rip the tissue
of his lungs.

"You leave Bittersweet, never contact Bliss again and
marry Terri Fremont."

What? His head was heavy, his mind unclear from the
raging pain, but he didn't understand. "No way. I can't—"
he forced out in a bare whisper.

"You know Terri's pregnant with your kid."

No! Impossible. He hadn't been with Terri since Bliss
had entered his life two months ago, but as he blinked
upward at the dark, swollen clouds and into the fury of
John Cawthorne's face, he felt a sickening sensation of ca-
lamity barreling, like the engine of a freight train, straight
for him.

"It's what you've always wanted, Lafferty—money the
easy way. Well, now you've got it. Just leave Bliss alone."

Bile crawled up Mason's throat and he turned his head
in time to retch onto the sodden grass of Cawthorne's land.

"The way I see it, you haven't got much choice."

Mason couldn't argue.

"Have we got a deal?" He spat his cigarette onto the
ground where it sizzled before dying.

No! Mason's nostrils flared and he tried to force himself
to his feet, got as far as his knees and fell back down, his

head smacking into the mud, his arm and chest searing with agony.

"Moron." Cawthorne's voice had lost some of its edge. "Come on, son. Think of your future. You've got a kid on the way. It's time to grow up. Face responsibility. And then there's that little matter of your sister."

Patty. Two years younger and beautiful, but oh, so messed up.

"She could use the money, even if you and Terri aren't interested, but you'd better talk to the Fremont girl first. My guess is that she's like most women and she'll want all the money for herself and your kid."

No! No! No! A burning ache blasted through his brain and his eyelids begged to droop.

"Now," Cawthorne continued a little more gently, "have we got a deal?"

No way! Mason's head reeled. He spat. Blood and mud flew from his cracked lips.

Cawthorne leaned down, the scent of smoke and tobacco wafting from him. "I'm giving you the chance of a lifetime, boy. All you have to do is say yes."

Mason closed his eyes. Blackness threatened the edges of his vision, but still he saw Bliss's gorgeous face. Cawthorne was right; he'd nearly killed her. If the old man hadn't shown up when he did, if he'd lost his grip only seconds earlier, if he hadn't followed her to the cliff... He swallowed and realized with an impending sense of doom that he had no choice.

"Well?"

Bliss, oh, God, I'm sorry. I'm so damned sorry. He felt more broken and battered than his injuries and realized that it was his soul that had been destroyed.

Through cracked lips, he agreed. "Yeah, Cawthorne," he finally mouthed, his insides rebelling at the very thought of giving her up. He skewered the older man with a glare of pure hatred. "We've...we've got a deal."

Now, ten years later, at that particular thought his stomach turned sour and he tossed the dregs of his drink into a straggly-looking fern positioned near the window.

So Bliss was finally returning to Bittersweet. With that little bit of knowledge, he knew that his painful bargain with Cawthorne was over. Though he should leave her alone, pretend that what had happened between them was forgotten, he couldn't.

He'd returned to Bittersweet with a single purpose: to gain custody of his daughter and provide a stable life for her. He shouldn't let anything or anyone deter him. Especially not Bliss Cawthorne. But there was that little matter of Cawthorne's ranch. Mason had always loved the place despite a few bad memories. Now, as luck would have it, he had a chance of owning it, maybe settling down with his kid and hopefully finding the peace that had eluded him for most of his life.

Except that he was going to see Bliss again, and that particular meeting promised to be about as peaceful as fireworks on the Fourth of July.

"I should have my head examined," Bliss muttered.

Oscar, her mutt of indiscernible lineage, thumped his tail on the passenger seat of her convertible as they raced down the freeway five miles over the speed limit. The radio blasted an old Rolling Stones tune as the road curved through the mountains of southern Oregon.

Oscar, tongue lolling, black lips in a smile that exposed his fangs, rested his head on the edge of the rolled-down side window. His gold coat ruffled in the wind and sparkled in the sun under a cloudless sky.

Bliss tapped out the beat of "Get Off My Cloud" on the

steering wheel and wished she'd never agreed to this lunacy. What was she going to do in the town where she'd
been so hurt, meeting half sisters and a bevy of step-
relatives she hadn't known existed, and watching as her
father, foolish old man that he'd become overnight, walk
down the aisle with his mistress.

"Unreal," she muttered as Mick Jagger's voice faded
and the radio crackled with static.

Oscar didn't seem to care. He was up for the adventure.
His brown eyes sparkled with an excitement Bliss didn't
share, and with a red handkerchief tied jauntily around his
neck, he looked ready for ranch life.

Bliss's hands tightened on the steering wheel. She'd
changed her mind about driving to Oregon six times during
as many days. Her father had recuperated and left Seattle
two weeks earlier, then just this past week had called to
tell her he was being married at the end of June. He wanted
her to come spend some time with him, meet her new family, and be a part of the festivities.

Great.

And what about Mason? her wayward mind taunted.
What if you run into him?

"The least of my worries," she lied as she stepped on
the gas to pass a log truck. She planned to avoid Mason
Lafferty as if he were the plague. Her hands on the wheel
began to sweat, and she bit down on her lip. She was over
him. Had been for a long time. So what if he'd been her
first love? It had been ten years ago—a decade—since
she'd last seen him or felt his fingers moving anxiously
against the small of her back.

At the old, erotic memory, goose bumps broke out on
her skin and she closed her mind to any further wayward
thoughts. Mason had never loved her, never cared. He'd
left without a second glance. Hadn't even had the decency

to stop by the hospital where she'd fought for her life after the accident. Hadn't so much as sent a card. In fact, he'd cared so much for her that he'd married another woman. He was the last man on earth she wanted.

An old Bruce Springsteen song, one she'd heard that painful summer, pounded through the speakers.

She snapped off the radio in disgust.

She wouldn't think of Mason. At least, not right now. Besides, she had other worries. What about the two women who were supposed to be her half sisters, for crying out loud? A nest of butterflies erupted in her stomach when she thought about the women she'd never known. Did she really want to know them? "Give me strength," she muttered under her breath.

She exited the freeway, her stomach tightening in painful knots. Memories, vivid and painful, slipped through her mind. The hills of pine and madrona looked the same as they had ten years ago. The landmarks—an old trading post and an abandoned schoolhouse—hadn't changed much. Barbed-wire fences surrounded fields lush with the spring rains, where cattle grazed lazily.

After a final rise in the road, the town of Bittersweet came into view. She passed by the old water tower that stood near the railroad station. Nearby, a white church spire, complete with bell and copper roof, rose above leafy shade trees surrounding the town square. Fences ranging from white picket and ranch rail to chain link cordoned off small yards within which bikes, swings, and sagging wading pools were strewn. The homes were eclectic—cottages and two-story clapboard houses intermingled with ranch-style tract homes and tiny bungalows.

In the central business district she drove past the old pharmacy where she'd ordered cherry colas one summer. She slowed to a stop at the single blinking red light in the

center of town and noticed that the old mom-and-pop gro-
cery store, once owned by an elderly couple whose names
she couldn't remember, had changed hands. It was now a
Mini-Mart. Time had marched on.

And so had she.

She hadn't belonged here ten years ago. She didn't be-
long here now.

Thoughts a-tangle, she drove on into the country again
and slowed automatically at the gravel lane that cut through
fields of knee-high grass. The gate was open, as if she were
expected, and the curved wooden sign bridging the end of
the lane read Cawthorne Acres. Her father's pride and joy.

John Cawthorne called this spot "heaven on earth." She
wasn't so sure. She wasn't seduced by the scents of honeysuckle and cut hay, nor did her heart warm at the sight
of the horses milling and grazing, their tails swishing
against flies. Nope. She was much happier as a city girl.
Margaret Cawthorne's daughter.

She slowed at the barn and parked near the open door.
Oscar jumped out his side of the car. She reached into the
back seat for one of her bags.

"Look, I thought I made it clear that I wasn't interested!" John Cawthorne's angry voice rang from the barn.

Bliss's shoulders sagged. The last thing her father should
be doing after his surgery was getting himself all riled up.
She dropped the bag, opened the car door, climbed out and
shoved the door shut with her hip. "Dad?" she called as
she walked into the barn. Dust motes swirled upward in air
thick with the odors of dusty grain and dry hay.

"Bliss—?"

Her eyes adjusted to the dim light and she saw her father
leaning heavily on his pitchfork. His jaw was set, his face
rigid and he was glaring at a man whose broad-shouldered

back was turned to her and whose worn, faded jeans had seen far better days.

"I think you probably remember Lafferty."

Bliss's stupid heart skipped a beat and her throat went dry. "Lafferty?" she said automatically, then wished she could drop through the hay-strewn floor. What was he doing here?

In the shadowy light, he glanced over his shoulder. Gold eyes clashed hard and fast with hers.

She froze.

Gone was any trace of the boyish charm she remembered. This man had long ago shrugged off any suggestion of adolescence and was now all angles and planes, big bones, hard muscle and gristle. A few lines fanned from his eyes and bracketed his mouth. His hair, though still blond, had darkened and was longer than the style worn by most of the businessmen in Seattle.

"Well, what do you know?" he taunted, turning on a worn boot-heel and giving her an even better view of him. The skin of his face and forearms where his shirtsleeves were pushed up was tanned from hours in the sun and the thrust of his jaw was harsher, more defined and decidedly more male than she remembered. A day's worth of whiskers gilded a chin that looked as if it had been chiseled from granite. "It's been a long time."

Not long enough! Not nearly long enough. "A good ten years."

"Good?"

"The best," she lied. She wouldn't give him the satisfaction of knowing that he'd hurt her.

"I knew you'd come," her father said and propped the pitchfork against the wall. He crossed the short distance between them and gave her a bear hug with arms that weren't as strong as they once had been.

"Did I have a choice?"

"Always."

She laughed as he released her. "No one has much of a choice when you set your mind, Dad. Mom used to say that stubborn was your middle na—" She bit her tongue and reminded herself that her mother, proud and ever-faithful, was gone. And her father was hell-bent to marry someone else.

"That she did," John agreed. "That she did."

The moment was suddenly awkward and Bliss, as much to change the subject as anything else, said, "I hope I didn't hear you shouting a couple of minutes ago."

"Me?" Her father's eyes twinkled. "Never."

She turned to Mason. "He's not supposed to get overly excited."

"I'll keep that in mind." Shoving callused hands into the back pockets of his jeans, Mason smiled, a sizzling slash of white that was neither friendly nor warm, just downright hit-you-in-the-gut sexy. Well practiced. A grin guaranteed to turn a young girl's heart to mush.

But she wasn't a young innocent anymore and all of Mason's wiles to which she'd been so vulnerable long ago, couldn't touch her. Not now. Not ever again. Her fingers curled into fists and her fingernails dug deep into her palms.

"Good."

His gaze raked up and down her wrinkled blouse and the tangle of her hair, only to pause at her eyes. "How've you been?"

As if he cared.

"Fine...I mean, great. Just great. Really."

"You look it."

She felt a blush climb up the back of her neck. "It must be because of all the clean living I do, I guess."

Mason laughed. "Right."

Her father snorted.

"You don't believe me?"

"I *know* you."

"Did know me. A long time ago. I—I've grown up."

"I noticed."

Bliss wasn't fooled by Mason's well-honed charm. Not a bit. How many nights had she cried bitter tears over this two-timing thoughtless bastard? In an instant, she wanted to strangle him and wasn't about to listen to any of his cheap compliments. She'd made that mistake before. Years ago he'd cut her loose and broken her heart; she'd never trust him again. Folding her arms under her breasts, she asked, "So what're you doing here?"

His smile only broadened as if he were amused by her discomfiture. *Amused!*

"Tryin' to buy the ranch out from under me, that's what he's doin'," her father said, his blue gaze blistering. "I told him I'm not selling."

"Why would you?"

"Because it's too much for him." Mason was matter-of-fact.

"Who're you to determine that? Just 'cause I had a little heart attack don't mean I've got one foot in the grave." Her father was as irascible as ever. Good. That meant he was getting better.

"Just think about it, okay?" Mason suggested. "And while you're at it, you might want to talk to Brynnie."

"Why?" her father demanded, suspicion flashing in his eyes.

"She's going to be your wife, isn't she?"

"Of course."

"Then you probably should ask her what she wants."

"I always do."

One of Mason's brows rose skeptically. "I'll bring you the offer. You can read it over."

John looked about to argue, but clamped his mouth shut.

With a nod to Bliss, Mason strode across the wedge of sunlight that had pierced the gloomy interior of the barn, shouldered open the door until it bounced against the wall and disappeared. A few seconds later a truck's engine roared to life and gravel sprayed from beneath heavy tires.

"No-account bastard," her father said as he reached into his back pocket and pulled out a plug of chewing tobacco. He started to bite into the black wad, then hesitated as if he'd caught the censure in his daughter's eyes. "It's just a little chew, Blissie, and since I can't smoke... Oh, hell." He shoved the dark plug back into his pocket. "What's Lafferty want this place for? He owns property all over the West." John hung his pitchfork on a peg near the door and walked outside where the breath of a breeze cooled the air. Leaves, lush and green on the apple tree near the front porch, turned softly in the wind.

"I was hoping you were down here taking it easy," she said.

"I am."

"I don't think working in the barn and arguing at the top of your lungs is what the doctors had in mind."

"What do they know?"

"Come on, Dad," she cajoled as they reached her car.

"Don't you start in on me, too. I've spent the last few weeks cooped up in bed, so I thought I'd come into the barn and clean up a bit. Nothin' more. Then Lafferty showed up." He glowered at the driveway. "I've thought about sellin' out, but it galls me to think that a no-account like Lafferty wants to buy."

"What do you care?" she asked and her father's eyes

flashed. "Weren't you the guy who always said, 'Money is money, as long as it's green'?"

"I know, I know," he agreed as Oscar explored the shrubbery around the house. "It's just that I care about this place, even if Brynnie doesn't."

"Why doesn't she like it?"

He shrugged. "Too many bad memories here for her, I guess." He settled a hip against her fender as sunlight bounced off the convertible's glossy finish.

"Because you were married to Mom?" Bliss asked, her heart wrenching.

"Even though your mother never lived here, it bothered Brynnie."

"Because you were married."

"I suppose."

Oh, God, this was going to be hard. A stepmother. One who had been involved with her father for a long, long time. Maybe this was a mistake. Maybe she shouldn't have come back.

"I'll look over the damned offer," he admitted, "but I'm not gonna accept it."

Oscar romped over, wagged his tail. As Bliss reached down to scratch him behind his ears, she glanced at the wake of dust that was settling on the long gravel drive.

"I know it was tough for you to come here," he volunteered, swiping at a yellow jacket that buzzed around his head.

"I'm worried about you," she admitted.

"Yeah, but it's more than that. You're curious as hell about Brynnie and the girls."

Lifting a shoulder, Bliss hoisted a bag from the back seat and hauled it toward the house. Her father carried a smaller case and followed her. "A little."

"A lot, I'll wager. Don't blame you." He eyed her as

he held open the front door and the scents she remembered—of floor wax, smoke and cooking oil—greeted her. She fingered the old globe, sending countries that no longer existed spinning.

She walked along the short hallway and pushed open the door. Her room was as it had been for as long as she could remember. Double bed, old dresser with a curved mirror, tiny closet. Rag rugs were scattered over an old, dull fir floor.

He dropped her small case on the foot of the bed.

"I'm drivin' over to Brynnie's for dinner later. You want to tag along?"

"No." She was surprised how quickly the word was out of her mouth, and hated the disappointment she saw in her father's eyes. However, the truth of the matter was that she still needed time to settle in and grow more comfortable with this new life that was being thrown at her. Seeing Mason again didn't help. Not at all. "Not—not tonight. Just give me a little time to catch up, okay?"

He started to argue, thought better of it and shrugged. "Whatever you say, kid. I just think it's time to make peace. I've made my share of mistakes in the past and now I'd like for you and your sisters to be part of a family." He scratched at the stubble silvering his jaw. "But I'll try not to push you too fast."

"Thanks, Dad," she whispered, her throat clogging at his kindness. Crusty as he was, he had his good points. Somehow she'd have to get over her feeling that he'd betrayed her mother. She only wished she knew how.

She walked to the window and forced it open. Returning to Bittersweet might have been a mistake. A big one. Not only would she have to deal with this new patchwork of a family, but also, she was bound to run into Mason again.

So? He was just a man. What they had shared was over a long, long time ago. Or was it?

Chapter Three

His first mistake had been returning to Bittersweet.

His second was seeing Bliss again.

"You're an idiot, Lafferty," he told himself as he parked on the edge of Isaac Wells's property just as night was threatening to fall. The woman had the uncanny ability to get under his skin. Just like before.

"Hell," he ground out, chiding himself for believing that he could see her and not care. He'd been thinking about her ever since leaving the Cawthorne spread—a place he intended to have as his own, if only to prove a point.

But he couldn't think of Bliss right now. He had too much on his mind. First he had to fight with Terri over custody of Dee Dee and secondly he had to find his sister. Patty had been in Bittersweet recently. Jarrod Smith had determined that much, and she'd come here to this scrappy piece of land owned by their uncle, a man who had turned his back on them years ago.

Isaac Wells.

A number-one bastard.

Who had now disappeared. Vanished, without a trace.

Mason climbed out of the pickup. In one lithe movement, he vaulted the fence and walked up the short, rutted lane to the dilapidated cabin that Isaac had called home.

An old wooden rocker with battle-scarred arms and a worn corduroy pad on the seat, pushed by the wind, rocked gently on the front porch. The old man had spent hours on the stoop where he'd whittled, read the stars, strung beans from his garden, and spat streams of tobacco juice into an old coffee can he'd used as a spittoon. He'd made few friends in his lifetime, but had unearthed more than his share of enemies.

So what had happened to him? Had someone killed him and taken his body? But why? Or had he been kidnapped? Or had he just taken a notion and up and left? Mason rubbed the back of his neck in frustration and wondered if Patty had been involved. "Hell's bells," he muttered as he scanned the countryside. Berry vines and thistle were taking over the fields, and the barn, which had never been painted, was beginning to fall apart. The roof sagged and some of the bleached board-and-batten siding was rotting away.

What the hell had happened here?

Foul play?

Or had an addled, lonely old man left in desperation?

No one seemed to know and everyone within fifty miles was frightened. Mysteries like this didn't happen in these sparsely populated hills. The town of Bittersweet and the surrounding rural landscape were far from the rat race and crime of the city; that was part of the charm of this section of Oregon. But Isaac's disappearance had changed all that. Dead bolts that had nearly rusted in the open position were being thrown, security companies contacted for new installments, and, worst of all, shotguns cleaned and kept loaded near bedsteads in the event that an intruder dared break in.

The townspeople and farmers were nervous.

The sheriff's department wanted answers.

And there was nothing. Not a clue.

Except for Patty.

Shadows lengthened across the dry acres that made up Isaac Wells's spread. Mason kicked at a dirt clod, then scoured the darkening sky, as if in reading the stars that were beginning to wink in the purple distance, he could find clues to the old man's disappearance. Of course there were none. Nor were there any celestial explanations for why Mason seemed destined to deal with Bliss Cawthorne again. He couldn't stop himself, of course, and truth to tell, he was inwardly grateful that she hadn't married another man and had a couple of kids.

Like you did.

He'd been foolish enough to think that by seeing her again he'd realize that what he'd felt for her all those years ago—some kind of schoolboy infatuation wrapped up in guilt—would have diminished; that he'd see her and laugh at himself for the fantasies that had haunted him over the years.

"Moron," he growled as memories of his youth, of that time in his life when he was searching, hoping to find something, anything to cling to, flitted through his mind. Boy, had he made a mess of it. He stretched out his left hand, felt the old scar tissue in his arm tighten and was reminded of the horrid, black afternoon when she'd almost died. Because of him. Though John Cawthorne didn't know the whole story and probably never would, the God's honest truth was that Mason had nearly killed her.

He shoved a wayward hank of hair from his eyes and

silently leveled an oath at himself. He'd been the worst kind of fool.

She'd turned into the beauty her youth had promised. Her hair was still a streaked golden blond, her eyes crystal blue, her lips as lush as he remembered. Her body was thin in the right places, and full where it should be. Yep, she'd matured into what he suspected was one hell of a woman, and the defiant tilt of her chin as she'd challenged him today in the barn had only added to her allure.

He looked around the outside of the small house, noticed the faded real-estate sign planted firmly in the grass and frowned. Who would want this scrap of worthless land?

"Damn it all to hell," he muttered as he headed back to his rig. He had enough problems in his life. Running his businesses, trying to convince Terri that Dee Dee was better off with him, and hoping to find his flake of a sister were more than enough. Now, like it or not, he would have to deal with Bliss.

Life had just gotten a lot more complicated.

"You know, Dad, I'm still having trouble with all this." Bliss slid a pancake onto the stack that was heaped on the plate before her father. She'd slept fitfully last night, her dreams punctuated with visions of her father strapped to an IV, of meeting women she didn't know and introducing herself as their sister and, of course, of Mason. Good Lord, why couldn't she get him out of her mind? It had been ten years since she'd been involved with him. A decade. It was long past time to forget him.

"What kind of trouble?" Her father slathered the top pancake with margarine, then reached for the honey spindle. Drizzling thick honey over his plate, he looked up at his daughter as if he expected her to accept the turn of events that had knocked her for such an emotional loop.

"You know with what. Brynnie. My half sisters. The whole ball of wax, for crying out loud. It's… Well, come on, Dad, it's just…well, *bizarre,* for lack of a better word." She shook her head, then winced as she poured them each a cup of coffee. After setting the glass pot back in the coffeemaker, she settled into the empty chair across from him.

"Not bizarre, honey. It's right."

"Right?"

"For the first time in a lot of years, I…I feel free 'cause I'm not livin' a lie." Blue eyes met hers from across the table. "Your mother was a fine woman—I won't take that away from her—but we weren't happy together. Hadn't been for a long time."

"I know." A dull pain settled in her heart. She'd felt the tension between her parents, known that theirs wasn't a marriage made in heaven, but still, they had been married and Bliss, though she hated to admit it, still believed in "till death us do part."

"She's gone, honey," her father said. "I would never have divorced her, you know."

"Only cheated on her."

He looked down and sliced his hotcakes with the side of his fork. "Guess I can't expect you to understand."

"I'm trying, Dad," she said, unable to hide the emotion in her words. "Believe me, I'm trying." Resting her elbows on the table, she cradled her cup in two hands. Through the paned windows she could see the barn and pastures. White-faced Hereford cattle mingled with Black Angus as they grazed on grass sparkling with morning dew.

The silence stretched between them, with only the ticking of the clock, the low of cattle, the rumble of a tractor's engine in the distance and an excited yip from Oscar as he explored his new surroundings, breaking the uneasy quietude.

John washed down a bite of pancake with a swallow of coffee. "Since I had the heart attack and looked the Grim Reaper square in his black eyes, I've decided to do exactly what I want with the few years I have left."

"And that includes marrying this...this Brynnie woman."

"Believe it or not, Bliss, she's got a heart of gold."

"And a string of ex-husbands long enough to—"

"She made some bad choices, I know. So did I. And if it's any comfort to you, I never ran around with another woman while I was married to your mother."

"Just Brynnie." Bliss couldn't hide the bitterness in her voice.

"Yes."

"Isn't she enough?"

He shoved his half-eaten breakfast aside and skewered his daughter with a look of sheer determination. "I know you don't approve. Can't blame you. But no one was hurt."

"What about Mom?"

"You mother and I... We had an arrangement."

"An *arrangement?*" Bliss sputtered, choking on a mouthful of coffee. "It's called marriage, Dad, and one of the vows a person takes when they get married is fidelity. To be faithful. It doesn't seem a lot to ask." She couldn't help the rising tone of her voice as if she were on the earth solely to defend Margaret Cawthorne's honor. Everything she believed in was being tested and though she was trying, really trying to understand, she was having difficulty. *Rise above it; it's not a big deal, Mom's gone,* her mind argued with the loyalty that burned bright in her heart and the belief that love lasted a lifetime.

Her father reached across the scarred maple table and

took her hand in his rough, callused fingers. "I'm sorry, Bliss, really. I never wanted to hurt anyone. Not you. Not Margaret. Not Brynnie. Seems it's all I do." He frowned, patted the back of her hand and picked up his fork again. "But now it's time to heal, to make some peace, to recognize the family that I have." His lips pinched together. "I wanted you to be a part of it, to meet your sisters, to find out about them. This is a chance for all of us to finally be a family."

"Of sorts."

"Yes. Of sorts."

Dear God, why did she feel like a heel? Someone had to make him face the truth. Now was one of the times she wished she really did have a sister or brother with whom she could share the burden of her father's problems. But she did have sisters, didn't she? Two half-sisters. Certainly they would add up to a whole one— Oh, for the love of Pete, this was making her crazy.

The sound of a truck's engine rumbled through the air, and from the porch Oscar gave an excited "woof." Bliss recognized the pickup from the day before and her heart did a little lurch when she spied Mason behind the wheel.

"Now what?" her father grumbled, looking over his shoulder and squinting against the sun rising over the hills.

"Trouble," Bliss predicted.

"Young upstart pup, Lafferty. Always pushing." He eyed Bliss speculatively. "You'd think with all he owns, he'd give up on this place." His jaw hardened slightly and his eyes thinned in anger. "Then again, maybe it's not the place that's got him so interested. Maybe it's you."

"I don't think so." Bliss remembered how easily Mason had left her ten years before, but couldn't drag her gaze away from Mason as he stepped out of the truck. Tall, lanky, hard-edged, with a walk that bordered on a swagger, he approached the front door. Tinted sunglasses shaded his eyes and a scowl etched deep grooves over eyebrows slammed together.

"I'll get rid of him," she said, wiping her hands on a dish towel and telling herself that she had the guts to face him.

"No way. He's as sticky as hot tar."

Bliss scraped her chair back and hurried to the front hallway just as he knocked. Yanking open the door, she faced him across the threshold and ignored the stupid, wild knocking of her heart.

A slow-growing smile wiped the grim expression from his face. "Mornin', Bliss."

"Hi." Dear Lord, was that her pulse jumping in her neck, visible in the V neckline of her T-shirt? Great! What a fool she was. A naive, stupid fool. She and Mason had been in love once, or maybe it was even puppy love, but what they had shared, that hot flirtation, was long dead. Yet she couldn't help the fluttering of her pulse or the urge to swallow against a suddenly dry throat. "Do you make it your primary objective in life these days to harass people?"

"Only a few special ones," he teased and she fought the urge to smile.

"Like Dad."

"Or you." He pocketed the sunglasses and stared at Bliss with eyes that were as seductive as cool water in a blistering desert at high noon.

"Wonderful." She managed a bit of sarcasm.

"Look, I just want to talk to your father."

"You talked to him yesterday."

"I know, but I'd like to finish the conversation."

"It's finished, Lafferty. Take a hint."

"I forgot to give him the offer." He glanced over her shoulder. "Is John around?"

"You bet I'm around," John answered, walking in his stocking feet along the dusty patina of the hardwood floor. "What is it you're lookin' for—as if I didn't know?" He glanced at his daughter and scowled. "I already told you. I ain't sellin'. No matter what the price."

Bliss lifted a lofty brow, encouraging Mason, if he had the guts, to draw her father into a battle he would surely lose.

Mason leaned a shoulder against the doorjamb.

"Since you and Brynnie are going to tie the knot, I thought you might want to retire, see a little of the world with your new bride, take it easy."

"You mean the old stud should be put out to pasture?" With a hoarse laugh and a scrape of his fingers against his empty shirt pocket where he searched by habit for a non-existent pack of cigarettes, Bliss's father shook his head. "One measly little heart attack isn't gonna scare me away from doin' what I want." He rapped his knuckles against his chest. "The old ticker's just fine and I'm gonna run this ranch like I always have." Again his fingers scrabbled into his pocket and he frowned when he realized that his cigarettes were gone, as his doctor had insisted he give up smoking after the heart attack. Bliss suspected that he still sneaked a puff now and again along with his chew, but she'd never caught him with a cigarette. Not that she could stop him from smoking. No one had ever been able to tell John Cawthorne how to live his life.

Mason reached into his back pocket and drew out a long envelope that he slapped into John's hand. "I think you'd better talk to Brynnie about this. In the meantime, here's a formal offer—for the acres in your name."

"In my name?" John questioned.

"Fair price. Good terms. Think about it." Mason slipped his sunglasses onto the bridge of his nose.

"Don't need to," her father insisted, but he didn't toss the envelope back at Mason as Bliss had expected. Instead, his bony fingers clamped over the manila packet.

Mason's gaze centered on Bliss. "I'll see you later," he said through lips that barely moved as he glared through his sunglasses, and Bliss had trouble drawing a breath.

John wagged the envelope at Mason. "Just remember that a few years back we had a deal."

"A deal?" Bliss repeated.

"That's right. Signed, sealed and delivered." Her father's smile was shrewd and self-serving and Bliss felt a sliver of dread enter her heart.

"I haven't forgotten." Mason's shoulders tightened. The skin over his face seemed to grow taut and his gaze, behind his tinted lenses held hers briefly before he turned and strode back to his truck.

Oscar bounded along behind him and Mason paused long enough to scratch the dog between his shoulders before climbing into the cab of his Ford.

"Pushy S.O.B.," John grumbled as the pickup tore down the lane. He was already opening the envelope, anxious to explore its contents, which surprised Bliss. For someone who was so vocally against selling the ranch—especially to Mason—John Cawthorne was certainly interested in the bottom line. But then, he always had been. That was how he'd made his money.

Scanning the pages, he walked into the living room, picked up his reading glasses from the fireplace mantel, plopped them on the end of his nose and then settled into his favorite battered recliner.

"You know why he's back in town, I suppose?"

"Other than to try and talk you into selling?" she bantered back.

"Seems he's decided to settle down here, be closer to

his kid." He glanced up, looking over the tops of his lenses. "Can't fault him for that, I suppose."

"No."

"But rumor has it he's trying to get back with his ex-wife. You remember her? Terri?"

How could she ever forget? "Of course, I remember."

"Good." He looked back to the pages again.

Why it should bother her that Mason was seeing Terri, she didn't understand, but the old wounds in her heart seemed to reopen all over again. Straightening a hurricane lantern sitting on the mantel, she said, "Okay, so what was this business about a deal between you two? As far as I knew, you didn't want anything to do with him."

"Still don't." Her father hesitated a fraction. "I had to do something to get him out of town. So I paid his medical bills and gave him the old heave-ho."

"Then he left to marry Terri Fremont," she said, feeling an odd sensation that something else in the past wasn't what she'd thought it was. But that wasn't much of a surprise, was it? Hadn't her entire life been a lie?

"I just gave him some extra incentive." He cleared his throat. "It wasn't too hard to figure out what was going on between the two of you and it worried me because I knew about the Fremont girl. So...I upped the ante a little, offered him a deal and he rose to the bait like a brook trout to a salmon fly."

"No—"

His lips pursed in frustration. "It was for your own good, Bliss. That's why I did it. Remember, he already had a baby on the way."

Bliss rested her hands on the back of the couch. "You shouldn't have gotten involved."

"He needed surgery on that arm of his and his kid needed a father."

"You're a fine one to talk," she sputtered. Then, seeing the pain in his eyes, she wished she could take the words back.

"Is that what you think?"

"Yes," she admitted, not wanting to hurt him, but knowing that the lies would stop with her. "You fathered *two* children with women you didn't marry."

"And I didn't want to see anyone, even a snake like Lafferty, make the same mistakes I did."

"But—"

"No buts, Blissie," he said, signifying that the conversation, as far as he was concerned, was over. He tilted his head to ensure that his bifocals were in the right position for reading. "Now, what have we got here?"

Bliss couldn't believe her ears. It was as if her father would use any means possible to get his way. She'd always known he was stubborn and determined, but this side of him was new to her and she wasn't sure she liked it very much.

"You know, for a man who swears up and down that he's not interested in selling this place, it's odd that you can't put down that offer." Bliss swatted at a cobweb that floated between the old blinds on the window and the ceiling.

"Just thought I'd see what Lafferty thinks the place is worth." With practiced eyes he skimmed the printed text and his eyebrows jammed together in concentration. "There's somethin' wrong here. The figures don't add up and... What in thunder? Is he out of his mind? This—" he snapped the crisp pages "—this is only for the north half of the property. I thought he wanted the whole place."

"Didn't you say that part of the ranch was in Brynnie's name?"

Every muscle in John's body tensed. His gaze shot up to hers. "What do you mean?"

"Well, if he wanted the whole ranch, he'd have to deal with her for her part."

"For the love of—" John scowled, rubbing the edge of the documents against the stubble of his chin and as he squinted, Bliss could almost see the wheels turning in his mind. "Brynnie's not like your mother, Bliss," he said, though his voice lacked conviction. "She wouldn't expect me to give up what I love."

"I'm not suggesting anything of the sort. And Mom would never—"

"Unless she got herself conned into it." Her father snapped the leg support of the recliner into place and climbed to his feet. Wadding the offer in his fist, he headed for the den. "I think I'd better call my lawyer."

"Why?"

"Just to make sure Lafferty doesn't try to pull a fast one."

"Damn it all to hell," Mason grumbled, stomping on the brakes as his pickup slid to a stop beside the carriage house of an old Victorian home in the center of town. Four stories counting the basement, painted gray and trimmed in white gingerbread with black shutters, the mansion had been divided into separate apartments sometime between the 1920s and now. There were two other units in the old carriage house as well, and for the next few months Mason would call the upper story of that smaller building home.

Climbing out of the cab, he spied Tiffany Santini, the widow who owned the place, clipping a few rosebuds from the garden. Tall, with dark hair and eyes, she was pleasant and pretty, the kind of woman who took to mothering like a duck to water. Mason didn't know much about her, but he liked the way she dealt with her kids—a teenage boy and a girl of three or four.

He waved and she smiled, hoisting a gloved hand as her little girl chased a black cat through the rhododendrons flanking the back porch.

Mason had decided to rent while he was negotiating for a ranch of his own and had chosen this complex over more modern units because he felt more at home in this charming older place, which had a backyard with a play structure that Dee Dee could use whenever she came over.

He walked up the outside stairs, unlocked the door and stepped into his living room. It was sparsely furnished with only the bare essentials. The hardwood floors were begging for throw rugs and the stark walls could have used more than a splash or two of color. But all that would come later—once he'd moved into a permanent place.

At Cawthorne Acres.

For the first time he wondered if his insisting on buying old John out was wise. True, Brynnie had come to him and he'd jumped at the chance to own a spread he'd fallen in love with as a kid, but now, with the old man's heart condition and Bliss thrown into the picture, he wasn't so sure that he'd made the right decision.

What was the old saying? Buy in Haste, Regret at Leisure. That was it. He hoped it didn't apply in his case.

In the kitchen he tossed his keys on the counter and reached for a glass. Pouring himself a stiff shot of bourbon, he tried to erase Bliss and the complications of dealing with her and her father from his mind. But it didn't work. Ever since seeing her yesterday afternoon and again this morning, he'd thought of her—even made an excuse to give Cawthorne his offer in person so that he could see her again.

Bliss Cawthorne, all grown up. He remembered her as

she had been ten years earlier with honey-blond hair and eyes as blue as cornflowers. She'd been a smart mouth at the time, a big-city girl who was pretty and damned well knew it. A dusting of freckles had bridged her nose and she'd been tanned all over from hours of swimming in the river.

Mason had been working for old man Cawthorne, and although all the other hired hands had warned him that the boss's daughter was off-limits, he hadn't been able to keep himself away. Which was where all the trouble had begun and ended.

He tossed back a long swallow of his drink and felt the alcohol burn a welcome path down his throat. Why did he torture himself with thoughts of her? Why couldn't he think of her as nothing more than a love affair gone sour?

Because you're a fool, Lafferty. You always have been, where that woman is concerned.

He finished his drink in another gulp and wiped his mouth with the back of his hand. Ten years. It had been ten years since he'd seen her. A decade of telling himself she meant nothing to him, but then, with one sidelong glance from her innocently seductive eyes, he'd come undone and last night, with the hot breath of a wind blowing the curtains in his room, he hadn't slept, but had envisioned Bliss's face as he'd stared through the window at the moon.

Now he remembered in vivid detail her expression when she'd answered the door. For a second he'd seen the glimmer of happiness in her eyes but it had been quickly hidden by a facade of anger.

Why the hell did it matter what she thought? She was just one woman, and John Cawthorne's daughter to boot.

"Idiot," he growled, contemplating another drink before screwing the cap on the bourbon bottle. He jammed the bottle back into the cupboard and slammed the door. Bliss.

Gorgeous, sophisticated and intriguing Bliss Cawthorne. Why hadn't she married, had a dozen kids and gotten fat? Why did she still attract him after all these years, all these blasted long, lonely years? "Grow up, Lafferty," he chided. He'd learned long ago not to entrust his heart to a woman. Any woman. Especially Bliss Cawthorne.

Besides, the old man was right. Inadvertently, Mason had nearly killed her years before. And there was more to it than that. He and Cawthorne had made a deal. A pact practically signed in Bliss's blood.

So cancel it, an inner voice suggested and he felt a grim smile tug at the corners of his mouth. He'd always believed in honoring his bargains, but Cawthorne had never played fair. So, technically, the deal was null and void.

Bliss, if she'd have him, was his for the taking.

He had only to figure out if he wanted her and for how long.

Chapter Four

"See that sorrel mare?" John Cawthorne leaned against
the top rail of the fence and pointed a gnarled finger at a
small herd of horses in the north pasture. The animals
grazed lazily, twitching their tails at flies while their ears
flicked with each shift of the wind.

"She's gorgeous." Bliss watched as the red mare's nose
lifted and her nostrils flared slightly, as if she'd somehow
divined that she was the center of attention.

"I want you to have her."

"What?"

"That's right. She's yours."

"But I live in Seattle, Dad. In a condominium that's
hardly big enough for Oscar and me." Bliss hazarded a
smile. "Trust me, the horse won't fit."

He chuckled. "I know, I know, but I reckon, now that
your mom's gone, you'll be spending more time down here
with your old man."

"And my stepmother." The words still stuck in Bliss's throat though she was trying, damn it, to accept this new and, she still thought, ludicrous situation.

"And hopefully, your sisters."

"If—and it's a pretty big if, Dad—I'm interested and they're willing to meet me halfway. What're the chances?"

"I don't know," he admitted, clearing his throat. "I just think it's all worth it. I'd hate for you—or them, for that matter—to miss out on getting to know each other."

"We might fight like cats and dogs."

"You might. Then again…"

She plucked a piece of clover from a clump near the fence post and twirled the purple bloom in her fingers. "Okay, okay, point well taken. Tell me about them."

"Well…" He stared off across the fields to a distance only he could see. "You know that Tiffany's older than you. She's a widow now. Works part-time as a secretary at an insurance agency in town. She's got a son Stephen— my oldest grandkid, mind you—almost fourteen and hell on wheels, the way everyone in town says. Then there's that cute button of a daughter of hers who's around three. My only granddaughter, so far."

He looked away quickly, as if bothered by the conversation, and Bliss fought back a feeling of having the rug pulled out from under her. She'd always thought that she would be the one to give her parents grandchildren—when the time came. As the years passed and her friends married and started families of their own, she'd heard her own biological clock ticking away.

"After her husband died, Tiffany moved down here to be close to her grandmother—you've heard of Octavia— Octavia Nesbitt?"

Bliss nodded. Who hadn't heard of Bittersweet's most prominent and flamboyant citizen? Octavia had inherited the Reed Estate years before, as she'd been nursemaid and caretaker of Bittersweet's oldest and most wealthy citizen. When Cranston Reed had died, he'd left his fortune to the widow Nesbitt.

"Well, when Tiffany's husband, Philip, died a few months back, she packed her kids into a U-Haul truck and drove south from Portland. She moved into an old house her husband had bought about a year back—it's been cut up into apartments that she rents out for a little extra money."

Bliss folded her arms over the top rail of the fence and watched spindly-legged colts frolicking beside their docile mothers. "So how is Tiffany with you?"

His eyebrows lifted and he bent down to pluck a long blade of dry grass from the ground. "Not great. In fact, she won't talk to me."

No big surprise there. "Do you blame her?"

He rubbed his chin. "Guess not. She didn't know much about me or that I was even alive for a long, long time."

"What?" Bliss couldn't believe her ears, then mentally kicked herself for being so naive. Hadn't she been hood-winked all her life? Why not Tiffany, as well?

"Her mother, Rose, finally told her the truth, I guess, but I didn't try to get in touch with her until a couple of months ago, after your mother passed on."

"Oh."

"Anyway, I tried to call her, you know, to break the ice, but she hung up before I could say anything other than my name." He placed the piece of grass between his teeth. "Guess she's a little ticked. As I said, Tiffany's mother told her that her father was dead, had died before they could get married—and then she did a quick reversal." He hes-itated, his thinning hair ruffling in the breeze. "Since I never showed any interest until recently...well, it's been hard for her.''

"Beyond hard," Bliss agreed, feeling a tiny pang of pity for the older half-sister she'd never met. "If I were her, I don't know if I'd ever forgive you."

He sighed. "You're having trouble now because I'm marrying Brynnie."

That much was true, but Bliss didn't want to think about it. Not now. She hardly dared ask her next question, but decided there was no time like the present. "So what about Brynnie's daughter. Katie? What does she think?"

"That's another story," he admitted. "Katie, too, just found out. Her mother told her a couple of weeks back that she wasn't Hal Kinkaid's daughter."

Bliss froze. "Wait a minute. Are telling me that Brynnie passed Katie off as—"

John lifted a hand. "She had no choice. I went along with it."

"But—"

"It was probably a mistake."

"One of many," Bliss whispered, wondering how deep were the lies that her father had perpetuated over the years. Her head spun with all this new information about a family she hadn't suspected existed.

"I know." He seemed suddenly tired and older than his years. "I've done a lot of damage. To you. To your mother. To the other women in my life. But I'm going to change all that by marrying Brynnie and claiming Tiffany and Katie as my daughters. If they accept me, I'll be a happy man. If they don't, well, I guess I'll just have to understand."

As if he could. No one had ever called John Cawthorne understanding. "I wish I could tell you that everything will turn out fine, Dad, but I'm not sure that's possible."

"It's all right." Her father managed a watery smile.

"I've given you a lot to think about. Maybe too much. But I've decided to finally live up to my responsibilities as well as make the most of the few years I've got left." A hawk circled lazily overhead, its shadow passing over the ground as John brushed an ant from the fence post. "Somehow I'm gonna make peace with my daughters and grandchildren."

"Are there more than Tiffany's two kids?" Bliss asked.

He glanced up sharply. "Katie's got a ten-year-old. Josh."

"So she's married?"

"No." He shook his head. "The guy left her pregnant and she wanted the baby, so she kept him."

"Does this never end?" she wondered aloud. Both her half sisters had children and she, who had always thought herself the mothering kind, had none, nor a husband or any prospects of one. Her mind wandered to Mason and she scoffed at herself. If Mason were the last man on earth, she wouldn't want him to father her child. She knew his true colors. He'd shown them once before and they were ugly and oh, so painful. Even now, ten years later, she still experienced a little burn in her heart when she thought of him and how deeply he had deceived her. *Bastard,* she thought unkindly, then told herself it didn't matter. Mason Lafferty was nothing to her.

"Tell me about Brynnie's other children," Bliss said, forcing her thoughts from Mason. She rubbed her hand across the top rail and a sliver pricked her finger.

"Three boys. Jarrod, the oldest, and the twins, Trevor and Nathan. Brynnie had her hands full with those three and little Katie, let me tell you." He grinned slightly as he stared at the mare, and not for the first time in her life Bliss wondered if John Cawthorne missed having sons, a boy to carry on his name. He nodded toward the mare. "You'll like riding Fire Cracker."

"Fire Cracker?" She plucked at the sliver with the fingernails of her other hand and heard a train rattling on far-off tracks.

Her father laughed. "Fire Cracker looks docile enough now, I suppose, but she's got a little bit of the devil in her." He slid his daughter a kind glance. "Like someone else I know."

Bliss rolled her eyes. "That was high school, Dad. I'm pure as the driven snow these days."

"Not if you're any daughter of mine," he said and slapped the top of the fence. "I'd better go see about the tractor. Seems to have a problem with the clutch."

"Just take it easy, okay?"

He waved off her concerns as she watched him walk back to the equipment garage, a tall shed of sorts where tractors, plows, harrows, bailers and God-only-knew-what-else were stored. As he disappeared into the interior, Bliss bit her lip. John Cawthorne was and always would be her father. A man she'd been able to depend upon. A man she loved.

A man who had lied over and over again. A man who, until recently, had led a secret life. A man she'd trusted.

She wondered if she ever would again.

Even though she was disgusted that he'd been such a liar as well as a cheat, she'd somehow ended up with a couple of sisters. How many times had she, as an adolescent, wished and prayed for a close sibling, someone to share dreams and worries with, a friend to shop and gossip with, another teenager who was as confused as she when she tried to understand the incomprehensible world of adults? Now, as a woman, wouldn't she love a new companion, another person who understood her hopes, dreams, ambitions, and concerns? Someone closer than a friend, a woman bound to her by blood?

Two, she reminded herself. Two women bound to her by blood.

But would either Tiffany or Katie want anything to do with her? Did she really want them to? She frowned as she finally managed to work the sliver free from her fingertip.

There was only one way to find out. Bliss would have to take the initiative and meet both her half sisters, whether they wanted anything to do with her or not.

Mason drummed his fingers on his desk in his den, which was really the second bedroom of his apartment. Tonight the room with its glowing computer monitor seemed empty. Hollow. Like his own damned soul.

It had been his night to see Dee Dee, but Terri had come up with another excuse to keep him from his daughter. Only half a mile away and it might as well be half a continent.

Just like Bliss—so near but so damned far. Completely out of reach.

"Where she should be," he reminded himself as he refocused on the illuminated screen, but try as he might, he couldn't concentrate on the spreadsheet for his ranch in Montana. Tonight he didn't give a damn. The numbers didn't mean anything to him now. Nothing did. Not when his daughter was being kept from him.

Or when Bliss Cawthorne was less than twenty minutes away.

"Stop it," he growled at himself and blinked to clear his head.

Restless by nature, he could never sit for long and had always worked off his excess energy in physical labor. But this evening had been different.

After his telephone conversation with Terri, he'd kicked

off his boots and jeans, donned sweats and running shoes and jogged six miles across hilly terrain. He'd returned sweating and overheated, his blood pounding, and had taken a cold shower, letting the needles of water spray against his skin as he'd rested his head against the tiles and willed his thoughts away from Bliss.

So what if she was close by? So what if she was still as intriguing as ever? So what if he still wanted her so badly he felt himself stiffen at the thought of her? She was still John Cawthorne's daughter and still off-limits. Way off-limits. He had enough problems in his life without the complication of a woman—especially that one.

Now, as he sat in his boxer shorts, a half-drunk bottle of beer in one hand, he stared at the ledgers on the computer screen and wondered how his life had careened so far out of control.

Oh, come on, Lafferty; it's your fault. You're the one who sent her out riding in that storm ten years ago, you're the one who took her old man's money and you're the one who got Terri pregnant. If your life's on an unwanted path, you've got no one to blame but yourself.

He took draft from his long-necked bottle. Ever since seeing Bliss again, he'd been distracted. Half-a-dozen times he'd reached for the phone to dial her number, only to stop before he picked up the receiver. Why call her? What could he say? The old torment gnawed at his soul. *"You nearly killed her."*

He snapped off the toggle switch, felt a sense of satisfaction as the screen faded, and took another long swallow. He remembered the first time he'd seen her as if it had been yesterday.

She'd been the boss's daughter, a pretty girl of nearly eighteen, who had come to spend a few weeks on her old man's ranch. He'd been twenty-four at the time, old enough to know better, young enough not to give a damn.

At first he'd wanted nothing to do with Cawthorne's daughter, or so he'd tried to convince himself. She'd been trilingual, for Pete's sake, danced ballet, rode polo ponies, played tennis, sailed, and was rumored to have a portfolio of investments that would have made a stockbroker's mouth water. In short, she hadn't been his kind of woman. No way. No how.

But she'd been fascinating. No doubt about it. And it hadn't just been her beauty. No, there was something more, something deeper that he'd sensed in her; and whatever that female essence had been, it had scared him. It had scared the hell out of him.

With eyes as blue as a mountain lake, cheekbones that a model would have killed for, pouty lips and an easy smile, she had caused most of the men who had worked for her father to think about risking their employment for a few hours alone with her. Including Mason.

Now he damned himself for being two times a fool, but the truth of the matter was that Bliss Cawthorne, curse her sexy smile and twinkling eyes, had gotten to him all over again.

It had taken less than ten minutes.

So what're you gonna do about it, Lafferty? his mind taunted as he peeled the label from his beer bottle.

There was only one safe answer—the same as it had always been. Stay away from the woman.

Trouble was, Mason wasn't known to take the safe path.

"So this is Bliss!" Brynnie Anderson-Smith-McBaine-Kinkaid-Perez breezed into the Cawthorne house in a cloud of sweet perfume laced with cigarette smoke. Her hair was a deep red beginning to streak with gray, her face tanned, her lips colored peach, her eyelids shaded in a soft pewter color. She wore jeans a size too tight and a white T-shirt that showed off her enviable chest. "Well, John, you're right again. She's beautiful." Brynnie winked at Bliss and extended a beringed work-roughened hand. "I've heard a lot about you. All good, mind you, all good."

"Same here," Bliss said, though what she'd found out about this woman had been recent and she wasn't holding her breath that the story her father gave her was the entire truth. Besides, not only had Brynnie wed more than her share of husbands, but she'd been a married man's lover. That thought was sour, no matter how hard Bliss tried to swallow it.

John captured Brynnie in a bear hug, and with his arm still slung over her shoulders, led them all through the kitchen and onto the back porch. A sweating pitcher of iced tea and several glasses were waiting on the picnic table.

"Looks like you were expecting me," Brynnie said.

"All Bliss's doin'."

"Thoughtful."

"Thanks." Bliss didn't know what to say. This was, after all, the woman with whom her father had been involved in an affair, the woman who had knowingly cheated on Margaret Cawthorne, the woman who had gotten pregnant with John's child while he was married.

Forcing a smile she didn't feel, Bliss told herself that discretion, if she could find it, was the better part of valor. Her mother was dead, had known of the affair and dealt with it in her own way. Somehow Bliss should do the same. But as she poured the tea into glasses, watching the slices of lemon dance, she felt a stinging loss, a pain deep in her heart, and she nearly slopped tea onto the table.

They sat in deck chairs in the shade of a larch tree. A breeze moved across the rolling acres, stirring the leaves and bending the grass of a field of hay not yet mown. The sound of sprinklers jetting water to irrigate the surrounding pastures vied with the distant hum of traffic far off on the highway.

"I know this is hard for you," Brynnie ventured as she set her glass on the table. Her fingernails were long, squared off and matched the peach gloss of her lips.

"Very."

"It's hard on everyone," John said thoughtfully, a hint of regret in his voice.

"Well, here goes." Brynnie looked Bliss straight in the eye. "Look, honey, I'm not proud of everything I've done in my life. Lord knows, I've made more than my share of mistakes and I'll probably make a few more before they bury me.

"Gettin' involved with your dad was inevitable, believe me, but our timing was always wrong. Well, maybe there never could have been a good time. But you have to believe me when I tell you that I never meant to hurt your ma."

Bliss didn't say anything. Her throat was too tight and her eyes stung with unshed tears.

"From all I've heard, she was a good woman. Deserved better." Brynnie's brown eyes shadowed with a pain she'd borne for years, but still, Bliss wasn't completely moved.

"She deserved the best," Bliss said. She slashed a glance at her father and noticed the hardening of his jaw, the determined set of his chin. Her mother had always said he was a stubborn man.

"I'm making no excuses, Bliss. Never claimed to be a knight in shining armor. Sure, I've made my share of mistakes just like Brynnie said. But then what man, or woman for that matter, hasn't?"

Bliss cast a mental glance at her own fractured love-life. Her first and, really, only love had been Mason Lafferty, and surely that relationship had been doomed from the start. With trembling hands, she lifted her glass and took a sip of tea. The cool liquid slid down her throat as she pushed Mason from her mind and concentrated on her father who had taken out his pocketknife and was avoiding her gaze as he cleaned his fingernails with a sharp blade.

"Unfortunate as it is, Blissie, your ma's gone now and Brynnie's divorced. Seems as if we're finally gettin' a break and this time we're gonna grab it. It's about time."

"Amen," Brynnie said and reached over to pat John's hand. Her rings sparkled in the sunlight and Bliss couldn't help but wonder how many of the jeweled bands had been given to her on her various wedding days by her ex-husbands and which, if any, had been gifts from her secret lover.

Brynnie's smile seemed genuine and for the first time Bliss caught a glimmer of what her father saw in a woman who was so unlike her socially upstanding and rigid mother. Brynnie seemed like someone who could roll with the punches and always land on her feet. Nonjudgmental. No false sense of pride. No matter what challenges life tossed this woman's way, Bliss guessed that Brynnie handled them and managed to end up grinning.

"I, uh, I hope you're happy," Bliss said, more for the sake of conversation than from conviction. In truth, hadn't everyone suffered enough? Reluctantly she conceded her father his point. It was time to make a stand, to recognize his other daughters, to find a place for all his family. She just wasn't sure that she could be a part of it.

"We will be happy, won't we, darlin'?" Her father nodded and his mouth turned up at the corners.

"Absolutely. That's all there is to life, isn't it? Being happy." Brynnie appeared to relax a little, although she avoided looking directly into John's eyes.

"As long as you don't hurt anyone in the process," Bliss interjected.

"Never intend to." John was adamant.

"Never," Brynnie agreed, clearing her throat.

Bliss couldn't remember when she'd been more uncomfortable. She took another long swallow of the tea and watched several honey bees flit from one opening rose blossom to the next. In the lacy branches above them a squirrel scolded noisily, and off in the distance a horse's whinny sounded over the rumble of a tractor chugging through the fields.

"You know, there's someone who's pretty darned anxious to meet you." Brynnie reached into a worn suede bag and pulled out a pack of cigarettes. "Do you mind?" she asked, and Bliss shook her head. "Good. I know it's a nasty habit and I should quit, but... Oh, well, what can I say? I just love to smoke." She shook out a long white filter tip, lit up and waved out her match. "My daughter, Katie, is dying to talk to you."

"Is she?" Bliss's stomach knotted. This was what she wanted, wasn't it? To see her half sister, even if it meant coming face-to-face with the fact that her father had been unfaithful to her mother. She found a little bit of pride deep in her own innards and managed to force some starch into her backbone. "I'd like to meet her, too."

The minute the words were out, Bliss regretted them. This was all happening way too fast. She sensed that she'd just hopped aboard an emotional freight train that was suddenly careening out of control.

"Good." Brynnie's grin was infectious. "I'll let her know and we'll set something up. If you're lucky you'll get to know her son Josh, as well." Brynnie's eyes sparkled. "My first and only grandchild so far, though I'm counting on a dozen more." She sighed and tapped ash onto the lawn. "I'm afraid that Josh, devil that he is, has got Grandma's heart twisted around his little finger."

"Several times," John said with a chuckle as the telephone rang.

"I'll get it," Bliss said, starting to stand, but her father, already on his feet, waved her back to her chair.

"Stay put. I'm expecting a call."

As she watched Bliss's father close the screen door behind him, Brynnie drummed her fingers nervously on the armrest of her plastic deck chair. "I worry about him, you know," she admitted, then dragged hard on her cigarette. "He makes light of that heart attack, but you can't convince me it was nothing. If it wasn't, he wouldn't have had to suffer through that god-awful surgery." She eyed the glowing end of her cigarette, then frowned regretfully. "I'll have to give these up," she decided, her brow furrowing. "I hate to, but I can't have them around the house tempting him." She slid Bliss a conspiring glance. "I guess I'll have to sneak one now and again. Just because I'm gonna get married, I can't give up all my vices." She bit anxiously on the corner of her lip. "This place...all the worries and work here, it's too much for him, don't you think?"

"I guess so. But he loves it."

"Lord, don't I know? But his health is the main thing, my big worry. He can't expect to put in fifteen- or even ten-hour days around here."

"No..." Bliss agreed, wondering where the conversation was leading.

"He's just got to sell." She took another nervous puff.

Bliss laughed. "I thought you knew him better than that."

"He just needs to be convinced." Brynnie licked her lips. "I guess that's my job. Uh-oh, now who's riling him up?'' she asked as John's voice filtered through the screen door.

"Dammit!" The receiver crashed into its cradle and the door was flung open so hard it banged against the house. "What the hell's going on?" John demanded.

"Now, honey," Brynnie said as she squashed her cigarette in the grass with the sole of her sandal.

"I can't believe you went behind my back," he charged.

"Oh, Lordy."

"So it's true!"

"John, just listen," Brynnie placated.

"To what?" Bliss was missing something—something important.

"I got off the phone with my attorney and he's been checking some things out with the county—the deeds and titles and records." Her father's expression was thunderous and he looked more like the hard-driven man she'd known as a girl. "It seems that my fiancée here has been doing some business that I didn't know anything about."

"I can explain," Brynnie said.

"You *sold* my ranch to Lafferty."

"My half," she said, standing and lifting a reddish eyebrow that dared him to argue the point. "And I'd do it again. Like that!" She snapped her fingers.

"Wait a minute," Bliss interjected. "I don't understand."

"It's simple. I deeded over part of the ranch to Brynnie for her and Katie—security if anything happened to me—and now I find out that she sold her parcel to Lafferty."

Bliss didn't move.

"John, now, don't get upset," Brynnie suggested.

"I'm already upset. Way past it, in fact. I think it's time you told me what the hell's goin' on." His face was a mask of raw anger, his lips tight over his teeth.

"I—I had to do something. While you were in Seattle, in a hospital bed because of your heart, I had a lot of time to think," Brynnie began, her fingers nervously scratching her throat. "Oh, Lord, I need another cigarette."

"Just finish." John scowled darkly, as if he were already reading his fiancée's mind.

"All right, I will. The truth of the matter is that I've spent too many years waiting for you as it is and I don't want to lose you. That heart attack scared me and I thought, well, I knew that you'd come back here and work yourself to death, so I...I knew that Mason was moving back here to be closer to his daughter. He'd always been interested in the place, so I called him up and sold my part of the ranch to him."

"Just like that," he challenged.

"Just like that." Brynnie didn't back down.

"I expected as much from him, but not from you, Brynnie. Never you. He hornswoggled you, didn't he?"

Brynnie swallowed back the tears in her throat. "No, John," she said. "This was all my idea."

John lowered himself onto a bench pushed up against the house. "But you know how much this place means to me."

"I'm hoping I mean more," Brynnie said, her chin trembling as she dabbed at her eyes with her fingertips.

John shook his head and Bliss decided they needed to be alone to sort this all out. "I need to drive into town," she said, "for some supplies. I'm setting up an office in the den and this looks like a good time. You two need to talk. Alone."

"No, please," Brynnie said. "Don't run off, we'll work this out—"

Bliss smiled and lied through her teeth. "I'm sure. Listen, it was great to finally meet you, but, really, I've got to

go. Bye, Dad." With a wave, she hurried into the house
and grabbed her purse.

   She was going to drive into town, all right, but her trip
had nothing to do with supplies. Nope. She was going to
track Mason Lafferty down and get the straight story.

   If the man was capable of anything other than lies.

Chapter Five

Bliss jammed on the parking brake in the shade of an
ancient oak tree and as the engine of her Mustang cooled,
she tapped her fingers on the steering wheel. Some of her
anger should have dissipated during the drive into town,
but it hadn't and even though she took the time to call the
phone company and locate Mason's apartment, here in this
huge Victorian manor, she was still ready to read him the
riot act.

Who was he to think that he could deal with Brynnie
behind her father's back? Why in the world was he so interested in the ranch? For once John Cawthorne was right.
There were dozens of other ranches Mason could purchase;
all he had to do was talk to a real-estate agent or two.

"Bastard," she muttered as she climbed out of the car
and slammed the door shut. She strode up the front walk,
past a rose garden and a sign that advertised an apartment

for rent. On the front porch, she punched the bell and heard the peal of melodic chimes.

Footsteps scurried inside the house and within seconds a little girl of about three yanked open the door. "Mommy," she called over her shoulder just as a woman with her black hair clipped into a makeshift French braid appeared. She was wiping her hands on a towel and smiled when she saw Bliss.

"Just a second." With a disapproving look at the little curly-haired imp, she said, "Christina, you know better than to open the door without me."

"But—"

"We'll talk about it later." She picked up the pouting child, balanced her on a hip and turned all of her attention back to Bliss. "What can I do for you?"

"I'm Bliss Cawthorne...a friend of Mason Lafferty's." That was stretching the truth just a little, but it didn't matter, did it? From the look on this woman's face, though, she might have said she'd just flown in from Jupiter.

"His...friend," the woman, obviously stunned, repeated. Maybe she had a thing for Mason, or was already involved with him. So who cared? Right now, all Bliss wanted to do was take Mason to task.

"I have his address, but not which apartment is his."

"Cawthorne?"

"John Cawthorne's my father," Bliss answered automatically, and wondered at the tension tightening the corners of the woman's mouth.

"He rents a unit in the back," the woman said, still eyeing Bliss with a sense of horror—or was it just curiosity?—for she managed a thin, though certainly not warm, smile again. "Upper level of the carriage house."

"Dee Dee's daddy?" the cherub with the dark curls asked.

"Mmm."

Dee Dee's daddy. The thought of Mason fathering a child did strange things to her. "Thanks," she managed to say, though she barely noticed what happened to mother and daughter as she walked around the corner of the house and along a tree-lined drive.

Would she ever have a child of her own? A baby? "Stop it," she muttered, ignoring that empty barb that pricked her soul as she thought about her childless state. She wasn't a hundred years old, for crying out loud. There was still time—plenty of it. She just had to find the right man. *Oh, right. Like that's going to happen anytime soon.*

Rounding the corner of the main house, she spied a second tall building with paned windows, black shutters, and the same gray siding as the main house. A private staircase led to the second story, and despite the perspiration on her palms, she marched up each step. She rapped on the door and was rewarded with Mason, all six feet of him looming directly in front of her.

"Well, Ms. Cawthorne," he drawled, his gold eyes silently appraising. "What brings you here?"

"We need to talk."

"Do we?" His smile slid from one side of his square jaw to the other.

"About Dad."

He leaned a shoulder on the doorjamb. "Come on, Bliss. I bet if you think real hard you can come up with a better topic than that."

"Do you?"

With that same amused, cocky smile, he stepped out of the doorway. "Come on in." As she passed he added, "How about something to drink? Soda? Coffee? Something stronger?"

"I don't think a drink is the answer," she said as she

tossed her purse into one of the few chairs in a room with glossy wood floors, windows opened slightly to let in the hot summer breeze, and walls paneled in yellowed knotty pine.

He left the door ajar, allowing a bit of cross ventilation as Bliss realized they were alone for the first time in a decade. Goose bumps rose on the back of her neck and the fragrances of honeysuckle and rose swept through the narrow room.

"Let me guess. You're here because I bought part of the ranch from Brynnie," he said, as if he'd been expecting her.

"Right out from under Dad's nose."

"She approached me."

"And you just couldn't say no, could you?" Bliss said, folding her arms over her chest.

"I didn't want to." The smile fell from his face and she noticed the fan of crow's feet at the corners of his eyes. "I've always liked the place. Dreamed of owning it years ago."

"And now there's a chance to get back at Dad."

"That wasn't the intention."

"Sure."

He crossed the room and stood directly in front of her. She'd forgotten how intimidating he was, hadn't remembered that the scent of him sent unwanted tingles through her blood. The temperature in the carriage house seemed to shoot upward ten degrees, and she found drawing a breath much harder than it had been. "Why, exactly, did you come over here?" he asked.

No reason to avoid the truth. "I think you manipulated this—this ridiculous situation. Somehow you convinced Brynnie that she needed to sell."

"I said, she came to me."

"You're lying."

"Ask her."

"Why would she sneak around behind Dad's back and—Oh!"

Quick as a rattler he struck, grabbing hold of her arm and yanking her toward him. "It was her idea."

"I don't believe—"

"Because you don't want to. Brynnie's a grown woman. She knew I was looking for a place and offered hers. We struck a deal." His face was so close to hers Bliss could see the striations of brown in his gold eyes, and watched as sweat dotted his forehead, darkening his hair. His nostrils flared and his lips barely moved. "I'm not going to deceive you, Bliss. There's no love lost between me and your old man. Never has been. But I didn't have to coerce Brynnie into selling out. She was more than willing."

"Was she?"

"Absolutely."

"You are a bastard, Lafferty."

His smile was cold and cruel, and his hand, rough with calluses, clamped in a vise-like grip over her wrist. But the scent of him, all male and musk and leather, filled the mere inches that separated his face from hers. "I wouldn't be throwing that particular word too loosely around here, if I were you," he warned. "It might hit a little close to home."

Frustration pounded in her pulse. Blast the man, he was right. Her father had sired two children out of wedlock. Two that she knew about. "Let go of me."

"If I only could," he said. Then, as if her words had finally registered, he dropped her arm and backed off a step. "Hell." With both hands, he plowed stiff fingers through his hair.

Idiot, she silently berated herself. How did it come to

this—that she was alone with the one man she wanted to avoid, the one man who could make her see red with only a calculated lift of his eyebrow, the solitary man who had touched her unguarded soul?

"Look, I didn't come back to Bittersweet to stir up trouble," he said.

"Too late," she retorted but decided, though her heart was thudding with dread, that there was no time like the present to sort out a few things with this man who seemed to be, ever since she'd glided into this part of Oregon, forever underfoot. "Just because you dumped me ten years ago and—"

"I didn't dump you."

"Ha." She shook her head and started gathering her purse. Coming here had been a mistake, and really, what had she expected—some kind of rationale for his need to buy the ranch? Or was it something more?

"I didn't mean to hurt you."

"But you married another woman," she said, the words, having been pent up for ten years, tumbling out of her mouth. "What do you call that?"

"A mistake."

The word echoed over and over again in her heart. But it was too late to hear it, far too late for apologies or explanations. "Listen, I shouldn't have asked."

"But you did."

"Never mind, I really don't need to know," she said, starting for the door.

"I should have called you. Shouldn't have been bullied into... Oh, hell what does it matter?"

She swallowed hard and turned to face him again. Maybe this was the time to sort things out. "When...when I got out of the hospital ten years ago, you were already gone," she said and saw a shadow of pain pass behind his eyes.

"Dad said you'd had some surgery yourself, then eloped to Reno."

A muscle worked in his jaw. "That's not exactly what happened."

"No?" She stood straight and met his gaze with her own. "The way I see it, you were two-timing me."

"Never."

Oh, God, how she wanted to believe him, to trust the honesty reflected in his eyes; to think, even for a minute, that he'd cared about her. But she couldn't. He'd been a liar then, and was a liar now. She was shaking inside and realized that the conversation was getting too personal. *Way* too personal, and Mason, blast his sorry good-looking hide, didn't seem afraid to open doors that had been locked for a decade. "I think you should back off with Dad."

"I thought we were talking about us."

"There is no 'us,' Mason. You took care of that. Remember?" She caught the door handle with one finger.

"It might be a good idea for me to explain."

"And I think it might be a good idea for you to go straight to hell, but I told you that already, didn't I? Ten years ago. If not, then consider the request retroactive."

"Damn it, Bliss, don't you think I've been there?"

She arched a cool brow. "I don't really care."

"Liar!" This time he reached forward so quickly she gasped. Strong fingers surrounded her arm.

"Obviously we need to talk a little more," he said, pressing his face so close to hers she noticed the furious dilation of his pupils, felt the warmth of his breath on her already-hot skin. Determination glinted in his eyes.

"I don't think so."

"There are things you don't know."

She tried to hold on to her rapidly disintegrating composure and yank her arm away, but his steely grip only tightened. Her heart began to thump so wildly she could scarcely breathe. "I'm sure there are, but I'm not interested in ancient history, Mason."

"Then let's talk about now."

"What about now?"

His gaze lowered to her lips and her breath stilled. A dozen memories, erotic and forbidden, waltzed slowly and provocatively through her mind. Her pulse ran rampant. Swallowing against a suddenly tight throat, she said, "Let me go."

"I made that mistake once before."

She yanked hard on her arms, but his hand only gripped tighter, his eyes glinting with sheer male persistence. "As I said, I think we should talk about us."

Her laugh was brittle. "Us. Now? You and me? You can't be serious."

"I've never been more serious about anything in my life," he said, though there were doubts in his eyes, as if he, too, remembered the pain and the lies. He pulled her closer to him and she knew in an instant that he was going to kiss her.

"This—this is a mistake."

"A big one," he agreed, his breath whispering across her face before his lips found hers in a kiss that questioned and demanded, that was fragile, yet firm. A kiss that stole the very breath from her lungs and caused her heart to trip-hammer madly.

Every instinct told her to stop this madness, to pull away; but another part of her, that silly, romantic, feminine part of her, wanted more. Her lips parted and his tongue slid quickly between her teeth, touching and tasting, dancing with her own.

Strong arms surrounded her and his hands splayed possessively over her back. She thought she heard a disturbance somewhere behind her, but discarded the sound as part of the rush of blood through her brain. Mason didn't stop kissing her and Bliss's heart, damn it, thundered in her chest.

Stop this lunacy now, rational thought insisted.

Don't ever let him go, her heart replied.

She heard a soft, wanting sound and realized it had come from her own throat. It had been so long, so damned long...and she wanted, needed, so much more.

"It's always been this way with you," he said as if disappointed, and she realized that their kiss had been a test, to see if he, like her, would respond.

"And it can't be." Though her breathing was as ragged as his, she was angry with herself for falling into his trap, for letting her body dictate to her mind. She couldn't, *wouldn't* let this happen again. "It...just can't."

Slowly he let go of her. Shoving his hands into the front pockets of his jeans, he cleared his throat. "I didn't mean to—"

"Of course, you did," she retorted. "You just didn't expect to be affected."

"So now you're a shrink?"

"Well?"

A muscle worked his jaw. "I was curious."

"So was I." She took a step even closer to him and tossed her hair over her shoulder. "But anyone can get caught up in lust. We did before, remember?" The words as they passed her lips, stung. She'd always thought she loved him, but she had to stop this destructive urge right now, because she wasn't about to take a chance on letting this man hurt her again. "And just for future reference, cowboy," she continued, "that kind of Neanderthal tactic might work on some of the women around here, but with me—"

"I'm sorry."

She couldn't believe her ears. Never had this man apologized to her. "What?"

"I came on too strong. You made me see red and then all of a sudden..." He leaned against the wall, sighed loudly, then before her eyes drew himself upright. "It won't happen again."

"You bet it won't!" she said, not sure if she was relieved or disappointed. Her pulse was still beating erratically and the taste of him lingered on her lips. "And as for my dad, just leave him alone, okay?"

His eyes narrowed. "Don't know that I can."

"Why not? What makes you want his place so badly?"

Mason shrugged as he held open the door and she passed through. "It's the right time."

"The right time for whom?"

"Brynnie, to begin with and, yes, me. I need a place down here. Cawthorne Acres has everything I want."

"Except a For Sale sign on the front door." She reached into her purse for her keys and as she extracted the ring, cut herself on a pair of nail scissors tucked into an inner pocket. "Ouch. Oh, damn." A drop of blood oozed from the tip of her forefinger and before she could do anything, Mason took her hand in his and eyed the wound.

"Let's see."

"It's nothing."

"Maybe."

"I said, it's..." Her voice faded as he slowly placed her finger to his lips. "Oh, no, don't—"

But his lips were warm, and the flow of blood was quickly stanched, the inside of his mouth so slick and seductive, Bliss could scarcely breathe. Why, oh, why did this one man still get to her? What was it about him she found so damned irresistible?

"I'm okay," she said, retrieving her hand.

"I know." He rocked back on the heels of his boots and had the decency to look uncomfortable. "I, uh, don't know what came over me."

He actually looked perplexed for an instant.

"Listen, Bliss," he said, clearing his throat and walking to the fireplace where he leaned against the mantel, as if he, too, finally realized the need for distance between them. "You'd be doing your father and Brynnie both a big favor by suggesting he sell the rest of his property."

"I think that's his decision. And now I have some advice for you. Just leave Dad and Brynnie alone. They have enough problems without having to deal with you."

"And what about you, Bliss?" he asked.

"What about me?"

"Should I leave you alone, too?"

"Absolutely." She tried not to notice the way his jeans settled low over his hips and the play of muscles in his forearms as he moved. Dark gold chest hair sprang from the V of his neckline, and she remembered exploring the springing curls that covered his nipples with young, interested fingers.

"I think you're afraid of me."

She laughed, and shook her head as she headed for the door again. "Don't flatter yourself, Lafferty. You don't scare me."

"Maybe I ought to."

"Maybe," she admitted. "But you don't." The lie hovered between them in the air for a few seconds until she turned and shoved open the door only to find a young girl, somewhere between eight and nine, hovering on the landing. "Oh."

"Dad?" the child asked, looking over Bliss's shoulder.

"Dee Dee." Bliss heard the smile in his voice and realized that she was staring at his daughter. With a fringe of brown hair and freckles bridging a tiny nose, Dee Dee looked from Bliss to Mason and back again.

"Bliss Cawthorne, this is my daughter, Deanna."

"Glad to meet you," Bliss said automatically, though she felt a stab of deep regret for the child she'd never had, had never had the chance to conceive with Mason.

"Yeah." Dee Dee chewed on her lower lip for a second. "Mom just dropped me off."

"And didn't stick around. Figures," Mason said, eyeing the street as if looking for Terri's car. "Are you hungry?"

"Starved. Can we go to McDonald's?" Dee Dee asked, her eyes suddenly bright with anticipation.

"Sure. You game?" he asked Bliss and she saw the girl's shoulders droop a bit.

"No...uh, no thanks," she said, not wanting to intrude on father and daughter. "Another time." She hurried down the stairs and offered a pathetic excuse of a wave. It wasn't Dee Dee's fault that she'd been conceived when Mason was dating Bliss, and yet Bliss didn't want to be reminded of the man's faithlessness.

She skirted the main house and made it to her car without looking over her shoulder. As she slid behind the wheel, she told herself it didn't matter that Mason had cheated on her, that he'd gotten another woman pregnant while he'd been seeing her, that he'd never loved her. He had an ex-wife and a daughter, and Bliss had her own life to lead—without him.

That night Bliss threw off the covers and glared at the digital readout on the clock near the bed. Two forty-five. Great. She'd been in bed since eleven and hadn't slept a wink. Ever since returning to Bittersweet, she couldn't wrench Mason out of her mind. Seeing him with his daughter hadn't helped. She'd been reminded of just how he'd betrayed her, how much she wanted a child of her own.

Outside, rain fell steadily from the sky; fat, heavy drops pummeling the roof, splashing in the gutters and dripping from the leaves and branches of the old oak tree that stood near her window.

Why hadn't he told her about Terri Fremont years ago when Bliss was falling in love with him? What was the reason he left Bittersweet without even stopping to say goodbye to her? Why was he back now and why was it so important that he buy her father's place? And why, oh, please, God, why, was she still thinking about him, wondering at her response to his kiss while hating herself for caring?

"Stop it!" she muttered, punching her pillow in frustration. She reminded herself for the millionth time that Mason Lafferty was nothing to her. *Nothing!*

So why was she thinking of him? Why? Why? Why? "Because you're an idiot," she told herself.

Knowing that sleep was impossible, she slid her arms through the sleeves of her robe and stepped into her slippers. Oscar, who had been curled up beside her, was already on his feet, stretching and yawning. He followed her into the kitchen and waited at the pantry door until she reached inside and tossed him a biscuit. While he crunched on his snack, she heated cocoa in the microwave.

Mason was a problem, but not one she could solve tonight. She needed to forget him and return to Seattle as she'd planned. Her father was recuperating at a rapid pace, and if he and Brynnie could quit fighting long enough to walk down the aisle and say their vows, then Bliss would leave Oregon and get back to her old life.

Her old, peaceful, and somewhat-boring life.

Sliding into a chair, Bliss cradled the warm cup in her

hands and let the chocolate-scented steam fill her nostrils and whisper over her cheeks. She'd told herself again and again that she was over—make that *long* over—Mason, but tonight, while the sky was thick with clouds and the outside air dense with rain, she wasn't so sure of her feelings.

Seeing Mason, touching Mason and kissing Mason had brought back memories, painful and tarnished. She'd spent ten years repressing her thoughts about him, trying not to compare him to other men she'd dated, hoping against hope that someday she'd never think of him at all, believing that he was just a summer fling—a schoolgirl crush. Nothing more.

Now, she was ready to second-guess herself. "Fool," she exclaimed, and when Oscar gave out a disgruntled "Woof," she laughed without any sense of satisfaction. "That's right, dog, your mistress is a first-class, A-one moron, I'm afraid."

Old feelings—excitement, anger, hurt and even a trace of first love—resurfaced. She remembered the tumbling, breathless feeling of hearing his voice or kissing him, or swimming nude in the nearby river with him. "Oh, Bliss," she whispered, stirring the hot chocolate and creating a small whirlpool in her cup, "I thought you were smarter than this."

The memory of the first time she'd seen him, tall and lean, covered in dust as he'd offered to lift her suitcases and trunk from the back of her father's truck, haunted her. And tonight, alone in the kitchen of the ranch house, with only the rain and Oscar to keep her company, that memory stretched out vividly before her. It had been ten years ago, but tonight, it seemed as real as if that summer had happened yesterday....

Chapter Six

Bliss sipped her cocoa and remembered that sultry afternoon when she had come to her father's ranch that summer. The housekeeper had called to John Cawthorne as he'd climbed out of his truck.

"Phone call for you, in the den," she'd said, standing in the doorway of the house and pushing aside clumps of dry dirt left from boots with her broom.

John, swearing under his breath, had dashed toward the front door and had left Bliss standing alone by the truck in the blistering sunlight. As she stood in the dusty gravel parking area near the garage, harsh, unforgiving rays pounded down on her crown and shoulders. She felt totally alone, a city girl plucked out of her nest and tossed here with a father who usually ignored her. As she reached into the bed of the truck for one of her bags, she silently wished, as she had since she could remember, that she had a sister or brother with whom she could share her misery.

"You must be John's daughter," a rawboned, slightly intimidating, cowboy drawled. He was tanned from long hours of hard work under the glare of the sun and his eyes, staring at her from the shade beneath the brim of his Stetson, were a light golden brown. Intense and unblinking, they stared at her in an uncompromising appraisal that caused her breath to catch and warned her that she should run now while she had the chance.

"That's right." Why did her tongue want to trip all over itself?

His grin was a slash of white against bronzed skin. "He's proud of you, let me tell you."

"Is he?" She smiled back, then blushed. This guy was way too old for her and she wasn't one to flirt, but there was something about him that made her want to linger. "Bliss Cawthorne," she said boldly, extending her hand and remembering the manners her mother had drummed into her head from the time she was a toddler.

"Lafferty. Mason Lafferty." He dropped the trunk and covered her soft small outstretched palm with his bigger, callused hand. His fingers were rough, covered with dust and warmer than the breeze that swept through the grassy acres. He tipped his hat and didn't apologize for the dirt that he left smudged on her skin.

"You work for Dad." There was something about him that nudged her curiosity; something that set him apart from the rest of the men who called John Cawthorne their boss.

"Most of the time." He hitched the trunk onto his back and started for the porch.

"And the rest?"

He glanced over his shoulder and winked at her so slowly she felt her knees turn to jelly. "Raisin' hell, if you believe the stories in town."

"Should I?" Lugging her suitcase, she struggled to keep up with his long, easy stride.

His gold eyes glinted. "Every word. Hey, don't carry that—I'll get it." He cocked his head toward the bag she carried.

"I can handle it."

"Can you?"

She knew she was being baited and she flushed. After all, this guy wasn't a boy; he was a man and he scared her more than a little. "I can handle a lot of things," she said, tossing her head. Margaret Cawthorne might have taught her daughter to be a lady, but she'd also instilled a fervor in Bliss to carry her own weight and be independent enough not to have to rely on any man, especially not a cowboy.

John walked out onto the porch. "Damned mechanics," he grumbled, then noticed Mason. "Take the trunk and the rest of her things into her bedroom—down the hall, second door on the right. Next to the bath."

"I can show him. I know where it is," Bliss said, feeling the fiery rays of the sun beating against the back of her neck. Heat shimmered in waves across the pastures, and dust, kicked up from the movement of cattle and horses in nearby fields, floated in the air. She was beginning to sweat and her blouse was sticking to her back and her heart was pounding so loudly she was sure everyone within ten feet of her could hear it.

"Good."

"When you're finished with the luggage, Lafferty, run down to the machine shed. The combine's acting up again, according to Corky, and the shop in town is overloaded. No one can look at the machine for three weeks at the earliest. Holy hell, how can you run a ranch like this?" Scowling and grumbling to himself, her father strode across the parking lot toward the machine shed.

Mason's jaw hardened. He held the screen door open for Bliss. "Your old man is gonna give himself a stroke if he doesn't calm down a little."

"It's just his way," she said, but felt an unspoken tension in the cowboy walking beside her. His muscles were suddenly strung tight, his knuckles showing white around the handle of the trunk.

Hurrying through the cool interior of the house, she bumped shoulders with him a couple of times and nearly tripped over her feet at the contact. Being alone with him was nerve-racking. She reminded herself that he was just one of her father's hands—a worker on the ranch. Right? So why did she feel instantly that there was something about him, something primitive and sexual, which bothered her and caused her already-flushed skin to break into beads of anxious perspiration? "You can put the trunk in the corner," she said, opening the door of her room and indicating a spot near the small closet.

"Whatever you say, princess."

She bristled at the name. "I'm not a princess."

His lips twitched. "Hmm. Coulda fooled me." He dropped the trunk on its end and hesitated long enough to make her uncomfortable. There was something in his eyes, something wickedly intriguing that warned her he was the kind of man to avoid; the kind of man a woman in her right mind wouldn't trust. "Anything else?"

"No, uh, I think I can handle the rest."

"You sure?" His voice was low and a little raspy, as if he'd breathed too much dust or smoked too many cigarettes.

She wasn't sure of anything. "Yeah. Don't worry about it."

With a wink that bordered on something far more sexual than she'd ever experienced, he left the room as quickly as he'd come in. She set her suitcase on the bed and opened the window. Suddenly the tiny bedroom seemed airless and hot. In the old mirror over the bureau she caught her reflection and nearly died. Her cheeks were a bright shade of pink, her blond hair wild, her eyes wide with an anticipation she'd never seen before.

The breeze that moved the curtains and filled the room didn't help much. Nothing did, she came to find out. Whenever she was around Mason, she couldn't seem to catch her breath or even untangle her thoughts.

In the days that followed, that summer ten years ago, she saw Mason enough, though most often from a distance. He roped steers, he branded stock, he castrated calves, he shoed horses and strung fence wire. The muscles of his back and shoulders, tanned from long hours laboring in the sun, moved fluidly as he worked, straining, then relaxing and drawing her eyes to the faded jeans that rode low on his hips. Dusty and torn, they offered a glimpse of a strip of whiter skin whenever he stretched, and that tantalizing slash of white, coupled with the curling golden hair on his chest, caused a warmth to invade the deepest, most private part of her, and she had to force her gaze away.

"You're being silly," she told herself on Tuesday evening when she was walking toward the stables and spied Mason leaning against a car—a yellow sedan—she didn't recognize. The driver was a pert woman with short dark hair, an upturned nose and doelike brown eyes that gazed upward through the open window to Mason's face. The car idled, exhaust seeping from the tailpipe, the thrum of the engine competing with the sounds of warblers and sparrows singing in the trees and fields.

Mason, wearing sunglasses and an irritated expression,

shook his head, and though Bliss's ears strained to hear the conversation she only caught snippets.

"...waited all night," the woman said.

"No one asked you to."

"...we had an understanding."

"Did we? Wasn't my idea."

"Mason, please—" The woman cast a sidelong glance at Bliss who increased her pace as she walked to the stables. The sun was hovering low in the western sky and the air was breathless and still.

Bored with listening to her tapes and reading old magazines, Bliss had decided to go for a ride. Her father had already pointed out the docile horses he wanted her to saddle, but Bliss had other ideas.

"Lousy son of a bitch!" The woman's voice blasted through the hot air.

Bliss turned toward the car.

The driver gunned the engine. Gravel sprayed. Mason leaped away from the fender as the car took off at breakneck speed down the lane.

Swearing under his breath, Mason swung his fist in the air in frustration. "Damn, fool—" He caught his tongue and threw his hat on the ground. Then, turning on a worn heel, he caught Bliss's eye. Rather than be the target of his wrath, she ducked around the corner of the stables and snagged a lead rope coiled around a peg near one of the doors. The last person she wanted to catch in a bad mood was Mason Lafferty. No way. No how. The man was enough trouble when things were going right.

Squinting against a lowering sun, she eyed the horses grazing quietly in the shade of a stand of oak. She wasn't interested in the docile palomino mare or lazy roan gelding her father had pointed out to her, and smiled when she spied the animal who had unintentionally captured her heart—a feisty pinto three-year-old. His eyes were an un-usual pale blue—the only blue-eyed horse she'd ever seen—and he was a show-off in front of the mares, always hoisting his tail high, tossing his head and snorting as he galloped from one end of the field to the other.

"Okay, Lucifer, I think it's time you and I got to know each other," she said as he snorted and pawed the dry earth. "Come on," she cooed, uncoiling the vinyl rope. "That's a boy."

Lucifer rolled his eyes suspiciously. He was wearing a leather halter. All she had to do was get close enough to snap the tether to the ring under his chin.

"It's all right," she assured him. She was only three feet away. One more step and—

He bolted. With a high-pitched squeal and a toss of his brown-and-white head, he galloped from one end of the pasture to the other, kicking up a cloud of dust in his wake. His odd eyes sparkled in the sunlight, as if he knew he was taunting her.

"Don't make me chase you," she warned.

"Why not? He loves a good fight. Especially with a female."

She stiffened at the sound of Mason's voice. Glancing over her shoulder, she ignored the sudden jump in her pulse and shot him a glance guaranteed to be as cold as ice. "Seems like you should know," she said.

"Can't argue with that," he admitted, though his jaw was hard as granite.

When he didn't stroll off, she asked, "Was there something you wanted?"

He was leaning against the gate, his arms crossed, elbows resting on the worn top board, eyes still shaded by aviator glasses. His hat was resting on a post and his hair, sun-streaked and ragged, brushed his eyebrows and the tops of his ears. "Just watching you."

She lied and told herself that the absolute last person on earth she wanted observing her was this sarcastic cowboy. "Don't you have *something* more important to do? You know, like work? Isn't there a cow to be branded, a horse to be shod or something?"

"Not just now. Besides, I wouldn't want the boss's daughter to get herself into some kind of trouble."

She made a disgusted noise in the back of her throat. "Don't worry about it."

He didn't bother to respond. Nor did he move. Bliss gritted her back teeth together and inched her chin upward in pride. She'd die before she'd let him witness her humiliation from this headstrong piece of horseflesh.

"Want me to help?"

"No!" Damn the man, he was enjoying this and making her so nervous she was beginning to sweat. "Give me strength," she muttered under her breath as she approached Lucifer again. In a louder voice she said gently, "Come on boy. That's a good—"

In another whirlwind of dust the colt again thundered away, bucking and showing off as if he and Mason were privately conspiring against her.

"Son of a—" she bit back a curse and stomped a foot, sending up her own pitiful puff of dirt and Mason, damn his soul, laughed outright. "I suppose you could do better," she challenged, then cringed as the words escaped her lips.

"Yep." In one lithe movement he vaulted the fence and gave a sharp, terse whistle.

Lucifer stopped short.

Another commanding blast from Mason's lips and the colt, ears flicking nervously, reluctantly turned. He hesitated, his nostrils flared, and Mason whistled a third time.

To Bliss's complete mortification, the colt trotted doc-
ilely to Mason, pressed his nose against the man's chest
and was rewarded with a piece of apple.

"Isn't that cheating?" she asked as Mason grabbed Lucifer's halter and with his free hand, slowly motioned for
Bliss to approach with the lead rope.

"Everything's fair in love and war and taming horses."
He glanced at her from behind his tinted glasses. He was
so close she could smell his aftershave as well as the dust
and odors of horse and leather that seemed to cling to him.
His jaw was gilded with a day's growth of beard and his
sleeves were shoved above his elbows to show off tanned
forearms where veins and hard muscles stretched beneath
his skin.

Swallowing against a suddenly arid throat, she turned her
eyes back to the horse.

"You have heard the expression before, right?"

"It was a little different." She snapped the lead onto the
metal ring on the colt's halter.

Mason lifted one dark eyebrow. "Well, around here we
make expressions fit the situation."

"So I see."

"Be careful with Lucifer."

"I can handle him."

"I hate to give you advice, but if you call what you just
did 'handling him,' you're in for a couple more lessons
from this guy."

"Am I?" She tossed her hair over one shoulder.

Mason patted the pinto on the shoulder. "You want me
to saddle and bridle him for you?"

Her smile was cool, though her hands were sweating on
the tether and her heart was beginning to pound erratically.
"I'll be fine," she said, clucking to the colt and heading
to the stables where she'd already picked out a saddle, blan-

ket and bridle. She didn't need any more help from the sexiest ranch hand on the place. All she wanted to do was ride to the river that cut through the north end of her father's property where she planned to take a long, leisurely swim. Nothing more...

But, of course, looking back on it now, she'd gotten way more than she'd bargained for. That night was the night she began to fall in love, the night when all the trouble really started.

"Oh, who cares?" she asked herself as she took a long sip from her cup. Life sometimes seemed to move in strange, fateful circles. Who would have thought that she would be here, at her father's ranch, drinking tepid cocoa at three in the morning? Back in Bittersweet. Involved with—no, not involved with—dealing with Mason again. "Fool," she muttered to herself as she tossed the remains of her drink into the sink and Oscar, panting, tagged along behind her to the bedroom.

She'd made a mistake with Mason in the past, but she wasn't going to repeat it. "Once burned, twice shy, you know," she told her mutt as Oscar slipped through the open door to her room and hopped eagerly onto her bed. "Okay, okay. Since you were already here earlier, tonight you can sleep with me, but that's it."

She slid beneath the sheet and sighed. The rainstorm had moved on, but she was still here, in bed with only a dog for comfort, and the nagging feeling that all the promises she'd made to herself wouldn't help where Lafferty was concerned. He was just one of those kinds of men that slipped under a woman's skin and wouldn't go away.

"Great," she thought aloud as she tugged at the covers. Well, she wasn't an ordinary woman. She was strong. Independent. Margaret Cawthorne's daughter. And she'd be damned if she'd let any range-rough cowboy change the course of her life or mess with her head. Mason Lafferty, damn him, could go straight to hell, for all she cared.

Mason towel-dried his hair roughly while barely glancing at his reflection in the foggy mirror. He hadn't seen Bliss in nearly a week and like it or not, he was going quietly out of his mind. He threw on slacks, shirt, socks and shoes, then walked though his apartment and thought it seemed emptier than before. His heels rang against the hardwood floor, echoing loudly enough to make the rooms seem hollow.

He snagged his jacket from a peg near the back door and slid his arms through the sleeves. He'd thought of Bliss off and on over the years, but had made a point to keep any lingering and provocative memories of her where they belonged—strictly in the past. Then again, he hadn't expected her to show up in Bittersweet, nor had he thought her old man would remarry so quickly on the heels of his first wife's death. Life, it turned out, was oftentimes stranger than fiction, and a hell of a lot more complicated.

Frowning, he thought of his own situation. How, as a small boy, he'd watched his father drive away in a beat-up old Dodge truck, the exhaust a blue haze in the coming darkness as the pickup rumbled away. He'd clung to his mother's hand, swallowing back the tears that burned in his throat, blinking against the rain that poured from the sky. He'd been five at the time, his sister, Patty, barely two. She'd sucked her thumb as she'd sat balanced on their mother's slim hip.

"It'll be all right," Helen Lafferty had said, her chin held high, her nose and eyes red from endless nights of crying. Mason had heard the fights, listened to his mother beg his dad to stay—to keep the family together, to stay with them. She'd forgive him the drinking. Forget the other women. Ignore his gambling.

But he'd left just the same.

"You go on to bed, Mason," she'd said, swiping at her tears. "I'll rock Patty to sleep out here on the porch."

Only years later did Mason realize that Albert Lafferty couldn't handle responsibility, a family, or just plain settling down. He'd never seen his father again and hadn't missed him.

"Yeah, right," he told himself now. His mother had never remarried and when she'd discovered she had breast cancer the year that Mason turned eighteen, she'd taken matters into her own work-roughened hands. Without insurance or a nest egg, she couldn't afford the operation that probably wouldn't have saved her life anyway. So, stoically, with no word to her children, Helen Lafferty had opened a bottle of sleeping pills, swallowed every one, and never woken up. She'd left Mason and Patty a simple note asking them to forgive her and begging Mason to look after his younger sister.

Well, he'd made one hell of a mess of that. Patty, he suspected, was in more trouble now than she'd ever been, and trouble, it seemed, was her middle name. As for Mason himself, his life had never been more complicated. He was considering suing Terri for custody of Dee Dee, Patty and old Isaac Wells were missing, he'd bought half the ranch and had old John mad as a hornet at him and, to top matters off, now Bliss Cawthorne, "the princess," had strolled right back into the middle of his life.

His back teeth gnashed together as he locked the door of his apartment behind him.

He wouldn't have believed that seeing her again would bring back a rush of memories he'd hoped to have forgotten. It seemed unfair to be haunted by the past, but then, he'd learned a long time ago that life was neither fair nor easy. Growing up in poverty, he'd developed a keen understanding of the fact that in order to even out the stakes in this life, a man had to have money and lots of it. His old man, when he'd been around, had taught him well. A few years later John Cawthorne had only reinforced that theory.

"Jerk," Mason growled and wondered where was the sense of satisfaction he'd been hoping to feel, why had the warm knowledge that he was finally getting even escaped him. Somehow, he suspected, this all had something to with Bliss and how he felt about her, how he'd felt about her in the past and what the future might hold for them.

Snorting in disgust at the turn of his thoughts, he headed down the stairs and to a space near the street where he'd parked his rig. Traffic was sparse on the quiet streets of town.

He should forget Bliss. She'd stumbled into his life at a time when the last thing he'd needed was involvement with the boss's daughter, but she'd been the most incredible woman he'd laid eyes upon in a long time and fighting his attraction to her had failed miserably.

Then he'd nearly killed her. He should never have let her take off on that horse in the middle of a storm. He should have risked her wrath and refused to let her saddle Lucifer. It would have been better to risk the old man's anger and lose his job than to have Bliss's life endangered.

But then he'd never been smart when it came to John Cawthorne's daughter. He hadn't been then; wouldn't be now.

Ten years after the accident, he was still drumming up excuses to see her, to be alone with her. Even as he climbed into his truck and silently swore that he'd keep his hands off her, he already knew that he was only kidding himself. Before the day was out, he'd find a reason to see her again.

"Hell, Lafferty," he told the eyes glaring back at him in his rearview mirror. "You've got it and you've got it bad." He threw his pickup into reverse, backed out, then nosed the truck onto the dusty pothole-strewn avenue. "Real bad."

Chapter Seven

Crossing the fingers of one hand, Bliss silently prayed and pushed a button on her new fax machine. "Let this work," she muttered as the machine hummed obediently. She'd tried to transmit the bid she'd been working on for two days to her office in Seattle with no success. This time she was in luck. "Thank you, God of All Things Electronic," she said as she filed her original away and heard the phone ring down the hall.

"For you!" her father yelled.

"Got it," she sang back, conscious of the irritation in John Cawthorne's tone. He and Brynnie were speaking again, but the situation was still tense and the wedding plans, though progressing, were in a constant state of flux. "Hello," she called into the extension.

"Bliss, hi, this is Katie Kinkaid. I, uh, thought you might want to meet for coffee or lunch or...well, whatever."

No time like the present, her mind prodded her, although,

deep down, she wanted to avoid this meeting like the plague. "Sure, I can meet you, or you might want to come out here. Delores made a killer batch of pecan rolls and I brought some French-roast coffee from an espresso shop in Seattle."

"You're on," Katie said with a lot more enthusiasm than Bliss felt. "I'll be there in half an hour."

"Great." Bliss hung up and told herself it was time to get to know her half sister, whether she wanted to or not. She straightened the den and told her father goodbye as he and Brynnie were off to talk to the preacher, who, Bliss hoped, was a decent premarriage counselor.

By the time Katie wheeled into the drive, Bliss had heated the gooey rolls, made a fresh pot of coffee and was halfway through the newspaper.

Katie rapped hard on the screen door, then let herself in, meeting Bliss in the hallway to the kitchen. She had curly auburn hair, pink cheeks and green eyes. "Hi." She seemed a little nervous but managed a cute grin. Extending her hand, she took Bliss's fingers in a crushing handshake. "I know this is hard for you. Jeez, it's hard for me and I really don't know what to say to you, but I think—I mean, the best thing is for us to get to know each other."

"I suppose," Bliss acquiesced, ambivalent. What do you say to someone who is the product of your father's infidelity? How do you accept them or they accept you?

"The truth of the matter is," the redhead said with refreshing honesty as she sailed down the hallway as if she'd done it a hundred times before, "I've been torn. From the minute I heard about you and realized that you were my sister, I wanted to meet you, but was afraid and embarrassed and, oh, it's just so damned complicated."

"Isn't it?" *Give the woman a chance, Bliss. She's obviously struggling with this as much as you are.*

In the kitchen Katie paused and eyed the rolls that Bliss had put on the table. "Mmm, smells great."

"Good. Sit, sit." Bliss waved her into a chair and poured them each a cup of coffee. She handed Katie a mug and watched as the younger woman spooned two teaspoons of sugar into her brew. "When Mom told me that John was my father I thought we should get together to shake our heads at our parents' stupidity if nothing else." She rolled her large eyes. "And I thought *kids* were hard to understand. You know, sometimes adults are ten times worse."

"You're probably right," Bliss agreed as she sat across the table, her back to the window. Outside the glass a robin was busy pulling up worms from the morning-damp lawn. Bliss didn't have to like the woman, just hear her out. Unfortunately, Katie seemed to be one of those bubbly, wear-your-heart-on-your-sleeve types that she found endearing.

"I have to admit, though," Katie said, sipping her coffee as Bliss cut the rolls apart and placed one of the sugary confections on a small plate, "after living with three brothers it was a relief to know that I had a sister—well, really, two sisters!"

Katie, all five feet two inches of her, cut into her pastry. She was small and wiry, with quick movements and the exuberance of a brushfire at the height of summer. No moss grew under this little woman's feet. "And what's your name?" she asked as Oscar, slowly wagging his tail, galloped into the room, only to slide to a stop at the table.

"Oscar. I've had him a couple of years."

"Well, you're just adorable," Katie said to the dog who wiggled at her feet. "Do you hear me? A-dor-a-ble." Without checking with Bliss, she tossed the mutt a bite of pecan roll, which he tossed and gulped in one swift motion. She wiped her hands and asked suddenly, "Do you have any kids?"

Bliss ignored the jab in her heart and shook her head. "No. At least not yet. Never been married."

"Neither have I, but I've got a boy—Josh. He's hell on wheels and the most wonderful thing that ever happened to me. I always say kids are the biggest blessing and curse of your life. You love them so much you worry about them day and night." She bit her lower lip and stared out the window, but Bliss guessed she wasn't seeing the horses grazing in the field grass or one of the ranch hands shoring up the ramp to the back of the barn. No, Katie was in her own private world—a world that seemed to revolve around her son.

Bliss felt the same tug on her heartstrings that had become a regular feeling whenever she thought of her own childless state. Ever since coming to Bittersweet she had been conscious of her biological clock. This wasn't a new experience. For the past few years as her friends and co-workers had become mothers, she'd felt her maternal instincts awakening, and she'd only wished she could have given her mother a grandchild while she was alive.

"Lately, Josh—he's ten going on sixteen—has been getting into a powder keg of trouble. I'm telling you, when school's not in session, look out!" Katie flung her arms wide, as if they'd been blown apart, before she finally turned away from the window and met Bliss's uneasy stare.

"Oh, I guess I came on like gangbusters, didn't I?" With a smile, she added, "I'm glad to finally meet you, Bliss, even though this is kind of weird for both of us. You know, I didn't know John was my real dad until just after his heart attack. For all those years I thought Hal Kinkaid was my biological father." She shook her head as if at her own folly and chewed on a bite of pecan roll. "He and I were never close. *Never*. But still, finding out that he wasn't the guy whose genes are running around in my body was a shock.''

"I imagine it was," Bliss replied, though, in truth, she couldn't imagine anything of the sort. The whole conversation was surreal in a way. What could she say to this forthright woman who seemed to have no qualms about talking about any subject under the sun, including her own conception, illegitimate though it was?

Katie propped one foot on the brace of one of the empty chairs scattered around the table. "It's really an odd sensation, you know," she admitted, "growing up believing one thing and learning that you were lied to and that everything you believed in is bogus."

Bliss only nodded. Her entire life, it seemed, had been a lie.

"Hal Kinkaid—the guy I thought was my dad—was a real jerk. I mean, a first-class bastard. Why Mom connected with him, I'll never know. He drank too much, always ran around on my mom, left her with a pile of bills. Strange as it sounds, I was relieved that he wasn't related to me."

"Yeah, but what about Dad?"

Katie shook her head and rubbed her arms as if she was suddenly chilled. "That's a tough one. Especially for you and your mom." She propped her chin on one hand and didn't argue when Bliss refilled both cups. She added sugar, and this time, a little bit of cream, watching in idle fascination as clouds rose in the dark brew.

"Thanks," the redhead said, taking a sip. "To think that John Cawthorne had two families. I can't say I have too much respect for him—well, or for Mom, either—but there it is. Now your mother's gone and they're finally getting married. What can I say?"

"It's...hard."

"Bingo. On one hand I think they should slow down, let

the rest of us catch our breath and deal with all this, and on the other I understand their need to be together. Who knows how much time they have?" Katie shrugged and blew across the top of her cup. "I just hope the rest of us— you, me, Tiffany and my brothers—can handle this. Well, and of course, I hope John can make Mom happy. She deserves it."

Bliss didn't comment, and Katie raised her hands as if to ward off physical blows. "I know, I know, you probably hate her for what she did."

"*Hate's* too strong a word," Bliss admitted.

"But you have to resent her."

That much was true. Wiping away a drip of coffee from her cup, Bliss said, "Let's just say I loved my mom a lot. She might not have been perfectly suited for my dad, but she deserved him to be true to her. It's him I'm having the problem with."

"Me, too," Katie admitted before taking a long swallow from her cup. "I just hope we can all work this out and be friends." She grinned. "I know, that's beyond optimistic, but it doesn't make sense for anyone to hold any grudges. What would that accomplish?"

"Nothing, I suppose," Bliss reluctantly agreed.

"Yeah, so go and tell your heart, right?" Katie laughed without much mirth. "This is one dandy mess."

"Touché."

"You know, this is probably hard for you to believe, but my mom wouldn't hurt a flea. Lord knows, she tried to break it off with your dad several times—or at least that's what she said—but they just couldn't stay apart. Every time she married another guy in an attempt to get over your father, she swore she'd have nothing to do with John Cawthorne, but then the marriage would begin to fail, probably because her heart wasn't in it in the first place, and John would come back to Bittersweet and it would begin all over again. I was too young and out of it to notice.''

''I don't want to hear this,'' Bliss said, her heart squeezing for her mother and the family they'd been.

Katie pursed her lips. ''Sorry. Tacky of me. My brothers say that I don't know when to keep my mouth shut, and I guess they're right.''

''No, I wanted to know, but it's… I don't know.''

''Painful. I get it. You feel like your dad betrayed your mother and therefore he betrayed you. I understand. I didn't mean to open up any old wounds.''

''No, no, it's all right.'' The last thing Bliss wanted was to alienate Katie, her half sister, a woman as unlike her as day was to night. But she found Katie Kinkaid refreshing and outspoken, relaxed and honest. No false pretenses. No worries about decorum or what the neighbors might think or say. In short, Bliss found herself warming to Katie whether she wanted to or not.

Katie sliced Bliss a curious look. ''I don't mean to pry, but since we're getting to know each other, I wanted to ask a couple of things.''

Bliss's back stiffened. ''Such as?''

''You visited here when you were growing up, didn't you?''

''The summers— Well, some of them.'' Unease knotted Bliss's already tight stomach.

''Then you know Mason Lafferty.''

It was a statement, and it hung in the air. Bliss had taken a bite of her roll, and it suddenly felt like a lump of wet cement wedged against the top of her mouth.

''He, uh, worked for Dad a long time ago.''

''Until he was fired,'' Katie said, then drained her cup again. ''You know, my brother Jarrod was his best friend at the time and thought John—er, Dad—oh, whatever he is—gave Mason a bum rap. There was something about a riding accident and you, right?''

Memories, as dark and dismal as that fateful day ten years past, scraped at Bliss's soul. She cradled her cup in her palms, as if expecting to gain some warmth from its heat. "I ended up in the hospital."

"Because of Mason?''

"No, in spite of him," Bliss admitted, thinking back to that storm-ravaged day and her wild ride to the north edge of the property.

Katie cleared her throat and Bliss came crashing back to the present. Her half sister was still staring at her, waiting for an explanation. "I took the horse out even though Mason warned me not to, that a storm was brewing.''

Katie picked at a raisin left on her plate. "Mason took the fall for you—well, so to speak.''

"I told Dad the truth, but he never believed me, thought I was covering up for Lafferty's—what did he call it? Oh, uh, his 'bad attitude, insubordination, pathetic sense of judgment and lack of respect.' That was it.''

Katie let out a long, low whistle. "That's not the Mason Lafferty I knew.''

"Me, neither," Bliss admitted, but her heart ached just the same, because Mason had used her and lied to her, left her for another woman—a woman pregnant with his baby.

"Ever since his divorce from Terri, he's become one of the most eligible bachelors in the county," Katie said, one eyebrow lifting.

"Is that right?" Bliss wasn't interested, or so she told herself. She drained her coffee cup.

"Well, that's just the recent consensus because he hasn't lived here in years. Just returned a few months ago so that he could be closer to his kid. In fact—''

"I know. He's trying to buy this place but Dad won't sell."

"Yeah, but my mom already owns part of the ranch and she's gone and signed on the dotted line."

"I know. She and Dad are fighting about it."

"Great," Katie said, frowning as she shoved aside her plate. There was a strange, uncomfortable silence for a few minutes and Bliss, to keep the conversation from becoming even more strained, cleared the table.

"Oh, damn." Katie glanced at the clock on the stove. "I've got to call and see if Josh is up. He's got a job doing yard work for Mrs. Kramer next door, so I don't want him to forget and take off on his bike or skateboard. Mind if I use the phone?"

"Not at all."

Katie scooted back her chair and plucked the receiver off the wall. Deftly she punched in the numbers and waited. "Darn it, either he's asleep or already took off— Josh, this is Mom, if you're there, pick up. Josh? Honey, if you're— Oh, about time. I was afraid you'd already taken off." She paused for a minute and then said, "No, don't go back to bed. You've got the job at Mrs. Kramer's, remember?" Another hesitation. "No, there's no way out of it. It'll only be for a couple of hours and I'll be home soon. You don't have to be over there until eleven—"

She stopped in mid-sentence and leaned against the wall. Absently twirling the phone cord in her fingers, she listened to all of her son's excuses.

"Okay, okay, just get ready. After you finish this afternoon you can go swimming and later I'll barbecue for dinner.... I don't know—how about hot dogs or hamburgers? Good." She waited and rolled her eyes. "See ya." She hung up and shook her head. "I'd better go before he takes off and ditches out of this job. A workaholic he's not, but

I guess he's pretty young." She was already heading for the hallway. "It was nice to get to know you a little better. Maybe…well, if we can convince her, we can visit Tiffany some day. You know about her, right?"

"My father's firstborn," Bliss said stiffly. "Yes. I've heard of her." But only recently.

"She moved back to Bittersweet a little while ago, just about the time school was out, and I saw her once to tell her about John and Mom getting married. She wasn't very anxious to talk to me—in fact, I'm not sure she can handle all this—" Katie gestured vaguely toward the interior of the house and waved her fingers. "Well, maybe none of us can, but I'm sure she just didn't know what to say to me, and she was having trouble with her boy and his uncle. The guy—J.D. Santini—seems to be butting into the kid's life. The whole Santini clan are kind of pushy, I think. Her father-in-law is the patriarch and head of Santini Wines, a big deal up in Portland. Her husband Philip worked for him and I think J.D. does, too, though he is, well, as I understand it, the black sheep of the family.

"Anyway, Tiffany's got her share of problems and I haven't worked up the nerve to call her again."

"You?" Bliss questioned. "Afraid? I don't believe it."

"'Intimidated' would be more like it," Katie admitted. "Tiffany's gone through some rocky times and I think she blames your—I mean, our—father."

"Maybe she's got valid reasons," Bliss suggested as she swiped bread crumbs from the counter and tossed them into the sink.

"Probably. But she's still our sister. I think we should give her another chance." She hesitated. "You gave me one."

Bliss lifted a shoulder. What could she say? It was impossible not to like Katie Kinkaid. "I'll try."

"Good." With a wave Katie was off, scurrying down the hallway like a whirlwind. Bliss followed her to the front door and closed it after Katie's tired old convertible rumbled down the drive.

Left feeling breathless, Bliss walked back to the den. Each and every day, her life became more complicated than she'd ever expected. Her father's impending marriage, her half sisters and Mason were more than she could expect to handle. Not at all certain she wanted to get to know either of her sisters any better, Bliss wondered if they'd ever come to terms with each other. Katie was a steamroller who seemed determined to take control of everyone's life she crossed, and Tiffany sounded cold and aloof.

"Don't judge," she warned herself, but she was still wary. She had to be careful. Years before, she'd cast caution to the wind when it came to relationships and it had cost her; it had cost her dearly. She'd lost her heart and nearly her life. She wouldn't make that mistake again. Not ever. Or so she tried to convince herself.

Chapter Eight

"So, is there a man in your life?"

Brynnie's question startled Bliss. She nearly dropped the pot of coffee she'd been pouring for her soon-to-be stepmother. Though she and John were still at odds about selling the ranch, they had buried the hatchet in shallow, soft soil. Everyone was treading lightly and Bliss wondered if the wedding would come off as planned.

"A man in my life? No, not really," she said, setting the glass pot back in the coffeemaker and handing Brynnie a steaming cup.

"A pretty girl like you? I don't believe it." Brynnie took a sip. "Mmm, that's good." She set her cup on the marred kitchen table and eyed her future stepdaughter. "You're an architect, isn't that what John told me?"

"When I'm working. Business has been a little slow lately."

"Good. You can spend more time here with your dad."

She added cream to her cup. "I would think, in a job like yours, that you'd work with lots of men."

Bliss swallowed a smile. "Too many."

"Uh-uh-uh. That's not the right attitude. By the time I was your age I was through with my second husband and on to my third." She laughed—a deep, throaty chuckle, made raspy by too many cigarettes.

"I guess I haven't met the right man yet."

"Of course, you have. You just don't know it." Brynnie blew across her cup and sighed. "You know, he might be right under your nose."

"Is that a fact?" The conversation made Bliss a little uncomfortable, but she couldn't help being intrigued by this woman who was so different from her mother. While Margaret Cawthorne had always been perfectly dressed, not a hair out of place, her smile somewhat immobile, her fingernails polished, her jewelry refined and understated, Brynnie wore tight jeans, T-shirts that had seen better days and costume jewelry that was outrageous and fun, rather than elegant.

Brynnie eyed Bliss over the rim of her cup. "I heard you saw Mason Lafferty the other day."

Bliss nearly choked on a swallow of coffee. This was a small town.

"I thought you two had some kind of, well—" she waved her pudgy fingers in the air and frowned "—chemistry, for lack of a better word."

Heat stole up Bliss's neck. That "chemistry" was none of Brynnie's business, and yet she'd probably already heard the story of her involvement with Mason from Bliss's father. "There was—once. It was a long time ago. It's over."

"Hmm." Brynnie chewed on her lower lip thoughtfully. "Some loves die hard. Never go away. Oh, they can be put on hold or people can pretend they don't exist, but it's all a big lie and one day you look in the mirror and face the fact that the love of your life might slip away if you don't do something.''

"Are you talking about you and Dad?" Bliss asked woodenly. This woman might soon become her stepmother, but, as far as Bliss was concerned, she had no right to hand out advice, especially on the subject of love.

"Right now, I'm talking about you." Brynnie drained her cup as John's boots pounded up the back steps to the porch. "You and Mason Lafferty. You can lie to yourself, if you want to, but it won't do any good. Besides, he's a good man and single."

Bliss bit her tongue to keep from saying something harsh about Brynnie being involved with her father while he was married.

"That marriage didn't seem to take. Over real quick. He and Terri split up years ago." She pointed an accusatory red-polished fingernail in Bliss's direction. "If you ask me, now that he's back in town, Mason Lafferty is the best catch in Bittersweet. Well, next to your father and my own boys, of course."

"Of course," Bliss said dryly as Brynnie shoved back her chair and the legs scraped against yellowed linoleum.

"My boys, now, they're good men, but land's sake, I pity the women they end up with." She shook her head. "I swear the twins were enough to nearly send me over the edge when they were in high school. But that's neither here nor now."

"Stay away from Lafferty, Blissie," John ordered as the screen door creaked open and he walked into the kitchen in his stocking feet. Pausing at the counter, he poured himself a cup of coffee.

"I'm not involved with Mason," she replied.

"I'm not blind, y'know. I see how you look at him."

"Give me a break," Bliss said, though she felt a blush steal up the back of her neck. Was it possible that she was so transparent?

"I shouldn't have to remind you that it was his fault you nearly—"

"No, Dad, you're wrong," she said vehemently. "Mason *saved* my life. I think we've had this conversation before." Bliss stood and tossed the dregs of her barely-touched coffee down the drain. Though she was furious with Mason for sneaking around behind her father's back to buy his ranch, she wasn't going to let John accuse him falsely. She slid her empty cup into the dishwasher. "Don't worry about me. I can take care of myself."

"Don't give me all that feminist mumbo jumbo. Women need men to take care of them. Good men," John said, then, the minute the words were uttered, he looked as if he wished he could swallow them back again.

Bliss blanched. She thought of her mother and the years of betrayal she'd borne; of Brynnie, in love with one man while marrying others; of herself, never quite over a silly schoolgirl crush on Mason Lafferty. "I...I don't believe that," Bliss said.

"Neither do I." Brynnie's eyes had filled with tears and her chin wobbled. "John—"

"Ah, blast it all, anyway." He rubbed a hand over his head, making his silvering hair stand on end. "What I meant was, Bliss, you could do better."

Just like your mother could have. The unspoken words hung in the air like forgotten cobwebs, visible one minute, hidden the next in the shifting light of mixed emotions.

"Well, uh..." Brynnie cleared her throat and dug into her purse for her cigarettes. "I heard you met Tiffany the other day."

"Tiffany?" Bliss repeated, still stung by her father's statement.

"Yes. When you visited Mason."

"You saw Mason and Tiffany?" John's mouth pulled downward.

"I don't think—" Bliss cut herself short as she remembered visiting Mason at his apartment. "Does Tiffany own an old Victorian in the middle of town?"

"Didn't you know?" Brynnie found her pack of cigarettes and shook out a filter tip.

"No, I..." So that explained the other woman's cool, stunned reaction to her.

"I ran into Octavia—that's her grandmother—down at the beauty parlor and she mentioned you'd been over."

"Is that right?" John said.

"I didn't realize she was Tiffany. I mean, I introduced myself and she didn't give me her name, just looked shocked and pointed out Mason's apartment."

"So you went visiting him?" He sighed wearily. "You're a smart girl, Bliss. I hoped you'd learned your lessons with that one."

"I have. But—"

Resigned, he waved off her excuses. "It's your life. Just use your head."

"Always do, Dad."

"Oh, honey, I wish I could believe that."

"Trust me."

"She's a grown woman," Brynnie reminded him. "And I'm not so sure either you or I are the right ones to be handing out advice." She struck a match and drew long on her cigarette.

John's jaw hardened. "I just don't want her to make the same mistakes I did."

"Or Margaret did," Brynnie said, shooting a geyser of smoke from the corner of her mouth.

"I won't." Rather than continue the no-win argument, Bliss headed for the den. She heard Brynnie defending Mason and her father going through the roof. The happiness he was certain he would find with his bride-to-be seemed to fade with each passing day, and Bliss doubted he'd find the peace he was so determined to have.

"You should never have sold out to him," her father was saying as Bliss walked the length of the house.

"It was my right."

"Like hell. I've half a mind to call the son of a bitch myself."

"Now, John, don't get all worked up...."

Bliss closed the door to the den behind her and leaned against the cool panels. What a mess. It seemed that John and Brynnie were forever at each other's throats. A match made in heaven, it wasn't.

But her part in it would soon be over; then they could fight it out like cats and dogs if they wanted to. Bliss only had to put up with a few more weeks of living with all this tension. Then, the Good Lord willing and true love, if that's what you'd call it, winning out, her father would be married. Bliss would return to Seattle.

For a reason she couldn't name, the thought of heading back to her apartment overlooking Puget Sound settled like lead in her heart.

Because of Mason. Because you can't forget him and because you haven't had it out with him. Face it, Bliss, what you really want while you're down here, is to find out why he abandoned you; why he ran away and why, when you cared for him him so deeply, he didn't return your love.

"All I'm saying, Lafferty, is that you had no right!"

Mason held the telephone receiver away from his ear as

John Cawthorne, swearing and yelling, told him seven ways to go to hell for buying out Brynnie's portion of the land. Though it had been days since the old man had found out, he was still furious and had, apparently, had another fight with his bride-to-be over the situation.

"I don't like anyone sneaking around my back, dealing with a woman, playing on her emotions. You're a snake, Lafferty, and I'll see your sorry backside in court, let me tell you."

"Fine."

"If you think I'm going to sell my part of the ranch, you'd better think again! And stay away from my daughter. You're not going to use Bliss to get to me!"

A quiet anger stole through Mason's blood. "I wouldn't."

"Sure. Like you wouldn't use Brynnie! Hell, Lafferty, you'd sell your own mother if you thought it would bring you a little profit in the future!"

Mason's jaw tightened and his knuckles showed white on the receiver at the mention of his mother's name.

"You're not going to pull a fast one on me, y'know," Cawthorne was yammering.

"Just think about the deal, Cawthorne," he said, managing to keep his voice calm though images of his mother, sad and old beyond her years, cut through his mind like razors. "That's all that matters."

"Like hell." Cawthorne slammed down the receiver.

"Great. Just great." Mason hung up and stood, stretching the tension out of the tight muscles of his back. Why the old man could get to him was a mystery.

Years ago, with Cawthorne standing in the rain, looming over him, offering him a deal for getting out of Bliss's life, Mason had been blinded by pain and had silently sworn he'd get even one day. Now the day was at hand, but the sweet taste of revenge eluded him.

He glanced at his watch. Not quite five, and he'd had a hell of a day even without John Cawthorne's verbal attack. Five cattle—three cows and two calves—had died of black leg on his ranch in Montana. The rest of the herd was quarantined, but there would still be losses—too many of them.

A foreman at the same ranch had fallen from the hay-mow, cracked three ribs and broken his ankle, and some neighboring rancher was screaming bloody murder about water rights. The neighbor had hired himself a local lawyer who had taken the case with a vengeance and was now threatening a lawsuit.

Then there was the matter of Patty. What had happened to her? It was strange that she'd quit calling him about the same time Isaac Wells had disappeared.

But John Cawthorne's phone call was the one that bothered him the most. Because of Bliss. Mason couldn't shake her out of his mind no matter how hard he tried. He'd always prided himself on being able to put each portion of his life into perspective, to give appropriate attention to the most pressing problems while letting others simmer until he was ready to deal with them, but Bliss dominated any other thoughts. Where she was concerned, he was beyond a fool.

"Get a grip," he growled as he squared a hat upon his head. He grabbed his jacket from a hook on the brass hall tree and decided to call it a day. It was after six and he needed a drink. A stiff one. Maybe even a double.

He yanked open the door and there she was. Bliss Cawthorne in the flesh. Her cheeks were flushed, her eyes troubled.

"I tried to stop her," Edie, his receptionist-secretary,

apologized helplessly, as if there was no way she could deter the intruder. Edie's earphones were still in place, the cord to her transcriber dangling from the headset.

"It'll just take a minute," Bliss said.

Mason doubted it. A minute? No way. An hour? He didn't think so. Whatever was weighing heavily enough on Bliss's mind to prod her down here looking for him, it would take a long time to hash out. "It's all right, Edie."

"But—" the secretary stammered, her feathers obviously ruffled.

"I'll handle it," Mason assured her as she glanced at her watch. "You can go on home. Just lock the door and have the answering service pick up."

"Are you sure? It's just that I have to pick up Toby."

"I know." He held the door to his office open and Bliss, looking suddenly as if she regretted whatever impulse it was that had driven her here, stepped inside. A cloud of her perfume trailed after her, but Mason refused to be affected by anything remotely feminine, even a scent that reminded him of long-ago years.

He closed the door softly and she nearly jumped.

"What's going on, Bliss?" he asked.

"I—I came down here because of Dad."

"You're sure about that?" He couldn't hide the skepticism in his words.

"Of course." She cleared her throat and her spine visibly stiffened as she impaled him with those incredible blue eyes. "I want you to back off, Mason."

"Back off?"

"Yeah, with Dad and his ranch. Surely there's another parcel you could buy." She tossed her hair over her shoulders. "Dad doesn't need this now—all this pressure. He's already had one heart attack and he doesn't need another.

He and Brynnie are at each other's throats because of this mess. Because of you.''

He propped himself on the corner of his desk and folded his arms over his chest. There was more to this than money and land; he could see it in her eyes and the set of her chin.

"I told you before, Brynnie wanted to sell," he reminded her.

"That was Dad's land."

"Which he had already deeded over to her."

Bliss took a step forward, placing herself directly in front of him and nailed him with a look that caused an uneven thumping in his chest. "You know, Mason, for years I've stuck up for you whenever Dad tried to pin that horseback-riding accident on you."

"Did you convince him?" he asked dryly.

"Never. But he knew what I thought."

He lowered his gaze to the semicircle of bone at the base of her throat where there was a pulse throbbing erratically. "And what was that, Bliss?" Mason asked boldly, painfully aware that her body was placed squarely between his legs, should he close them. His throat was so dry he had trouble concentrating. "What did you think?"

She paused and her gaze shifted. "I was the one who rode out in the storm. You saved me."

"Did I?" He wasn't convinced. Too many years of carrying a load of guilt around.

She didn't answer and through the frosted, pebbled glass of his door, he noticed the lights dim in the outer office. Edie had left. He was alone with Bliss. His palms began to sweat. His thighs, straddling the corner of the desk, began to ache.

"Just stay away from Dad and Brynnie, okay? Don't cause trouble between them."

"You want them to be together?" he asked. "Given all the circumstances, I would have thought—"

"I want my father to be happy," she interrupted. "That's all. He's...he's already had one heart attack."

"Which is the reason why Brynnie sold." He rubbed his knees with his hands and felt a tightening in his groin, the start of arousal. He should just cut the lights and escort Bliss and her air of self-righteousness out the door. But he didn't. He couldn't. Being alone with her—so close that he could smell her skin, see the faint freckles bridging her nose, witness the sweep of her honey-brown lashes against her cheeks—was his undoing.

Her eyes narrowed a fraction. "They've been fighting about it, you know."

"No one twisted Brynnie's arm."

Her eyes locked with his, and he felt a catch in his throat. "What is it with you, Lafferty? What is it you have against my father?"

He should have been prepared for the question and been able to deal with the silent accusations in her gaze, but he wasn't. Damn it, whenever he was near her, rational thought slipped away and he saw her as he remembered her best, naked as the day she was born, swimming in the rippling current of the river, her hair dark and damp, her skin flushed from the icy water, and her nipples, round pink buttons visible beneath the shimmering surface.

"What is it you have against me?"

"What?"

"You're not here because of 'dear old Dad,'" he said, seeing a spark of passion and the hint of pain in her eyes. "You're here because you wanted to see me again."

"Don't flatter yourself, Lafferty."

"Admit it, Bliss."

"I came because of the ranch—"

"Bull. You just don't know what to do with me."

"What?"

"Strangle me or kiss me."

"That's ridiculous!"

"Is it?" he asked, his heart thumping, his body hard with arousal. The scent of her perfume was tantalizing, the smell of her hair damned near drove him out of his mind. "You've never married."

She froze and the color in her face drained quickly. "Does it matter?" she demanded, then shook her head. "Listen, don't answer that. It's not important—"

"It is to me."

His words echoed through her soul, and she reminded herself to tread carefully, that this was a man to be wary of, a man she couldn't trust, a man who had stolen her heart years ago, only to ruthlessly toss it away.

She stepped away from him and rubbed her arms at the sudden chill in her bones, and he, as if understanding the need for distance between them, stood and walked around the edge of the desk to the window. Still, he was waiting for an answer. So why lie about being single? "Okay. Just for the record, Lafferty, I never found the right guy, okay? I've dated, sometimes seriously, been asked a couple of times, but never felt that I wanted to throw away my independence on some guy who...whom—"

"You didn't love."

Oh, God, it was as if he could read her mind, so she turned her back to him, tried to think. "Yes...I suppose that's it." He always had a disconcerting way of slicing right to the point. She heard him shift and leave his place at the window. His footsteps thudded dully on the carpet. She felt his hands upon her shoulders, his breath warm against the nape of her neck, and she stiffened. Her idiotic pulse had the nerve to skyrocket. Worse yet, his hands, work-roughened but gentle, felt so natural as they gently rotated her to face him.

"So why didn't you fall in love, Bliss?" he asked in a whisper that wafted through her hair and reverberated through her mind. Oh, Lord, he was too close and oh, so male.... She noticed the shadow of his beard, dark gold and rough against his square, uncompromising jaw.

"What?"

"I asked, why didn't you fall in love?"

I did. A long time ago. With you. And you hurt me. Oh, God, Mason, you hurt me so badly. She swallowed hard and licked lips that had become dry in a second. "I, uh, I guess I'm picky." Dear God, was that her voice that sounded so breathless—so filled with a desperate yearning she didn't want to name? "What—what about you?"

"I fell in love with the wrong woman."

Terri Fremont. His ex-wife. Of course. "I see."

"Do you?"

He was too close, *way* too close. She needed to escape, but her feet wouldn't move.

"Terri and I are divorced." His lips turned downward and a private pain pierced his eyes. "We have been for a long time. Ours wasn't exactly a marriage to write home about."

Her heart squeezed even though she'd told herself over and over again that she didn't care about Mason Lafferty, that he could rot in hell, that he was a selfish bastard. "I suppose not."

His mouth twisted and his hands, still upon her shoulders, didn't move. "You know, I never meant to hurt you—"

Oh, no, he was going to apologize! Again! This man who could barely admit to making a mistake. Bliss couldn't take it, didn't want to hear anything he had to say about what had happened between them. "Don't, Mason," she begged, staring into eyes as gold as an October sunset. "Just don't, okay?"

"I thought I should explain what happened."

"I know what happened, and guess what? It doesn't matter anymore," she said, her tongue tripping over the untruth. "I said what I wanted to say."

"Liar."

"Pardon me?" she asked, inwardly telling herself it was time to leave, to get away from him.

"I think you have a lot more to say. More questions that beg to be answered." He stepped even closer, touched the side of her face with one callused finger. Just being alone with him and breathing the same air he did caused her chest to constrict and her heart to pound in a silly, useless cadence.

"Bliss—" His hands captured her shoulders. His expression, harsh only minutes before, seemed suddenly haunted and weary. "Just...just believe that I never meant to hurt you."

She swallowed against a sudden lump in her throat as she witnessed a ghost of pain cross his eyes.

"I am sorry," he whispered.

"I know." Oh, Lord, now tears were burning against her eyelids but she forced them back. She'd wasted too many tears on this man years ago. "Believe me, Mason," she said, lying through her teeth again as anger overcame sadness, "it doesn't matter. It wasn't that big a deal. If you think I spent years or even months pining for you, you're dead wrong. I went home to Seattle, pulled myself up by my bootstraps and was dating Todd Wheeler not long after you finished saying 'I do.' So don't flatter yourself into thinking I cared a whit about whom you married or even when."

She tried to pull herself from his grasp, but his fingers clamped possessively over her arms. His amber gaze—hot, wanting and intense—pinned hers. No, she thought desperately. *No! No! No!* This was wrong. So very wrong, and yet, despite the denials screaming through her brain, she couldn't breathe, couldn't think, could only stare at his lips—blade-thin and hard. It took little effort to imagine what they would feel like against hers, how his mouth would open and his tongue would slide so easily past her own lips and teeth, searching, seeking, touching....

"If I could do things over—"

"What?" she asked, tearing her gaze from that sexy slash that was his mouth. "What are you saying, Mason? That you'd change the past? How? Sneak around so that I wouldn't find out about Terri? Keep me from riding out to the ridge in the storm?" *Make love to me like I begged you to?* Oh, God. "What?"

"No, I—"

"I don't want to hear it!" Now she sounded like a spoiled teenager, but she didn't care. She had to find a way to break away from him, away from the sweet seduction of his touch. This was all happening way too fast and much too late. "Look, Mason, as I've said, it just doesn't matter anymore."

"Like hell." Their gazes clashed—innocent blue and rugged gold. Like metal striking metal.

"No— Oh, Mason—"

He dragged her against him and as she gasped, his lips crashed down on hers. Urgent. Wanting.

She voiced a soft moan of protest that went unheeded.

His mouth was hard and warm and molded so effortlessly against hers. He smelled of leather and aftershave, musky and male. A part of her let go—after ten long, heart-wrenching years.

His lips were as sensual and insistent as they had been years before, and she was just as lost to him now. In the warm interior of his office, a decade had melted away.

Don't do this, Bliss. Don't let him use you again!

But she couldn't stop herself.

His mouth moved over hers with a wild abandon that touched the deepest part of her. Within a heartbeat her traitorous body began to respond, and desire, hot and long-slumbering, awoke with a vengeance. She could hardly breathe, her knees threatened to buckle and her mouth opened willingly under the sweet, gentle pressure of his tongue.

Somewhere in the back of her mind she knew she was making a horrid, life-altering mistake, but she didn't care. For the moment, she only wanted to close her eyes and drown in the seductive whirlpool of his taste, his smell, his touch.

With a moan, she started to wind her arms around his neck. Then, as his fingers toyed with the hem of her T-shirt, she realized that she was falling into the same precarious trap that had snared her ten years earlier.

He used you before.

He'll use you again.

He never loved you and never will.

"I—I can't," she managed. "W-we shouldn't... Oh, Lord, this—this isn't a good idea," she whispered, lifting her head and feeling dizzy. Her eyelids were at half-mast, her blood flowing like lava.

"I know." He kissed her—a soft, teasing brush of his lips over hers.

She melted deep inside. "I don't think—"

Another feather-light kiss to the corner of her mouth. "Don't think."

Sweet heaven, how she wanted him. Her legs turned

wobbly. "Listen, Mason, please, I can't do this." Forcing the unwanted words over her tongue, she pushed him away with all her strength. She was breathing hard, her chest rising and falling with each breath, her anger pulsing in her ears. "What we had was over a long time ago. I thought you understood that a few minutes ago, but if you missed the message let me give it to you loud and clear, okay?" Somehow she found the strength to say what her heart so vehemently denied. "I don't believe in reliving the past."

"How about changing the future?"

Her heart stopped for a crazy minute and in her mind's silly eye, she saw herself walking down an aisle in a white dress, swearing to love him for the rest of her life, becoming his wife and bearing his children. Mason's babies. A part of her heart shredded when she remembered he already had a child, one that had nothing to do with her. Tears touched the back of her eyelids and she said dully, "We have no future." And that was the simple truth. They both knew it. "Look, don't…don't you have an oil well to drill, or some tractors to sell, or some livestock to brand?"

A slow, sexy smile spread across his face. "I was just about to call it a day." Reaching behind her head, he snapped off the lights. "Maybe you and I should have dinner or drinks," he suggested, and a part of her longed to be with him, to forgive him, to be confident enough to make love to him without the need to think of becoming his wife.

"I—I don't think that would be such a good idea."

"Scared?" he taunted, and a spark of amusement flared in his eyes.

"No way."

"Then, why not go out with me?"

Because I can't take a chance. I don't want to get hurt, and I can't trust myself when I'm around you! "I…I have plans.'' Even to her own ears, her excuse sounded feeble. ''With Dad.''

He hesitated, his silence accusing her of the lie. His jaw slid to one side. ''Then I'll take a rain check.''

''Fine. Right.''

''I'm serious, Bliss. Any time you want to see me, drop by.'' Amber eyes held hers for a second. ''You know where I live.''

''Yes. At Tiffany's.''

He nodded and touched her lightly on the arm. ''Any time.'' A tremor stole through her at the thought of being alone with him at his place. He opened the door and she walked through with as much dignity as she could muster, but all the way down the stairs to the first floor, she felt her lips tingle where Mason had kissed her and her cheeks, where the stubble of his beard had rubbed against her skin, were slightly tender. Oh, Lord, what was she getting herself into? She shoved open the front door and heard Mason's keys jangling in the lock but she didn't wait for him to follow her.

Quickly, she hurried outside to the sidewalk. The flow of traffic was lazy in the late afternoon and in the town square across the street, women pushed baby buggies or watched their children play on equipment in the park. She thought she spied Tiffany Santini pushing her daughter on a swing, and again her heart twisted at the thought of children.

Tiffany threw her head back and laughed as the imp in the swing said something she found hilarious. Tiffany's black hair gleamed in the sunlight, and mother and daughter seemed carefree and incredibly happy.

Someday, she silently told herself. *Oh, sure, and when is that going to happen? Remember, Bliss, you've got a long way to go. You're twenty-seven years old and still a virgin.*

Chapter Nine

"So tell me, Lafferty, what is it you're afraid of?" Jarrod asked. He peeled the label from his bottle of beer while some old country ballad wafted through the smoky interior of the bar. From the back room, billiard balls clicked while conversation at the few odd tables scattered around the room was punctuated by laughter. A television mounted high over the bar was tuned in to a baseball game, which the bartender watched as he polished the battered old mahogany with a white towel.

"'Afraid of'?" Mason took a swallow from his long-necked bottle and let the beer cool his throat. He didn't like lying; wasn't much good at it, but knew that once in a while it was necessary. This was one of those times. "Nothing."

"Bull." Jarrod eyed him with the calm of a cougar advancing upon a lamb. He leaned forward. "You're scared that Patty's involved up to her eyeballs in old man Wells's disappearance."

"I don't know how." That much was the truth, though he couldn't help suspecting that Patty, with her penchant for trouble, knew something about their uncle's vanishing act. What, he couldn't imagine, but then Patty always kept him guessing. He never knew what to expect from his muleheaded sister.

"Yeah, and I'm the Pope."

"Why would I pay you a lot of money if I already knew the answer?"

"*That's* what I'd like to know." He hoisted his empty bottle and signaled to a bored-looking waitress. "Hey, Tammy, how about another one?" He motioned to Mason. "For him, too."

She nodded a head of overbleached and kinky-permed hair, and Jarrod swung his gaze to his friend again. "I get the feeling that you've led me on a wild-goose chase, Lafferty, and I don't like being played for a fool. You know that."

"Look, I don't know where Patty is and I sure as hell can't begin to figure out what happened to old Isaac. As much of a pain in the butt as he was, most of the people in this county think it's a blessing that he's gone, but I'm not one of them."

Jarrod snorted as Mason drained his beer. "Right."

The waitress, slim in her blue jeans and white T-shirt, deposited two more bottles on the table. "Anything else?"

"Not just yet," Jarrod said, flashing her a smile that was known to break women's hearts.

She, today, wasn't in the mood. "Just let me know," she said sourly and took the empties.

"You got it." Jarrod rolled the new bottle between his palms.

Jarrod had phoned Mason, invited him for a drink, and Mason had agreed. He needed something—*anything*—to get his mind off Bliss. But he wasn't too keen on being grilled by his old friend.

Jarrod checked his watch. "Look, I've got to go, but there's one more thing."

"Shoot."

"It's about Mom."

"Brynnie?"

With a sharp nod, Jarrod settled back in the booth. "She's in a pile of trouble because of her deal with you about her acres of the ranch. Old man Cawthorne is fit to be tied and he wants blood. Yours and Mom's."

"So I heard."

"Yeah. He feels that she betrayed him."

"What do you want me to do about it?"

Jarrod rubbed his jaw. "I don't know. Maybe sell the ranch back to her." At the tightening of Mason's jaw, Jarrod sighed and shook his head. "Hey, you know there's no love lost between the man and me. I'd just as soon spit on Cawthorne as talk to him, but he's gonna be my stepfather—like it or not. And for some unfathomable reason, he makes Mom happy. Or he did, until she up and sold out to you. Now he's hot under the collar, furious with her, and she's got her back up. They're barely talking and they're supposed to be tying the knot."

"Sounds like a marriage made in heaven," Mason observed.

"There is no such thing," Jarrod replied, finishing his drink and reaching into the back pocket of his jeans for his wallet. "You, of all people, should know that. This one's on me, Lafferty." He tossed a few bills onto the table.

"I'll buy next time."

"Nope." Jarrod climbed to his feet. "Just be straight with me."

"Always am," Mason said, inwardly cringing at the lie.

"Good." They walked outside where a summer breeze was chasing down the dusty streets and a million stars were visible over the faint glow of the sparse streetlights. "So, are you going to give me a hint about where that sister of yours could be?"

"If I knew that, I wouldn't have to hire you."

One side of Jarrod's mouth lifted. "But you're holding back. I can feel it. Don't you know that confession's good for the soul?"

"Got nothing to confess."

"That'll be the day." Jarrod opened the door of his pickup and paused. "By the way, I heard through the grapevine that you've been seeing Bliss again."

The muscles in Mason's shoulders bunched. "That grapevine's all twisted the wrong way. She won't have anything to do with me."

Jarrod pulled on his chin and hesitated for a second before dispensing his advice. "Just tread softly. Old man Cawthorne's already on the warpath."

A smile tugged at the corners of Mason's mouth. "So I'm supposed to back off?"

"Just be careful." Jarrod slid into the seat and jammed his keys into the ignition. "And be smart. Bliss is a classy lady."

"I noticed."

"She deserves the best."

"Don't we all?"

Jarrod started the engine and his mouth tightened. "Don't use her, okay? I know you have a thing—some kind of personal vendetta—against her old man, but don't use her to get back at him."

"Don't worry about it." The last thing in the world he wanted to do was hurt Bliss, but he damned sure wanted to make love to her. And that was a problem—a problem that had been with him since the first time he'd seen her so many years ago, a problem he couldn't begin to solve.

But then again, he was a firm believer in the old "Nothing ventured, nothing gained" theory. Now was as good a time as any to test it.

On Bliss.

Astride Fire Cracker, Bliss craned her neck and peered over the edge of the ridge. Full from the spring runoff, the river far below slashed wildly over stones and fallen trees, carving a rushing swath through the stony canyon as it had on the day she'd nearly lost her life at this very spot.

Her heart began to pound and her hands sweated on the reins as the memories of that fateful afternoon ricocheted through her mind. She remembered Mason's warnings as clearly as if he'd just uttered them....

"Don't be a fool."

Too late, she thought. She'd always been a fool for Mason Lafferty. They'd been so young, so innocent, and so afraid of falling in love.

It seemed as if everything and nothing had changed. Slowly she dismounted.

The wind stirred, rustling through the trees and causing wildflowers to bend in its wake. Bliss sighed for all the could-have-beens until she noticed the shadow creeping slowly beside her. Squinting against the sun she saw Mason, tall astride his horse, rangy and rugged as the mountains that towered around them.

Her heart squeezed as it always did when she was alone with him, and a tiny voice inside reminded her that he was the one—he had forever been the one—who was wedged deep in her heart, be he bad, good or indifferent. "Mason," she said, surprised that her voice had lost some of its timbre.

"Thought I might find you here." He swung down from his gelding and let the horse roam free.

"Did you? Why?"

"Because, like it or not, Bliss, I know you."

Her throat turned to dust but she wouldn't be so easily seduced. "No, Lafferty, you don't know a damned thing about me. Not anymore."

Slowly he sauntered toward her. "When you weren't at the house and Delores said you'd taken off riding, I thought I'd be able to catch up with you. So I, well, 'borrowed,' I guess you'd say, one of the horses in the stables and rode out here. After all, this is the scene of the crime, so to speak."

"'Crime'? You mean accident." Oh, God, his eyes were such an incredible hue of gold.

He lifted a shoulder. "Whatever." The corners of his mouth twisted. "I—" His gaze centered on hers and she knew in an instant that he was searching for her soul. "I thought there were some things you and I should get straight."

"Like what?" she asked warily and wished her pulse would slow a little. So he'd followed her out here, so they were alone together in the dying sunlight, so her throat was as dry as a desert wind, so what?

"I wanted to say that I didn't mean to hurt you."

Somewhere nearby a crow cawed loudly.

She stiffened. "You didn't."

"Of course, I did." He closed the short distance between them.

Trying to back away, she nearly stumbled but his hands, rough and large, caught her and held her upright. His fingertips were warm through the light cotton of her blouse and she felt them press intimately against her ribs, as if there were no barrier, no flimsy piece of cloth separating his skin from hers.

"Terri didn't mean anything to me, Bliss," he said, a muscle jumping in his jaw.

"Then why did you sleep with her?"

"It was before I met you. Before I understood."

"Understood what?"

He hesitated for a second. "What caring about a person is all about."

Oh, God, she wanted to believe him. But there was too much time, too many lies. "Mason, you don't have to explain."

"Like hell." Shifting clouds covered the sun in a soft, thin veil.

"It doesn't matter. Not anymore."

"It matters to me." A lick of lightning flared in his eyes and in that split second she knew he was going to kiss her. Not just once, but many times, with a pulsing passion that was certain to be her downfall.

She tried to pull away, but his hands held her fast and when his lips claimed hers the whimper of protest forming in her throat turned into a soft moan of pure female wanting. Dear God, she'd waited so long for this. Much too long. Kissing him seemed so natural, so right, and yet... His tongue slid easily between her teeth and beyond, searching and teasing, tasting and flicking against its mate.

Bliss was lost. All thoughts of denial swiftly fled. As the horses, bridles jangling, grazed on the summer grass and a hawk circled lazily in the cloudless sky, Mason kissed her eyes, her cheeks, her throat. Her skin quivered with each brush of his lips and she couldn't protest as his weight pulled them both to the soft carpet of grass covering the ground.

"I told myself to forget you," he whispered.

"I know. I did, too."

"But I couldn't."

She didn't argue, didn't bring up the fact that he'd married another woman. Right now, alone on this grassy ridge, with an outcropping of stone near the edge and the forest so close, she closed her eyes and gave in to the sensations that she'd denied for oh-so-many years.

Her heart thundered; her skin was on fire. Strong arms held her fast, firm lips loved her as if she were the only woman on earth.

As the wind picked up, he lowered himself over her and the intimacy of his weight pressed against hers felt so right. Kissing each patch of her exposed skin, he drew her closer. With deft fingers, he unbuttoned her blouse and the warm air of summer touched her skin.

Slowly he kissed the dusky hollow between her breasts before he brushed his lips across a lace-encased nipple. "Bliss," he whispered as she arched her back. "Sweet, sweet Bliss."

A yearning, feminine and wanton, swirled deep inside her and seeped into her blood. He lifted one breast from the lacy bounds of her bra, and her nipple puckered in expectation.

"Mason—" she cried as his mouth found her nipple and gently suckled. "Oh..." She should stop this madness, stanch the heat flowing wildly through her blood, halt the driving need that was causing her to want him so badly.

"That's it, darlin'," he murmured as his hands moved to the waistband of her jeans. "Let go."

"I—I can't."

"Sure, you can." His mouth was wet velvet, smooth and slick, his tongue wantonly teasing her as he slid her jeans over her hips.

Somewhere in the back of her mind she knew she should

stop him, that letting him touch her was downright dangerous, but as he trailed his tongue along her bare skin she melted inside and passion ruled over reason. His lips were hot, his breath a warm summer breeze that rolled over her, and she trembled deep inside.

This was wrong. So how could it feel so right? Through her panties his lips and tongue touched her, parting her legs, creating a hot pool of lust that ached for all of him. "Mason, please..." she rasped as he teased at the elastic of her underwear with his teeth.

He slipped his hands beneath the silk. "Trust me," he said, and her heart nearly broke. Hadn't she trusted him with her love—with her very life—ten years ago?

Slowly he touched her. With infinite care he explored and caressed while his lips pressed anxious kisses to her abdomen. She closed her eyes and the world seemed to swirl on a new and separate axis. He rimmed her navel with his tongue and she felt perspiration soak through her skin. She knew nothing more than the feel and smell of him. Closing her eyes, she gave in to the storm of desire sweeping through her, moved under the gentle tutelage of his fingers, cried out as the world spun out of control and the universe, stars and rainbows, collided behind her eyes.

"That's my girl," he whispered, as she quivered and his arms surrounded her. He kissed her gently on the stomach, then held her close.

Her mind reeling, she looked up into his gold eyes. "But—" she cleared her throat "—what about...what about...you?"

With a cynical smile, he drew her even closer, his nose pressed to the crook of her neck. "Another time, darlin'," he promised, then kissed the side of her throat. "Another time."

* * *

Despite the open windows, the air inside the house was airless and hot. Most of the tension was due to the fact that Brynnie had come over to make amends with her intended, but some of the frustration Bliss was feeling was because she hadn't seen Mason in several days. She didn't understand what had happened to them up on the ridge—why he hadn't made love to her—and she hadn't been able to think of much else.

"A curse, that's what it is," she told Oscar, and the dog, seated on a chair, his chin between his paws, wagged his tail. "Men. Who needs them?"

As for her father, John Cawthorne wasn't ready to reconcile with Brynnie. He obviously felt betrayed and bamboozled and kept reminding the woman he supposedly loved that she was some kind of traitor.

"Oh, I give." Bliss threw down her pencil and walked from the den toward the kitchen. As she passed the dining-room windows, she heard the sound of tires crunching against the gravel in the driveway.

For a split second she thought Mason might have come by the house and her heart did a stupid little leap, but she glanced out the window and spied Katie, all business, striding to the front door. Disappointment settled upon her, though she couldn't explain why. Just because she hadn't seen Mason in a few days was no reason to get a case of the blues. Oh, she was being such a ninny. What did she care about him? Who cared if she spent her nights sleeplessly remembering how he kissed her and caused her insides to tremble?

The bell rang just as Bliss yanked open the door. Oscar let out a few excited barks and scrambled to the doorway, jumping wildly on Katie as she breezed into the house. "Hi," Katie said a trifle breathlessly. "Is Mom here?"

"In the kitchen."

"Good." Katie hurried down the hallway to find her mother stirring a bowl of strawberries, sugar and pectin together as she made freezer jam. John was sitting at the table reading the paper.

"Katie!" Her mother looked up and beamed. "What brings you out here?"

"I, uh, thought it might be a good time for Bliss to meet Tiffany." She glanced at Bliss. "I know it's kind of sudden, but I'm not working today and Josh is over at Laddy's, so I thought if you have the time…"

Bliss cleared her throat and noticed that her father, looking over the tops of his reading glasses, was staring at her. There was something akin to hope in his eyes. "Are you sure she wants to meet me?"

"I don't know," Katie replied honestly.

"Why wouldn't she?" John demanded.

"Oh, Dad, come on. If you can't figure it out, I'm not going to spell it for you."

"You're a wonderful person and—"

"And I'm your daughter. Your *legitimate* daughter—the one you claimed."

"We're all adults, now," he said stubbornly. "And she's got a couple of kids. I'm their grandfather."

Grandfather. Bliss held back the argument that was brewing in her mind. Her father was a grandfather—three times over—and though she had trouble with the concept, he didn't. A little spurt of jealousy flowed through her veins. For most of her life she'd thought she would be the only bearer of Cawthorne grandkids. If she could. That was still a question. It was funny, in a bitter way, how life had turned out, and again she felt an empty space, a small hole in her life—one that only a child could fill.

"That's why I think we should talk to Tiffany. See her face-to-face," Katie said.

"Maybe you should slow down a mite." Brynnie patted Katie's hand and Bliss felt a lump forming in her throat. Though she and her mother hadn't been the touch-and-hug kind of mother and daughter, they'd been close, and seeing this display of affection between Brynnie and Katie brought to the surface a part of her she'd tried to suppress—the part of her that missed Margaret Cawthorne so badly that sometimes she still fought tears. "Tiffany might need a little more time, you know, to get used to things."

"It's been over thirty years," John interjected.

"But not for her." Brynnie took a chair at the table so she could face Bliss's father. "You know she might not come to the wedding. You'll have to accept that."

"Don't know if I can." Taking off his reading glasses, he rubbed one hand over his face and Bliss was struck by how he'd aged in the past few years.

"Look, let's not get all tied in knots about it," Katie said. "Just tell me how the wedding plans are coming along."

"Humph!" John pushed his chair back.

"They're fine." Brynnie shot him a look that dared him to argue, but for once, John Cawthorne held his tongue.

In the ensuing silence, Bliss glanced at the calendar. Only a few weeks until her father said "I do" for the second time in his life. Somehow, Bliss had come to terms with her father and his new bride. She had to find a way to lock away her past with him, to concentrate on the future so that she could honestly wish him happiness and maybe some kind of peace that had eluded him for most of his life.

"The invitations went out last week," Brynnie was saying. "The flowers are ordered, the cake is gonna be beautiful and if I can only get those miserable caterers to come up with a decent meal for a price that wouldn't make a millionaire's eyes pop out of his head, we'll be set."

Katie glanced at her watch, then at Bliss. "Why don't you take a ride into town with me and we'll grab a soda or something?"

Bliss hesitated, but just for a second.

"Okay," she said, involuntarily squaring her shoulders as if readying herself for battle. "Let's go."

Katie didn't need any further encouragement. Within minutes they were out the door and on the road in Katie's old rattletrap of a convertible. Despite her seat belt, Bliss clung to the door handle. The car was an older model with a big engine and it practically flew past the dry fields and rounded hills. Telephone poles whipped by and Bliss's hair tangled in the wind. The radio was on and the pounding beat of an old song by The Who rocked through the speakers.

"I hear that you and Mason Lafferty are an item," Katie said as she took a corner so fast the tires squealed.

"An item? Where'd you hear that?" Bliss was trying to hold her hair into a ponytail with one hand while clutching the door with the other. The last topic of conversation she wanted to deal with was Mason.

"Mom. She seems to have an ear to the ground."

Or a nose for gossip, Bliss thought. "There's nothing going on between Mason and me."

"Why not?" Katie cast her half sister a grin. "You have to admit he's hot."

"Oh, for the love of... Hot?"

"That's the term the kids use. Josh is always telling me who's hot and who's not in the fourth grade."

"This isn't elementary school." And yet her heart pounded like that of a schoolgirl whenever she heard his name.

"I know, but, as I told you before, Mason's one of the most eligible bachelors in these parts."

"I'm not in the market," Bliss said, as if to convince herself. "Why don't you date him?"

"Naw. Known him all my life. He hung out with my older brother, Jarrod, so even though he's sexy as all get-out, I'm immune." She eased up on the gas as she approached town. A wooden sign welcoming visitors to Bittersweet needed a new coat of paint and the railroad tracks that had run parallel to the road curved toward the spindly-looking trestle bridge that spanned the river. Flat, single-story strip malls had sprouted on the outskirts of town, while in the older section, near the town square and Mason's office, shops with false western-style fronts rose two or three stories.

"Do you know his wife?" Bliss asked as Katie nosed her car into a parking spot.

"Terri? Sure." She turned off the engine and tossed the oversize key ring into her purse. With a shrug, she added, "She's okay, I guess. After the divorce, she moved to— Colorado, I think. Either Boulder or Aspen or... Well, it doesn't matter. A few years ago she moved back here with Dee Dee, her and Mason's daughter."

Bliss remembered the girl with the soulful eyes.

They walked across the hot sidewalk where tiny particles of glass reflected in the sunlight. Katie opened the door of a coffee shop with her hip and waved to a waitress in a checked blouse and brown pants.

She seemed to know everyone in the place, from an old man with one leg and a charming smile, to a five-year-old blond girl who burst out of the rest room and careened into Katie's waiting arms. "Cindy Mae West, what're you doing here?" Katie asked with a wide grin as she scooped up the urchin.

"Havin' ice cream with my dad."

"You'd better go eat it before it melts." Katie hugged the child and set her on the black-and-white tiled floor. Like a shot, the kid bolted to a booth in the corner where her father was smoking a cigarette and a caramel sundae was dripping over the side of its dish.

Katie and Bliss sat in a booth near the windows, ordered soft drinks, and after they were both sipping from their sodas, Katie, green eyes sparkling, said, "Go ahead. Ask me about Mason." As if she saw the protest forming in her half sister's eyes, she added, "And don't give me any back-talk about not being interested. I'm a journalist, you know, write part-time for the *Rogue River Review* and you just happen to be one lousy liar, Bliss Cawthorne."

That much was true, and since Katie had already guessed that she was, at some slight level, emotionally involved with Mason, there was no reason to argue the point. "All right. So I'm interested. A little."

"A lot, I'd think."

"A little."

"Okay, okay. The way the story goes is that Mason had an affair with Terri Fremont years ago. She got pregnant and he, after losing his job at John's, er, your—well, my dad's place, too, I guess. Gosh, this is complicated. Anyway, Mason married her and moved to Montana or somewhere. His sister—you remember Patty, don't you?" When Bliss shook her head, Katie waved her hand as if to dismiss the girl. "She was a wild one and Mason felt like he had to take care of her after his mother died. Anyway, she moved in with Mason and Terri, and I suspect there was hell to pay. Then Terri miscarried and the marriage was in trouble. The baby was all they had in common, the only reason they had walked down the aisle."

"Miscarried?" Bliss repeated, jolted. "But Dee Dee..."

"Deanna. I know. She came along right after the miscarriage, I guess." Katie's face twisted thoughtfully. "I don't exactly know all the details, probably no one does, but I'm sure... Well, I think I've got the story pretty much straight." She took a long sip through her straw. "As I said, I really don't know Terri that well and Mason's pretty tight-lipped about everything concerning his private life. All I'm sure about is that the split wasn't amicable at all. They were separated for a couple of years and ended up getting a divorce. Terri, who hired some hotshot attorney from Portland, came out smelling like a rose."

"How's that?" Bliss asked, knowing she shouldn't be listening to such blatant gossip, but she couldn't help herself. When it came to Mason, she couldn't seem to learn enough. The thought rankled her. She detested women who were forever trying to find out more about certain men, but here she was, pumping her half sister for information on the one guy she should forget about.

Katie swirled her drink with her straw, and shaved ice danced in the glass. "Because by that time Mason had done well for himself. He'd saved for years, bought a ranch in Montana, discovered oil on the property and then started buying other places. He threw himself into his business as if he had something to prove. Worked twenty-hour days if you can believe the local gossip. Terri left the marriage a wealthy woman—well, wealthy by Bittersweet standards. I doubt if she'd cause much of a stir in New York or L.A." Katie tossed down her straw and gulped down the remainder of her drink.

"What about his sister?"

"Patty?" A dark cloud passed behind Katie's eyes. "Don't know," she admitted. "She has a place over near the river, but she's gone a lot. Very private person—kind of weird, I think. Never got over her mother's suicide."

Frowning slightly, Katie glanced at her watch and found a way to change the subject. "I think we should talk to Tiffany."

"Now?" Bliss was stunned.

"No time like the present." Katie dropped a few dollars onto the table and pretended that she didn't hear Bliss's protests that she would pick up the tab. "Come on." Katie was already on her way to the door.

With trepidation as her companion, Bliss slung the strap of her purse over her shoulder. "Don't you think we should call her first? Give her some time to get used to the idea?"

"Probably." But Katie shouldered open the door and walked briskly toward her convertible. "Trust me, she won't be that shocked. I already introduced myself a couple of weeks ago."

"But—"

"Come on. You're not a coward."

"No, just cautious."

"Oh, I don't believe that one for a minute. No daughter of John Cawthorne's is cautious."

"Okay, okay." There seemed to be no talking Katie out of her half-baked plan, and Bliss reluctantly climbed into her half sister's disreputable car. "You know, she might not be all that interested in meeting me."

"Never know until you try." Katie jammed the car into gear.

Bliss settled back in the seat and sighed. The truth of the matter was that she wanted to know more about her older half-sister, and if the truth were known, the fact that Tiffany was Mason's landlord only added to her interest.

"This could be the best thing that ever happened to you!" Katie took a corner a little too fast and Bliss slid in her seat.

Or, Bliss thought, *it might just be the worst.*

* * *

The air-conditioning was on the fritz and Mason's office was an oven. Even with the windows partially open, the room was stuffy and warm. Sweat collected around his collar and hairline, and he thought of dozens of reasons to take the rest of the day off. But he couldn't leave quite yet.

Edie was in the outer office and, as the door between their rooms was ajar, he heard her humming to herself as her fingers flew over the keyboard of her computer.

"So I'm not sure where I'll be," Terri said over the phone. "Bob has a place up on Orcas Island and it's absolutely beautiful in the summer."

"Dee Dee needs a permanent home."

"So you've said."

"Terri, for once, think of her."

"Like I don't?" she replied, her voice elevating an octave. "Do I have to remind you that I've raised her almost single-handedly these past eight years?"

Here we go again. "No, Terri, but I've told you I'd like her to live with me."

She snorted. "Forget it, Mason, I'll let you know what I decide. Remember, you've got her for a couple of hours tonight. I'll drop her off later."

"Wait a minute—"

Click.

"Terri? *Terri?*" But she'd hung up. "Damn it all to hell." He kicked at the wastebasket and sent it flying against the far wall.

"Are you all right?" Edie asked.

"Just fine," Mason growled as he slammed down the receiver and fought the urge to swear a blue streak. His head pounded and if he thought it would do any good, he'd drive over to Terri's place and— And what? Scream and yell? Beg and plead? Threaten? No way. The only thing Terri understood was money. Lots of it. He had to calm down and work this out with a cool head and an open checkbook.

Slowly counting to fifty, he stood and stretched his spine, balled and straightened his fists. His desk was cluttered and now, where the wastebasket had spilled, papers had spewed onto the floor. He picked up the can and retrieved the trash and vowed never to let that woman get to him again.

He'd spent the better part of the day going over profit-and-loss statements, dealing with attorneys and accountants, and wrestling with decisions about his business, his daughter, and, of course, Bliss. He'd foolishly thought he could forget her. Wrong. It seemed that with each passing day he was more obsessed with John Cawthorne's daughter.

Cawthorne. He was another headache in and of himself. A real head-case, that guy.

Resting a hip on the corner of his desk, Mason spied the deed to Cawthorne's ranch on top of one stack of papers. Brynnie had signed it, the thing was legal, all he had to do was record the transaction with the county.

Or sell it back to her.

Hell, what a mess.

He rounded the desk, found a bottle of Scotch in the cupboard by the window, unscrewed the cap and took one long, fiery swallow. As the liquor burned a welcome trail down his throat, he discovered that all of his anger with the old man had evaporated, and the vengeance he'd nurtured over the years—the need to prove himself to Bliss and her father—had faded with time. He didn't need Cawthorne Acres. Unfortunately what he did need, he realized with a sinking feeling, was Bliss.

"Get a grip, Lafferty," he chastised. She was still off-limits. Always would be. And he had other problems to deal with. If he wasn't going to settle down at the Cawthorne ranch, he needed a place big enough for himself, Dee Dee, and a housekeeper-nanny. *Or a wife.*

He took one more tug off the bottle, screwed on the cap and shoved it back where it belonged. A wife? No way. He'd tried that once before and look what a mess he'd gotten himself into. *Yeah, but you married the wrong woman. You knew it at the time.*

He folded the deed and slipped it into the inner pocket of his jacket just as the phone rang.

"Jarrod Smith, on line one," Edie called through the open door.

"Got it." Mason picked up the receiver. "Hey," he said, "what's up?"

"It's Patty." Jarrod's voice was grim, without any trace of humor whatsoever. "I think I've found her."

Chapter Ten

"I've got a bad feeling about this," Bliss thought aloud, but Katie, determined that the sisters should meet, was threading the car into the slow stream of traffic that ran through Bittersweet. "You know I already met Tiffany once."

"I heard. Mom said Octavia told her about it."

"Tiffany never said a word about who she was or that we were sisters or anything."

"She was probably shocked."

"Beyond shocked. Way beyond," Bliss said, remembering the horrified look in her half sister's eyes when she'd mentioned who she was.

"Well, she should have said something, but didn't. We'll give her a second chance." Katie gunned through a yellow light, then eased up on the throttle as they passed hundred-year-old churches with spires and bell towers and wound down tree-lined streets flanked by stately old manors.

"She's Mason's landlady," Bliss ventured.

"Mmm." Katie sent her a sidelong glance. "Thought you didn't care about him."

"I don't, much."

Katie didn't say a word, but looked as if she were swallowing an I-knew-it-all-along smile.

Bliss's stomach tightened as Katie turned the corner to the street where both Tiffany and Mason lived. She told herself that her paranoia was ridiculous as Katie parked at the curb in front of the ornate Victorian house.

Bliss steeled herself for her meeting with her other half-sister. A sprinkler sprayed jets of water over the parched lawn and a black cat sunned itself on the pavement of the driveway near a basketball hoop. Bliss didn't know what to expect. It had been over a week since she'd stopped by looking for Mason and had inadvertently introduced herself to Tiffany, and in that time she hadn't heard a word from her. At Katie's swift pace she walked up the brick path to the porch. Once at the front door, there wasn't any time for second guesses. Katie pressed the button for the bell.

The door opened and Bliss stood face-to-face with her older sister again. Tiffany Nesbitt Santini looked no more like her than Katie did.

Chin-length black hair framed a heart-shaped face. Eyes, a soft brown, were surrounded by thick lashes and tanned skin stretched tautly over high, sculpted cheekbones. Her mouth was wide, full-lipped and set in a tentative smile.

"Katie," she said, shifting her curious gaze to the petite redhead. The smile faded a little.

"Hi." Katie seemed suddenly nervous.

"And Bliss." Tiffany's grin disappeared. "I wondered when you'd figure it out and be back."

Bliss's heart did a nosedive. Any warmth in Tiffany's

eyes had disappeared and there was a slight stiffening of her backbone. "I thought we should meet."

"We did," Tiffany replied.

"No. You met me. You didn't give me your name."

"You didn't bother to ask."

"I know, I didn't think of it."

"Because you were anxious to find your 'friend' Mason."

Boy, this woman had a wicked tongue. Bliss gave herself a swift mental kick for agreeing to Katie's screwball plan. The least they could have done was given Tiffany the courtesy of a telephone call.

"Can we come in?" Katie acted as if she didn't sense any of the nuances of the conversation, as if she didn't feel the tension simmering between her half sisters. But it was there, evident in Tiffany's cool stare and frosty demeanor.

"If it's not too much trouble," Bliss added, half hoping she'd refuse them and this ordeal would be over. So Tiffany didn't like her. Big deal.

"Sure. Why not?" Tiffany's voice had all the warmth of the inside of an igloo.

A million reasons why not, Bliss thought, but pressed on.

Guardedly, the eldest of John Cawthorne's three daughters stepped out of the doorway and allowed them both to pass. Katie, as if she knew the place, took a right into an old parlor with gleaming hardwood floors covered partially by a floral-print carpet and wing chairs. A small camelback sofa was set in front of a marble fireplace and cushions covered the bench seats of two bay windows.

"I didn't expect company," Tiffany explained.

"Mommy? Who is it?" a small voice called from the second floor.

"Ms. Kinkaid—you don't know her, honey. She's here with a...a friend."

A flurry of footsteps heralded the entrance of Christina. Her eyes were wide like her mother's and her black hair shone nearly blue as she careened into the room. Tiffany's harsh countenance softened a bit. "I think you've both met my daughter."

The smiling cherub flung herself into her mother's waiting arms, but she eyed Bliss with unveiled suspicion, much as her mother did.

"Well, uh, wow, this is awkward, isn't it? Where are my manners? Please—" Tiffany waved toward the chairs "—have a seat. Can I...offer you something to drink?"

"Naw. We just had a soda downtown," Katie said as Tiffany set Christina onto the floor and the little girl barreled out of the room. The sound of small footsteps scurrying up the stairs reached Bliss's ears. Katie made an idle gesture with one hand. "I thought it was time we all got together."

"I've been thinking about it, too," Tiffany admitted, her cheeks flushing slightly. She fiddled with the chain on her watch. "I know I should have said something the other day when you, Bliss, came looking for Mason, but...well, you took me by surprise and I didn't know what to say. Then, as the days passed, I decided I didn't have to do anything until I was ready."

"Or someone forced your hand," Katie said with a shrug.

Tiffany nodded and splayed her fingers in front of her. "Look, I believe in telling it like it is, so to speak, and I've got to tell you straight-out that I don't like what's happening."

"You're not the only one." Bliss was so uncomfortable, she wanted to climb out of her skin and disappear. Instead, she sat on one of the cushions in the window seat overlooking a side yard filled with heavy-blossomed roses and a rusting swing set.

Katie plopped onto the couch. "Have you made any decisions yet?" she asked Tiffany as she ran a finger around the stitching on one arm. "About the wedding? You know that Dad—or John, or whatever it is I'm supposed to call him—really wants you to come to the ceremony."

"I got the invitation. And he called. But I don't think so. You know, just because he's had a change of heart, or some kind of personal epiphany or whatever it is, I can't just forget all the years that I didn't know of him." She wasn't smiling and looked as if her mind was cast in concrete. Bliss suspected that no one pushed Tiffany Santini around.

Katie was just as stubborn. "I can't make up your mind for you, but—"

"No buts about it. I'm not going. And you're right— you can't make up my mind for me."

Amen, Bliss thought, but Katie, forever the steamroller, plunged forward. "Don't you think it would be a good idea if we all tried, if possible, to bury the hatchet, so to speak?"

Tiffany lifted an already-arched brow. "Why?"

"Family unity. Solidarity. All that stuff."

Bliss's stomach clenched.

"Solidarity," Tiffany repeated with a little cough. "*Family* unity. That's rich." With determination flashing in her dark eyes, she settled onto the ottoman of one of the overstuffed chairs. "Let's understand each other. You want to go, Katie, because, after all, your mother and father are finally getting married. And Bliss—" she turned those wary eyes in her middle sister's direction "—it makes sense for you."

"But not you?" Bliss asked, trying not to appear as nervous as she felt.

"No, not me, and I don't think I really have to explain myself."

"Why don't you try," Katie suggested.

A flash of anger flitted through the eldest's eyes. "Okay, if that's what you want. It's been hard for me, okay? And all this nearly killed Mom. She lied at first, told me my dad was dead. I guess that way she thought I wouldn't feel so abnormal, but the truth of the matter was that I was born illegitimate, unwanted by a father who preferred another woman over my mother."

"No!" Bliss gasped. "Dad didn't know Mom until after—"

"Doesn't matter." Tiffany held out her hands to cut off Bliss's protest. "Katie asked and I just answered truthfully. I think there've been enough lies as it is."

Bliss gulped. It was time to leave. Past time. Obviously, Tiffany didn't have any of Katie's need for family unity.

But Tiffany wasn't finished. "I know what the local story is. My grandmother filled me in. It goes something like my mother didn't love John Cawthorne, didn't want to marry him. Nor did he want her. I was the result of a fling." She rolled her eyes and shook her head. "Anyway, for all my mom's tough words, I learned later from my grandmother that it about killed her when he married a rich woman from San Francisco, a woman of breeding, so to speak, and then you came along and were treated like a princess."

Heat soared up Bliss's cheeks and for a second, hot tears touched the back of her eyelids.

"I wasn't going to say anything," Tiffany added, as if she could see the pain ripping through her half sister. "But you two asked. The way I see it is that my mother struggled to raise me, and she taught me never to depend upon a man—any man. She never married, refused to even date much, and was of the opinion that most men were rats or even worse. When things got tight, there was Grandma to depend upon.''

''Aunt Octavia,'' Katie clarified. ''She's not everyone's aunt but everyone calls her that, and she *is* Tiffany's grandmother.''

''Yep, and she somehow helped keep my mother sane, I swear, during those…well, the rough years.''

Bliss rubbed her sweating palms on her pants. ''You mean when Dad married Mother?''

''Yeah. But I thought it was because my dad had died.'' Tiffany nodded and plucked at the fringe on the cushion of the ottoman. ''Anyway, she got over it—at least I thought she did. Then, when I married Philip, she nearly didn't come to the wedding. He was older, and Mom was certain he was a father figure to me, the only father I'd ever known. She read all sorts of self-help books and told me that I was mixing up love and security and— Oh, well, it doesn't matter. I'm sure you didn't come here to hear my life story, so put away the violins and handkerchiefs. I'm not really bitter, just not interested in the prospect of dealing with a dad I've never known.''

''But you live in the same town as him. It seems silly to ignore your own father.'' Katie was nothing if not dogged.

''Let's get one thing straight,'' Tiffany retorted. ''He never was my father. It takes more than getting someone pregnant to earn that title.'' She glanced out the window, then added, ''Maybe that's a selfish way to look at it, but too bad. As for John Cawthorne's wedding—what's that all about? Brynnie's said those supposedly sacred words more times that anyone should. I think they should run off and elope. Have some kind of reception when they get back." Hearing herself, she rolled her eyes. "Like I care."

"You might more than you want to admit," Katie ventured.

Before Tiffany could answer, the front door flew open. Thud! The doorknob banged hard against the wall.

"Stephen?" Tiffany was on her feet in an instant.

"Yeah?" a voice cracked, and in the foyer a boy in his early teens appeared. His hair was black and shaggy, his brown eyes filled with distrust. Every visible muscle appeared tense, as if he expected to make a run for it at any moment. He would be handsome in a few years, Bliss supposed, when his jaw had become more defined and his face had caught up with his nose.

"I think you'd better meet someone," Tiffany said, taking his tense arm and propelling him into the parlor. "This is Bliss Cawthorne. John's daughter."

His eyes narrowed. "Another one? Cawthorne? You mean 'the princess'—"

"Actually, she's my half sister," Tiffany said quickly, as if to cut off whatever derogatory comment he was about to make. "She's lived in Seattle with John and his wife."

The princess. The second time she'd heard it in a few minutes. So that was what they'd called her behind her back, what they really thought. Why had she so stupidly agreed to come here? Because Katie had practically shanghaied her, that was why.

Stephen's gaze was positively condemning. "Oh." He didn't say anything for a few long seconds, but Bliss was instantly embarrassed that she was the legitimate daughter, the one who bore her father's name, the odd woman out, so to speak. "Well, aren't you the lucky one?" he finally whispered, sarcasm lacing his words. "What do you want from—"

"Don't, okay? Just don't say it," Tiffany warned.

Tossing a hank of black hair out of his eyes, Stephen shifted from one dirty sneaker to the other. "So, can I go now?"

"*May* I, but sure."

Bliss could almost feel the boy's relief.

Tiffany let go of his arm. As he bounded up the stairs two at a time, he didn't give his mother or her guests so much as a backward glance.

"I think it's time I got back," Bliss said, standing. She saw a movement through the window and spied Dee Dee, Mason's daughter, sitting in a patio chair. Wearing cutoff jeans and a sleeveless T-shirt, she lazed, one foot resting on the opposite bare knee as she flipped through a magazine and petted a black cat that was curled up in her lap.

The girl seemed pensive and slightly sad, Bliss thought.

Glancing at her watch, Katie scowled, tiny lines forming across her forehead. "Oops. You're right. I've got to scoot and pick up Josh from his friend's house so that I can get him to baseball practice. Well, uh, gee, I really don't know what to say, except maybe thanks for letting us come by and bend your ear," she said to Tiffany.

"No problem." Tiffany walked to the door, but didn't ask them to return as they stepped onto the porch. "And just for the record, tell *your* father that if he wants to talk to me, he can call himself, or stop by—not that I have any interest in dealing with him. But I think it was underhanded to send you two."

"It wasn't his idea," Katie assured her. "It was mine."

Tiffany didn't reply, just arched a disbelieving brow as she closed the door.

"Boy, that was a good idea," Bliss mocked.

"What do you mean? I think it went well, all things considered." Together, Katie and Bliss walked beneath the shade trees and around the corner of the main house, where Bliss caught another glimpse of Mason's daughter.

"Are you kidding?" Bliss couldn't believe her ears and decided right then and there that Katie Kinkaid was an eternal and somewhat-myopic optimist.

"I suspect that deep down she likes you," Katie added.

"Oh, right."

"I mean it."

"Then I'd hate to see how she treats an enemy."

"Don't worry about it." Katie slid a pair of sunglasses onto her short nose. "If there is a problem, and, for the record I don't think there is, you'll win her over. It'll just take time." She opened the car door, but Bliss hesitated.

"Just give me a second, okay?"

"What for?" Katie glanced at her watch.

"I'll only take a minute." Bliss was already heading along a path winding through a rose garden and arbor. Butterflies and bees flitted in the air as she turned from the side of the house to the backyard where Dee Dee was still perusing a slick teen magazine.

"Hi," Bliss ventured, not sure why she wanted to connect with this kid, but knowing deep down that it was important.

Dee Dee looked up, but didn't smile. "Oh. Hi."

"Saw you out here reading and thought I'd see what you were up to."

"Waitin' for my dad."

"He's not here?"

"Naw." She shrugged as if she didn't have a care in the world, but a shadow of worry slid through her eyes and Bliss suspected Deanna Lafferty was used to hiding her feelings. "Mom just dropped me off."

"Is he expecting you?"

Again a lift of one shoulder. "Who knows?"

"Can you get into the house?"

"Tiffany will let me in." She chewed on her lower lip and looked at the main house. "It's okay."

"You're sure?"

Her expression changed and Bliss read "Yeah, and what's it to you?" in the set of her jaw. Great, she was making friends left and right today. "I'm fine, okay?"

"Sure. See ya around." With a wave, Bliss was off and she caught a glimpse of Tiffany at the kitchen window. The pane was open and Tiffany seemed to be washing dishes or something, but Bliss guessed she'd heard the entire exchange. Good. At least Dee Dee had an adult to keep an eye on her.

"What was that all about?" Katie asked, once Bliss had settled into the passenger seat of her car.

"Just checking."

"On Mason or his daughter?"

"Dee Dee seemed unhappy."

"Don't blame her. Terri's talking about pulling up stakes again, this time to Chicago, and Dee Dee doesn't want to be so far from her dad."

"But Mason just moved here."

"I know." Katie edged into traffic. "That might be the reason. Terri might not want to be so close to her ex."

"But it would be best for their daughter to be close to both parents."

"I'm not judging. Just telling you what could be happening." Once outside the town limits, Katie lead-footed it, leaving Bittersweet in a trail of dust. She fiddled with the dial on the radio, came up with an oldies station that was playing "Ruby Tuesday" by the Rolling Stones, and while Mick Jagger sang through the speakers, she drove like a maniac past the fields and hills that led back to the ranch. Exhaust spewed from the tailpipe and the wind streamed through Bliss's hair, but she barely noticed.

Her mind was on Mason's doe-eyed daughter, and she felt a twinge of remorse that she'd ever been jealous of the sad girl.

"You know," Katie said, oblivious to the turn of Bliss's thoughts. "Tiffany's got her own set of problems, what with J.D. Santini and all."

"Her...brother-in-law, right?"

"One and the same. Kind of a cross between James Dean and the Marquis de Sade, if you ask me."

"That bad?"

"Well, not really, I suppose. Good-looking, sexy, with an attitude that won't quit. He's not cruel, I don't think, but he's certainly a thorn in Tiffany's side. Ever since her husband, who was quite a bit older, died, he's been calling giving Tiffany advice on how to raise the two kids."

"I'll bet she likes that," Bliss replied with only a trace of derision.

"Not a whole lot, no."

"I don't think she'll be coming to the wedding," Bliss said.

"Uh-oh." Katie eased up on the throttle when she spied a sheriff's cruiser speeding in the opposite direction. She checked the rearview mirror to make sure the deputy hadn't decided to make a quick U-turn and tail her. "Oh, she'll come, all right. I know she appears kind of stuffy and re-served when you first meet her, but trust me, she'll warm up to you, and if nothing else, curiosity will entice her to the ceremony."

"I don't know." Bliss wasn't convinced. She wasn't even sure about Katie's feelings. "Tiffany seemed to resent me."

"Of course she does, but she'll get over it. I already told

you I think she's gonna like you, but give it a little time, will ya? Remember, Bliss, you're the one kid our father claimed. You grew up privileged, while Tiffany and I had to scrape by. Now, it never really bothered me because I didn't know that John was my father until a little while ago and we had a big happy, if poor, family, but Tiff, she's lived with a real downer of a mother who lied to her, and it sounds like now that she knows the truth, her mom's made no big deal that she's still bitter about it. Never married. Wouldn't take a dime of support from John."

"How do you know this?" Bliss asked, as Katie cranked on the wheel and the convertible rolled into the driveway of the ranch.

"Mom."

"Brynnie knew?"

"She and John have always been close and I know that probably bothers you, but...well, there it is...." Her voice faded as she stared through the bug-spattered windshield. "Uh-oh. What's going on?"

Bliss had been looking at her half sister but as she turned she spied an ambulance, its lights still flashing starkly. Parked at an odd angle near the front door of the house, the white-and-orange emergency vehicle loomed before Bliss like a specter. Her heart nearly stopped. "Oh, God. It's...it's Dad!" she cried, her throat closing and fear congealing her insides. "He's had another heart attack!"

"You don't know anything of the sort—" But Katie stepped on the brakes. The convertible skidded to a stop only feet from the ambulance.

Bliss's heart turned to stone.

Paramedics were wheeling a gurney out of the house. Wheels rattled and creaked, and an ashen-faced John Cawthorne lay on the thin white mattress.

"Dad!" Bliss was out of the car in an instant.

Brynnie, sobbing hysterically, was following close behind the gurney and Oscar was yapping and bounding, confused by all the activity. Horses and cattle grazed lazily, unaffected by all the human drama, and a few of the ranch hands were standing around, grim-faced, their hands in their pockets, their cheeks bulging with chewing tobacco. From somewhere—probably the dash of the ambulance—a radio crackled and the entire scene seemed surreal. Bliss's legs felt like lead as she ran toward her father. Her heart was beating a dread-filled cadence and her eyes burned with tears she didn't dare shed.

"What happened? Is he all right? Where are you taking him?" she asked, surprised she wasn't shrieking.

"Slow down and stay out of the way." The shorter paramedic sliced her a look that brooked no argument. "We're taking him in to town, the medical center. If the doctors there think he needs more specific care, he'll be transported to the hospital in Medford."

The hospital. Mom had died in Seattle General. Dad had nearly lost his life, as well. "Oh, my God."

"He's gonna be all right," Katie predicted, but beneath her freckles her skin had turned the color of the sheets draping her father's thin body.

Let him be all right, Bliss silently prayed as she grabbed one of John's hands.

"Please, miss, stand aside," the round paramedic with thinning blond hair ordered. Bliss stepped back and let her father's fingers slide through her own.

"I'm his daughter," Bliss said.

"So am I," Katie added.

"Just stand back and let the men do their jobs." Mason was striding from the front porch. Bliss's gaze touched his and she saw fear in his eyes; fear and something else—something deeper and more personal. He looked so big, his shoulders so wide. His jaw was tense, his expression hard and determined.

"Oh, John, I'm so sorry, so damned sorry," Brynnie wailed as she, still trying to pull on her sandals, followed the attendants. "Not now, dear God, not now!"

"Everyone give us some room!" The paramedics were loading the gurney into the back of the ambulance.

"It's his heart, I just know it. He can't breathe," Brynnie said, her eyes and nose red.

No! This couldn't be happening. Not after he'd survived the first attack. Bliss swallowed back tears. "I'm coming, too."

Brynnie climbed inside and Bliss was about to do the same when Mason grabbed her arm. "You can ride with me." She wanted to fight him, but didn't. Right now she needed his strength. She didn't kid herself that he cared about her, but it didn't matter; not until this crisis had passed.

"What—what are you doing here?" she asked, but deep in her heart, she knew the answer. He'd come to see her father; there had been an argument. John Cawthorne had lost his cool and his already-weakened heart had quit working.

Sirens wailing, the ambulance took off.

"I can drive," Katie offered, her face ashen as she glanced at her watch. "I just have time to pick up Josh and then we can—"

"Don't worry about it, I'll take her," Mason interrupted.

Bliss was already on her way to his pickup. She couldn't think, couldn't believe that this was happening. First her mother's painful death, then her father's heart attack. Had he survived only to die a few months later? *Please, God, no. Not now!*

As she reached the door of Mason's truck, she stopped,

and the damning truth hit her as hard as a belly punch. She sagged against his rig and turned on him. "Don't tell me, Lafferty. You're the reason my dad's had another attack."

"I don't know," Mason admitted, his face grim as he hurried to his pickup. Mason opened the door for her, then slid behind the wheel. "I told you this place was too much for your father." He slammed his door shut and switched on the ignition.

"So you had to come by and badger him again." Fear and anger took hold of her tongue. "I don't know what it is with you, Mason, but you should leave him alone."

"Believe me, I am," he said, jamming the truck into gear.

"Oh, sure, and that's why you came out here to pick a fight with him."

"I didn't pick a fight, Bliss." He popped the clutch and the truck took off. "In fact, if you want to know the truth, I came out here to sell the place back to Brynnie for what she paid for it."

"What?"

"That's right," he said, slipping his aviator sunglasses onto his nose. "I'm out of this mess with your father. As far as I'm concerned he can do whatever he wants with his ranch. I don't want it."

Chapter Eleven

"Wait a minute. You don't want the ranch? After all this legal maneuvering and arguing and angst?" Bliss couldn't believe her ears. "Come on, Mason, what happened? You came out here to sell back Brynnie's share to her and what—my dad collapsed? Give me a break."

"Believe what you want to believe." His lips barely moved as he spoke.

The interior of the pickup was hot. Stuffy. Too close. Bliss cranked down the window and looked away from Mason's sharp-honed profile. She couldn't think about him and the last time they'd been together; not now, not when her father's life was in question. In the distance, the horrifying shriek of the ambulance's siren sliced across the arid fields.

Mason slid her a glance. His mouth was tight, his jaw hard, his knuckles white as he gripped the steering wheel.

She took a deep, calming breath. "Okay, okay, no more accusations," she said. Nervously Bliss stared through the dusty windshield. Her throat clogged and she couldn't help but wonder if at this very moment her father was fighting for his life or if, like her mother, he'd slipped away. She bit her lip and crossed her fingers. Surely she wouldn't lose him. Not now, she thought, echoing Brynnie's words. "Just tell me what happened."

"I thought we—you and I—needed to talk, so I stopped by, looking for you," he said. "I wanted to speak to you first before I offered John and Brynnie the place back. But you weren't around and Brynnie invited me in for a glass of iced tea. So I decided to wait.

"I was in the kitchen talking to her when John came in from working outside." He slid a glance in Bliss's direction. "I don't mean to scare you, but he didn't look all that great. He was red in the face and sweating like nobody's business. He took two steps into the house, saw me and stumbled. I caught hold of his arm and we both ended up on the floor." The corners of Mason's mouth turned down. "Your father lost consciousness. Brynnie dialed 911 and I tried and failed to revive him."

"Oh, God," she said, feeling tears burn behind her eyelids. As angry as she'd been with her dad, she loved him, didn't want to lose him. "I—I should have been there."

"There wasn't anything you could have done. John won't slow down—you know that as well as I do. He's not happy unless he's going twice the speed of sound."

"You don't think he's going to make it," she said, stunned.

"Don't give up." Mason placed a hand on her shoulder. "You know your dad. He's a fighter. He was still breathing, his heartbeat still strong when the paramedics arrived." He offered her the hint of smile. "If anyone can beat this, it's your old man."

"I hope you're right," she whispered, wrapping her arms

around herself. She stared out the open window and fought tears. It wasn't like her to cry, yet right now, knowing she might lose her only surviving parent, she wanted to break down completely and shake her fist and scream and tell the whole world that it wasn't fair.

Mason's hand was comforting and she wished there was time for him to fold her into his arms and tell her everything would be all right, that her father would live a robust life, that somehow she'd learn to accept John's bride as well as the half sisters she hadn't known existed. And that, crazy though it seemed, they would all be one big happy family. Of course, it was a pipe dream.

"I, uh, saw Dee Dee today," she said, as much to break the silence as to keep her mind off her father.

"Today?"

"At Tiffany's."

He checked his watch. "Terri said she'd drop her off for a couple of hours, but it was supposed to be later this evening. Are you sure?" Concentration furrowed his brow as they reached the outskirts of town.

"Yes, I spoke with her."

"For the love of Mike, that woman!" His mouth flattened over his teeth. "Look, I'll drop you at the clinic, then check on Dee Dee, but I'll be back."

"Fine," she said, knowing that he had to look in on his child, but feeling disappointed nonetheless. All too quickly she was becoming dependent upon his strength.

At the clinic, Mason gunned the truck into a parking space near the ER entrance. Bliss was out of his pickup before it had completely stopped moving. "I'll be back," Mason promised, then drove off. Bliss nodded and straightened her shoulders. She'd get through this. Somehow. No matter what happened.

She strode through the automatic doors and found Brynnie, ashen-faced, wringing a shredded tissue in her hands. She was seated on the edge of one of the well-used plastic couches in the waiting area.

"How's Dad?" Bliss asked.

"I don't know anything," Brynnie responded as she dabbed at the corners of her eyes. Mascara ran down her cheeks despite her best efforts. "The paramedics seem to think it was just heatstroke, but the doctors are running tests anyway. Oh, Lordy, Bliss, I don't know what I'll do if I lose that man. I've loved him so long, and now...now that we finally have the chance to be together, he might..." She dissolved into tears, and Bliss, unable to resist, wrapped her arms around the older woman as Brynnie sobbed in earnest.

For all her faults, Brynnie did seem to love John Cawthorne, and Bliss had trouble disliking a woman who cared so deeply.

"I should never have sold part of the ranch to Mason. I thought it would help, but it backfired on me. John will never forgive me."

"Sure, he will. Mason says he'll sell it back to you."

"I know, I know, but I'm afraid it's too late. John will never trust me again."

"Shh. You don't know that."

"Where is Mason?"

"He had to check on Dee Dee, but he said he'll be back soon."

"He's a good man, Bliss. No matter what your father says."

"I know."

People came and went as the minutes ticked by. After nearly half an hour, Mason returned with his daughter in tow. She looked small and frail beside him; her eyes were wide, wary, and stared at Bliss as if she were some kind of oddity.

Mason guided his daughter to a chair by the windows where potted plants were growing in profusion and a rack of well-used magazines was propped against a post. After one last suspicious glance cast in Bliss's direction she dug into her oversize bag and drug out a thin paperback novel. Mason nodded at Bliss, but stayed near his young charge.

"What's taking so long?" Brynnie asked, gnawing on her lower lip.

"Don't worry. It always takes a while. Dad will be fine," Bliss assured the older woman, all the while wishing she could believe her own words and aware of Mason's gaze boring into her. "He wouldn't miss your wedding for the world."

Brynnie laughed despite her tears and blew her nose so loudly she woke a baby who was sleeping in his mother's arms in a nearby chair. The mother smoothed the baby's curls and softly hummed a lullaby to quiet the child who nestled even closer and sighed as his eyelids drooped again.

Bliss looked away from the tender scene. Ever since returning to Bittersweet it seemed that everywhere she went she was faced with shining examples of motherhood and was constantly being reminded of her own childless state.

"I...I need a cigarette," Brynnie admitted and eyed the No Smoking sign with distaste. "You know, nowadays, they make you feel like a criminal just because you need a little hit of nicotine. Big deal."

"Well, this *is* a health-care facility."

"Yeah, I know. And I've tried to quit, but old habits die hard. Even the ones that will kill you." She laughed again, coughed a bit and patted the edge of a tissue against the corners of her eyes.

"Go ahead. I'll wait in here," Bliss said, relieved that

Brynnie seemed to be calming a bit. "If there's any news I'll come find you."

"Promise?"

"Absolutely."

As Brynnie walked outside, Mason said a few words to Dee Dee, then crossed the room. He hitched his chin toward the windows and beyond, where Brynnie was rifling through her purse. "She's not so bad, now, is she?" he asked.

"Brynnie?" Bliss sighed as she watched Brynnie shake out a cigarette and light it with trembling hands. "No. I guess not. She loves Dad." Bliss bit her lower lip. "That much is obvious. And Mom is gone, but... I had this belief that marriage should last forever, that two people could be faithful for a lifetime, that... Oh, I don't know." She shook her head. Right now, nothing mattered except her father's health.

Mason rubbed his jaw. "I would never have guessed you for a romantic."

"I'm not a— Look, I just believe in commitment."

"Hard to come by these days."

She cringed inside because she knew he was telling the truth. "People just don't try hard enough."

He eyed her speculatively, but didn't say a word, and she suspected he thought her incredibly naive. So let him. She had her convictions.

The woman with the sleeping baby was called into one of the rooms. She disappeared for a few minutes, then returned not only with the infant, but also with a girl of about twelve with a cast that ran from her fingers to her shoulder on her right arm.

"Ms. Cawthorne?" a nurse paged.

"Just a minute."

"I'll wait out here with Dee Dee," Mason said.

Bliss waved to Brynnie, who took one last drag and stuffed her cigarette into the sand of an ash can filled with other used cigarettes. She hurried inside. "Come on, I think they're going to let us see Dad now," Bliss said, shepherding the older woman down a short hallway to a bed surrounded by hanging sheets.

Her father, pale and gaunt, eyes slightly sunken, lay staring at the ceiling. His thin hair was mussed, his expression grim and angry. "What the hell am I doin' here?" he demanded.

"You—you collapsed," Brynnie said, choking back tears. "Oh, baby, are you all right?" She nearly stumbled against the metal railing of the bed to reach for his hand. Her fingers laced with his despite the IV dripping into the back of his wrist.

"I'll live," he grumbled, apparently not too happy about the prospect. "Seems that every time I wake up I'm in some damned hospital."

"A habit you'd better break," Bliss said.

Brynnie patted his arm tenderly. "I talked to Mason and he's made me an offer to buy back the ranch and, oh, John, if that's what will make you happy, I'll do it. I—I had no business trying to tell you what to do or make you do what I wanted even if it was for your own good. It was stupid of me to sell out. Stupid, stupid, stupid!"

"We'll see," John said with a sigh. He looked as if he'd given up on life, and a little part of Bliss died. Too many times in the past her father's anger had taken hold of his tongue and he'd been rash, unreasonable and sometimes nearly cruel, but she'd love to see some of the old fight in him today. Instead, he looked old and beaten down.

"The paramedics were right," a doctor said as he pushed aside the curtain. "Heatstroke." The name tag on his white coat identified him as Dr. James Ferris. He eyed John's chart. "Has anyone suggested to this guy that he should slow down?"

"Bah!"

"Only his cardiologist," Bliss interjected and was rewarded with a warning glare from her father. "And a few other doctors."

"So this is a hearing problem, eh?" the doctor joked as he picked up his patient's chart and made a note.

"Listening problem," Bliss corrected.

"I hope you're having fun at my expense," John retorted grumpily. "Now, when can I get out of here?"

"Tomorrow, if you're lucky." The doctor clicked his pen and jammed it into his pocket. "I still want to run a few tests and talk to your doctors in Seattle."

"What do they know?" John complained.

"You listen to them." Brynnie's lips were compressed with new determination. "I'm not about to become your widow before I get to be your bride."

"Hogwash. I'm not dying."

"Not yet," the doctor said. "And probably not for a while. But I want you to stay overnight for observation."

"Doesn't seem like I have much choice in the matter."

"You don't," Bliss said, straightening one of the crisp sheets covering her father's thin body. He'd always been such a robust, strapping man, but now he seemed frail.

"I'll stay with you," Brynnie promised.

"He's going to be moved to a private room. We've only got a couple here, but one's empty and I can't see sending him to the hospital in Medford. The room's on the other side of the admitting desk and down a short hallway. Room three. You can wait for him there if you want to."

"Oh, go on. Go home." John grimaced as he shifted on the bed and Bliss was reminded that he was a terrible patient, hated being sick or laid up, had no tolerance for anyone who tried to wait on him. But at least she caught a glimpse of the man he used to be, the man who'd spent his life giving orders rather than receiving them. Good luck to the nurses who had the night shift.

"I will in a minute," Bliss said, patting her father on the shoulder.

Brynnie didn't budge. "I'm sticking around. You couldn't get rid of me if you tried, John Cawthorne." A heavy-set nurse had to walk around her to check Bliss's father's blood pressure, temperature and IV drip. Brynnie glanced up at Bliss. "You run along, now. I'll take care of your dad."

"I don't need anyone taking care of me."

"See, he's getting better already." Brynnie winked at Bliss. "I think someone's waiting for you."

"Who?" John demanded. "Oh, for the love of Mike, don't tell me that Lafferty's here!" Color boiled up his neck and cheeks.

"Oh, calm down, or I'll call that doctor and have him admit you for the rest of the week," Brynnie warned.

"I'll see you later, Dad." Bliss brushed a kiss against her father's temple and he patted her hand.

"You're a good kid."

"Remember that when I insist you follow doctor's orders." Feeling as if an incredible weight had been taken off her shoulders, she hurried to the waiting area where Mason had taken a seat and was involved in an argument with a preteen boy who sat stubbornly next to Katie. Dee Dee was still in her chair, legs crossed, pretending to be absorbed in her book, though her eyes peered over the tops of the pages as she watched her father.

"You have to show some respect, Josh. Not only for your mom, here, but other people as well."

Josh—Katie's son, Bliss assumed—was pouting and at

Mason's crisp words his lower lip protruded another half inch.

Katie saw Bliss and was on her feet in an instant. "How's John?" she asked, her face a mask of worry.

"He'll be fine. Heatstroke." Bliss filled them in on the details and Josh dug at the carpet with the toe of his worn sneaker. Katie introduced her reticent son, then pummeled Bliss with questions while Mason, arms crossed in front of his chest, expression dark and serious, listened intently to every word she said. There was a part of him she didn't know, couldn't understand, a mystery that she hadn't unraveled. Would she ever? she wondered and found herself staring at the hard slant of his jaw and the thin seam of his mouth. Did he care for her as she had begun to care for him? Or was his interest solely because of the ranch and this need she sensed in him—a need to outdo the man who had fired him years before? How much of John Cawthorne's speculation—that Mason was only using her as a way to get to her father—was true?

He was offering to sell his portion of the ranch back, wasn't he? How bad could he really be?

"Well, I'm going to see him as soon as he's in his own room," Katie said, ignoring any advice to the contrary.

"Ah, Mom," the boy whined.

"You, too, kid. He's your grandfather."

"Yeah, right. Since when? A few weeks ago? Big deal." Josh tossed a wayward lock of hair from his eyes and scowled as if the world had wronged him.

"It is," Katie insisted.

"Yeah, so where was he before? Huh? He knew you were his kid and he just looked the other way." Josh rolled his eyes expressively. "Real great guy."

"All that's changed."

"Come on, there's nothing more we can do. Let's get out of here," Mason said. "Dee Dee, are you ready?"

She looked up and her lips pursed for just a second. "Sure." Then, as if sensing her father's disapproval, she tossed her book into her bag and was on her feet.

"I'll take you both to dinner," Mason announced.

"You don't have to," Bliss protested.

"I *want* to."

"I'm not hungry." Dee Dee fidgeted with the strap of her bag. She glanced at Josh and rolled her eyes. "Besides, Mom said she'd be back by now."

Mason's jaw clenched. "I know, but she was supposed to—"

"Wait a second," Katie, ever vigilant, interrupted. "Why doesn't Dee Dee come over to our place for a while? Josh and his friend Laddy just finished building a tree house and the neighbors have a litter of eight puppies. I'll call Terri and square it with her."

Dee Dee's eyes lit up. "Puppies? Oh, Dad, could I?"

"I don't know—"

"Please, Daddy," Dee Dee begged, and Bliss watched as Mason's heart melted.

"Don't you have plans later with your mom?" Mason asked.

"Mom and Bob." Dee Dee's nose wrinkled at the thought.

"Don't worry. As I said, I'll give Terri a call on my cell," Katie said, zipping open her purse and scrounging for her phone. "She can either pick her up at my place or I'll run her home. It's no big deal."

Mason, it seemed, couldn't deny his daughter anything, and in a matter of minutes the change of plans was arranged and Dee Dee remained with Katie and Josh.

Nonetheless, Mason wasn't pleased as they left the hospital. "Damn that woman, why can't she make a plan and stick to it?" he muttered, then shot Bliss an apologetic glance. "Not your problem."

"I don't mind."

He ran stiff, frustrated fingers through his hair. "Terri's talking about moving again," he admitted, once they were walking across the parking lot. Heat shimmered in waves from the hot asphalt and the air was still even though it was late afternoon.

"Where?"

"The San Juan Islands, I think, or Chicago. It depends on Bob." He slid his aviator glasses onto the bridge of his nose and she couldn't see his eyes, but his entire demeanor had stiffened.

"Bob is—"

"Her fiancé or live-in or whatever you want to call it. He's older, has kids my age and... Oh, hell, I don't like the situation. I moved down here to be close to Dee Dee, have a little more influence in her life, and wouldn't you know, Terri's decided to take off again." He opened the door of the truck and helped Bliss inside. The vinyl seat was hot to the touch even though he'd left the windows cracked, and an angry yellow jacket was buzzing loudly, pounding its striped body against the windshield. Mason slid behind the steering wheel, swatted the bee out the open window, then twisted on the ignition.

Bliss glanced at the clinic and sighed.

Mason slid a glance her way as he eased through the parked vehicles. "Your dad will be okay, you know."

"How would I?" she asked.

Mason snorted. "John Cawthorne's too stubborn to give up the ghost that easily."

"You didn't see him after the heart attack in Seattle."

He couldn't argue. Didn't.

"It scared me."

"I didn't think anything scared you."

She let out a hard laugh. "If you only knew."

They drove back to the ranch in silence as the sun lowered over the western mountains. A tiny breeze kicked up and crickets began their twilight songs. Mason parked by the garage and walked her into the house. It was odd being alone with him here, in her father's home, and she suddenly felt tongue-tied and awkward.

The house was too close, too reminiscent of another time and place. She helped herself to two sodas and carried them outside to the back porch. Shadows lengthened across the lawn.

"What will you do if Terri does move again?" she asked, unscrewing the top from a bottle of cola and handing it to him.

"Fight her, I suppose." He took the drink and rolled the bottle between his hands. "I can't follow her across the country, but I need to be close to Dee Dee. I made a mistake letting Terri take her away from me in the first place. I should have demanded that she stay in state. We lived in Montana then...." He frowned and took a long swallow. "Doesn't matter. It's all water under the bridge. It wasn't my first mistake." His eyes found Bliss's. The back of her throat tightened, just as it always did when he looked at her so long and hard. "I've made a lot of them."

She fumbled with her bottle, but finally twisted off the cap. "We all have."

He leaned a shoulder against the post supporting the overhang of the porch. "My worst was losing you."

"Wh-what?" Her head snapped up and she nearly dropped her soda.

"You heard me." He smiled ruefully. "What do you think buying this place was all about?"

"I thought you wanted it to prove a point. With my dad. He fired you a long time ago, humiliated you, and you thought that by buying this place you could get back at him."

"That's part of it, I guess. But it wasn't really his land I was after. It was his daughter."

She froze, not certain she understood everything he was saying. "Look, what happened between us was a long time ago."

"Was it?" He took a long swallow from his drink and she watched his throat work.

"Yes."

"What about now?"

Oh, God. "Now?"

He set his drink on the porch rail, removed hers from her grip and placed her untouched bottle next to his. Then, standing only inches from her, he didn't touch her, didn't inch even the slightest bit closer, but said, "I want you, Bliss. As much as I ever have."

There it was. Hanging in the air between them. A statement so direct and frightening that Bliss didn't know what to say. She wanted to step away, to put some distance between herself and this man who knew just what to do to upset her world, but she didn't, and she held her ground, staring up at him and wishing he would take her into his arms and kiss her as she'd never been kissed before.

"You didn't," she finally said. "You...you had your chance and you left me."

"Wrong." His gaze centered on her lips. "I always wanted you, Bliss," he said, his voice so low it was barely a whisper. "I just didn't know how to go about it."

"You're lying," she accused, but saw the naked truth etched in his features, the pain of baring his soul.

"I wish it was different with us, but it isn't."

"That's how it has to be."

"No way."

She looked up at him, saw the passion stirring in his eyes and felt a trembling deep within her. The world seemed to shrink. Mingled fragrances of dry earth, bleached grass and blossoming Queen Anne's lace didn't diffuse the scents of leather, soap and aftershave that clung to him, nor did the coming twilight dim his blatant sexuality.

What was wrong with her? Why would she fall for his lines all over again? What kind of fool was she?

She only hoped that he would leave soon and she would be away from him and would no longer notice the hard angle of his jaw, the dark secrets in his eyes or the way his jeans hung so low on his hips.

He was, after all, just a man.

But the only man who had ever been able to turn her head around and get under her skin.

Well, that had happened years before; a lifetime ago, it seemed. This time around, she was older and hopefully wiser.

He reached forward and she thought—hoped—that he would pull her into his embrace. Instead, he brushed a lock of hair from her cheek. At the feel of his fingertip, she trembled. Quicksilver images of his body, naked and hard, glimmering with sweat as he'd made love to her, flitted through her mind.

"Take a ride with me," he suggested.

"A ride?"

"To Cougar Creek. Come on, Bliss. What have you got to lose?"

Just my heart. She swallowed hard. "Nothing."

Didn't he know how dangerous being alone together would be? Didn't he care?

"Good." He stuffed his hands into the back pockets of

his jeans. "We can take us a thermos of coffee, or a bottle of wine."

"Could we?" she teased, warming to the idea.

His grin was infectious. "You know," he added, "I thought I recognized Lucifer in the south pasture. I suppose he's still a mean son of a gun."

"The meanest. Dad says Lucifer's still a handful but not as young or as full of the devil as he once was."

"None of us are."

She noticed a shadow chase through his eyes, as if he, too, was remembering the fleeting past they'd shared so many years before. Suddenly she was leery. Being alone with him was tantalizing, but oh, so perilous.

"I—I don't know. It's been a long day and—"

"Coward."

"I'm not—"

"So you still remember how to ride, city girl?" His voice was teasing, but deeper-sounding than usual.

The air between them grew thick. "I think I can manage."

"Good." His smile was positively evil. "Then what are we waiting for?"

Chapter Twelve

By the time she'd called the hospital to check on her father, perked a pot of coffee, poured it into a thermos and wrapped a few cookies in aluminum foil, the sun had settled behind the mountains and twilight had descended. The first few stars were winking in a lavender sky, and a half-moon hung lazily over the horizon.

Mason was waiting for her in the paddock near the stables. Two horses, Lucifer and Fire Cracker, who was snorting and pulling at her tether, were saddled and tied to the fence.

"It's, uh, getting late," Bliss said, and Mason slid her a knowing smile.

"Don't tell me you've become so much of a city slicker that you're afraid to be out past ten? No one's going to mug you out here, you know."

"I was thinking of the horses. In the dark, they could step in a rabbit hole or stumble or—"

"They're both more surefooted than either you or I," Mason said, opening the gate. He untied the animals, took the thermos, cup and foil package to tuck into one of the saddlebags. "Come on." Climbing astride Lucifer, Mason quickly pulled on the reins before the stallion tried to turn his head and take a nip out of Mason's leg. "No, you don't." Mason chuckled and shook his head. "Still full of it, aren't you, boy?"

Bliss laughed as Lucifer rolled his blue eyes and tossed his head in frustration. "I don't know who I feel more sorry for. You or the horse."

"The horse, definitely. I'm going to show him who's boss."

"This I gotta see." Bliss's worries evaporated as they rode through a series of connecting paddocks and corrals, then took off through a huge field of yellow stubble. The horses loped easily over the rolling ground while grasshoppers and a covey of quail fluttered out of their path.

Bliss, despite her worries, felt suddenly lighthearted and free. All her concerns about her father's health, his upcoming marriage, her newfound sisters and mostly her volatile relationship with Mason, vanished in the clean air that tore at her hair and stole the breath from her lungs. Life was good, if complicated.

They rode through the pine trees and along a deer trail that wound upward to a craggy ridge overlooking the creek. A hawk soared high in the violet sky as stars winked and the moon cast the ground in shades of silver. Somewhere in the distance an owl hooted, only to be answered by a coyote whose cry was nearly drowned by the rush of water slicing through the canyon.

Mason climbed off Lucifer and the horse shook his great head, rattling the bit of his bridle. "This place hasn't changed much."

"No," Bliss admitted, as she slid to the ground. While the rest of the world had careened into the future in a mad rush of fax machines, telecommunications, computers, and cellular phones, out here the land was the same as it had been for centuries. Fewer wild creatures roamed the hills, and Native Americans no longer claimed this part of the world, but the geography itself seemed unmarred by civilization.

He poured coffee into the cup, handed it to her, then took his from the lid of the thermos. They sat in silence, steam rising from their drinks as they let the dark mantle of the night surround them.

"So tell me about Dee Dee," she said when the silence became uncomfortable and she found herself sliding glances at his profile. Damn, he was sexy. Crooked nose, high cheekbones, hard jaw, dark beard-shadow and heavy eyebrows over intense eyes gave his face character while his body was lean and muscular, rawhide-tough and strong.

"A great kid. Despite her parents."

"You must've done something right."

"I don't know what."

She sipped from her cup and the hot brew burned a path down her throat. Dear Lord, what was she doing here, alone with Mason beneath the stars, as a summer breeze played over the land?

He turned to face her and her heart kicked into a faster, more potent cadence. "So—so what happened between you and Terri?"

"Not much. That was the problem."

"Oh."

"Your old man convinced me that I should leave and marry her, that she was pregnant with my kid."

"Wasn't she?"

"Apparently not." His words were bitter and harsh.

"But Dee Dee—"

"Wasn't *the* baby. That one, I suspect, never existed."

"What?" Bliss was stunned.

"Oh, Terri claims she miscarried, and before I knew what hit me, she was pregnant again. I think she lied about the first pregnancy because she and I... Well, we weren't together much and then you came along. All of a sudden she turned up pregnant and then you nearly were killed in the accident. Your dad offered me money—more money than I'd ever had before—to disappear and do the 'right thing' by Terri, so I did. Then she 'loses' the baby. Before I can figure out if I should divorce her, she's pregnant again."

"With Dee Dee."

"Yep." He took a long swallow from the thermos lid. "And that pregnancy was one of the best things that ever happened to me." He lifted a shoulder. "But no matter how much you love your kid, if there're no feelings between you and the mother, then the marriage is doomed."

Bliss felt empty inside. All the years of envy and jealousy and misunderstanding were such a waste, such a horrid, painful waste. "If only I'd known," she said with a sigh. "No wonder there's so much bad blood between you and Dad."

"He never thought I was good enough for you," Mason said. "I was a poor kid who had to look out for his younger sister, a screwup who had no business being involved with his daughter, 'the princess.' The accident only proved him right."

"It didn't."

"In his mind, Bliss." He took another gulp of his coffee and tossed the dregs into the grass.

"Well, not in mine."

"Is that so?"

"Mmm." She caught the gleam in his eyes and her pulse jumped.

"Don't tell me you didn't regret getting involved with me."

"Okay," she teased, smiling. "I won't."

One side of his mouth lifted, revealing an off-center slash of white. "You're a maddening woman, Bliss Cawthorne."

"So I've been told."

He was suddenly serious. "You know, I never meant to hurt you."

"You didn't," she lied.

"I wish I could believe you." He leaned back on his elbows and stared at her. "If I could change things—"

"You wouldn't. You have a beautiful daughter, a successful business... What more could you want?"

"I already told you earlier."

"I want you, Bliss," he'd said. Not *I love you.* Not *I want to marry you.* It was more than she should have expected.

"I don't know," she said as the breeze ruffled her hair. She reached forward, spanning the small distance between them, and touched the back of his hand with her fingers. That one gesture was her undoing. The heat of his skin, the cords running along the back of his hand, caused her blood to ignite. She felt her pulse begin to throb, saw his gaze shift to the hollow of her throat.

With a groan, he moved closer. His fingers linked through hers and an intimate heat, like none other she'd ever felt, passed from his skin to hers.

Stop this, Bliss, while you still can. But it was too late. She was mesmerized by the depths of his eyes, the curve of his lips, the flare of his nostrils. He pulled her next to him and his mouth, wet and hard, found the pulse point in her neck.

No! No! No! a part of her screamed.

Yes, oh, yes! a deeper, more feminine part responded as Mason's fingers twined in her hair. His lips tasted and touched, pressing soft kisses along the column of her throat. "I've wanted you for so long," he whispered in a voice that was rough with need. "So damned long." His lips found hers again, and desire, new and hot, danced wantonly through her blood.

She couldn't think, could scarcely breathe as his hands lowered and he cupped both breasts in his rough hands. Bliss's heart nearly stopped as he buried his face in the cleft, and through the thin cotton of her blouse his breath fanned her skin.

Somewhere deep within her a wanting, warm and moist, began to awaken. A night bird sang a soft song and a breeze stirred the long grass and madrona leaves. Her head lolled back and passion, so long denied, awakened in a rush that stole the breath from her lungs.

"Bliss," he whispered against her throat before lifting his head and staring into her eyes again. Even in the darkness she saw streaks of brown in his golden gaze, witnessed his own apprehension before he lowered his head and kissed her full on the mouth.

She couldn't resist. Her blood pounded in her head and the touch and smell of him invaded her senses. His tongue flicked against her teeth, then delved farther. And yearning, like a silken cord, unwound deep in her core and spread throughout her body. She knew she should stop, that touching him, allowing his hands upon her body would only lead to disaster; but being with him was too seductive, and when he lifted her blouse from her jeans, she didn't stop him. Nor did she protest as one by one, the buttons were undone and her skin was exposed to the breath of the breeze. She felt the lapels part as the soft cotton slid over her shoulders and his fingertips traced the path of the fallen fabric.

"So beautiful," he murmured as he tugged on her bra strap and bared her breast to the pale light of the moon.

She could barely breathe and rational thought escaped into the night. The air was warm and silky, his touch forbidden and so, so wanted. He kissed the tip of her breast, watching as her nipple puckered willingly. Her spine curved as if pulled like a bowstring, and silently she offered herself to him.

His hand was rough and hard against her nipple, his fingers callused as he lifted her breast and brought it to his lips again. Slowly he laved the little bud, teasing and tasting, breathing fire over her wet skin.

A needy moan escaped her lips. Heat roiled deep between her legs. Desire swept through her blood and she was certain her heart, pounding so loudly it echoed against her ribs, would surely break. She couldn't give in to him, but had no will to stop his lovemaking. "Bliss—" he whispered across her nipple, and some final wall of resistance inside her crumbled. "Tell me to stop."

"I—I can't," she admitted.

For a second, he lifted his head. His jaw tightened and he stared straight into her eyes. She reached forward and unbuttoned the top fastening of his shirt. His teeth gritted and he grabbed hold of her wrist with fingers that felt like steel. "You're asking for trouble."

"I know." Her voice was low and husky. She slid another button through its hole.

"Listen to me—oh, for the love of—" He drew her into his arms and locked his mouth over hers as she pulled his shirt from his waistband and in one swift movement he discarded the unwanted clothing. Bliss's hands explored his body, the corded muscles of his shoulders, the mat of curling hair on his chest and the taut planes of his abdomen.

He let out a low, primeval sound when she touched his nipples with her fingers and his lips became more demanding. He reached for the waistband of her jeans, yanked hard enough that her button fly gave way in a series of pops and the denim slid easily over her hips and thighs.

"Bliss. Sweet, sweet Bliss," he whispered, lowering himself, kissing each of her breasts and the hollow between them, then moving lower to the flat of her abdomen where he circled his tongue slowly around her navel.

A spiral of heat and need wound through her insides as his tongue slid along her skin. "Mason, oh," she cried as his hot breath invaded the thin lace of her panties. She wriggled against him and he kissed the lace and the downy curls beneath it. "Please," she begged in a voice that was not her own. "Please, oh, oh, ooh!"

His tongue worked magic through the fragile barrier of lace and she closed her eyes, her entire body centered where he touched her. Desire throbbed between her legs. She moved against him, silently begging for more until at last he stripped her of that last shred of clothing and kissed her intimately.

The world seemed to collide with the stars. She gasped for breath and convulsed. She was on fire, needing more. Wanting only this one man. Her body, slick with sweat, convulsed again and again before he kicked off his jeans and parted her legs with his knees.

"We should stop—"

"No!" *Oh, God, please, no!*

"But I can't. Bliss...I can't—" He lifted her buttocks and thrust into her, hard and deep, breaking that fragile barrier she'd held on to for twenty-seven years.

She let out a cry of ecstasy and pain.

He quit moving, his eyes wide. "Lord, Bliss, you're a virgin!"

"Was," she said. "Was. Oh, Mason, please don't stop, don't ever stop." Her fingers pressed deep into his shoulders.

"But—"

"I want you," she said, opening her eyes and staring into his. "I've always wanted you."

"And I want you. Oh, darlin'—" He let out a groan of surrender and then began to move, slowly at first, then faster and harder as Bliss's pain vanished and she matched his tempo. Her heart thundered, her breathing came in short anxious gasps, her body arching up to his. His hands held tight to her buttocks, drawing her closer as the world swirled in a vision of light and color.

"Bliss...I..." His voice trailed off and she watched sweat run from his temples. Somewhere deep inside a dam broke and she jerked in a contraction of joy. With an ecstatic cry, he went still atop her just as her spirit soared to the heavens and the kaleidoscope of colors behind her eyes became a warm blaze of light.

I love you, she thought desperately, but bit her tongue before the hasty words could reach her lips. This was sex, nothing more. The loss of her virginity, yes, but still just a coupling of two people who were not in love.

Stupidly, tears burned behind her eyes because she'd always thought that when she gave herself to a man, it would be for the time-honored and glorious emotion called "love."

He cradled her face in his big hands and looked deep into her eyes. "Bliss...?" He kissed her forehead and cheeks and must have tasted the salt of her tears. "Are you all right?"

"Perfect."

"Yes," he said with a reverence that touched her heart. "You are."

Oh, God, was he serious? "If you only knew."

"I do." Twirling a strand of her hair around his finger, he slid to the side of her and with one leg possessively pinning her against him, added, "What I didn't know was that you were still a virgin."

A stain of embarrassment washed up her neck in hot, humiliating waves.

"You should have told me."

"Oh, sure. At this age." She managed a thin smile, but didn't tease an answering grin from his lips. "It's probably some kind of world record or something."

He levered up on one elbow and stared down at her. "I doubt that we should call Guinness."

"Good. Then it doesn't matter."

"No?" Still he was skeptical and with one hand he reached forward and touched her nipple with one long finger.

"I think it was long past time to give it up," she said, clearing her throat.

"So why not earlier? And don't give me that line about not meeting the right man, 'cause I won't buy it."

"All right, maybe I just didn't trust anyone, okay?"

"But you do trust me." He didn't mask any of the skepticism in his words.

"As I said, it was time, don't you think?"

"That's your call, Bliss." With a wicked grin he pulled her into the crook of his shoulder. His breath stirred her hair as he spoke. "What I think is that we—well, make that I—should have been more careful. I didn't have...protection.''

She stiffened and stared upward where leaves of low-hanging branches shifted in the moonlight. The smooth beauty of the moment was shattered. ''Believe me, you don't have to worry about any disease from me.''

''Nor me,'' he admitted. ''I was tested last year. Twice. Since then I've been careful. Until now.''

''Don't worry about it.'' She tried to pull away from him, but he held her fast.

''It's you I worry about,'' he said, as if he hated the words. ''I didn't mean for this to happen.''

''Neither did I, but there it is.'' She was near tears again. This should have been the happiest, most definitive moment of her life. Instead, she wanted to melt away. Already he regretted making love to her. ''We're both adults. You didn't force me into doing anything I wasn't ready for.'' With renewed energy, she pulled away from him. ''Let me go, Mason.''

''I can't.'' He held her fast. ''Why me, Bliss?''

''I told you it was time.''

''It's more than that.''

''Meaning what?'' she demanded. ''That I was waiting for you? Is that what you think?''

''I don't know what to think,'' he admitted, staring at her as if for the first time. ''But you're over twenty-five and—''

''Don't remind me, okay?'' she said jerkily. Yes, she'd been a virgin, and no, she didn't have a husband, or children, or any reason to think she would anytime soon, and though those things bothered her, she wasn't going to let them get her down. She was young, had a career, a life in Seattle. She didn't need Mason's pity.

No, only his love.

"Bliss, I didn't mean to imply—"

"Look, you don't have to say anything, okay?" She wrenched away from him and this time he let her go. Quickly, before she broke down altogether, she snatched up her clothes and dressed, sliding her legs into her panties and jeans, still feeling new and achingly feminine. As she buttoned her blouse, she whistled to her horse and Mason, still naked as the day he was born, grabbed hold of her hand.

"What the hell's going on?"

"Nothing," she lied.

"Bliss, I think we should talk."

"Maybe we should have talked more before we...we—"

"Made love?"

Oh, God. Her throat tightened and she blinked against a wash of tears. She couldn't face him, didn't want to cry like some fragile female, some spoiled *princess,* for heaven's sake! She had to get away, had to avoid saying something she would regret. "I—I have to go."

"You're running away," he accused.

"Like you did?" The minute the words were out, she regretted them. She saw the tensing of each of his muscles, the dark fury in his eyes. "Forget I said that. But don't accuse me, okay? Maybe I am running away. I don't know. But I need time, Mason, to think all this through."

"Ten years wasn't enough?"

She glanced up and stared into eyes as clear and amber as priceless Scotch. "I guess not." She pulled her hand away and though her heart was breaking, managed a sad smile. "Goodbye, Mason," she said, hating the finality of the words.

"It was good, but now it's over?" he asked, taunting her.

"It was good, but it never really began." She swung into the saddle and didn't look back. She couldn't. Because if she saw him again, all hard sinew, muscle and bone, his face chiseled and strong, she'd never be able to look away again. She loved him, that much was certain, and it was a cross she would bear for the rest of her life.

Chapter Thirteen

"You had to do it, didn't you?" Mason glared at his reflection in the steamy mirror, scraped away a swath of shaving cream and whiskers and mentally kicked himself for having made love to Bliss.

Though he'd had no conscious plan to seduce her, he hadn't been able to stop himself from spending more time with her, from seeing her, from suggesting the evening horseback ride to the ridge. Pursing his lips, he tried to avoid cutting himself as he finished shaving, then washed his face. He was standing naked in front of the mirror and had the fleeting thought that if Bliss were in the room, he probably should wear a towel wrapped around his waist, or his boxer shorts.

He stiffened just at the thought of her and ground out several oaths. What was he thinking? Why the devil would Bliss ever be in his bathroom in the morning? Just because they'd made love didn't mean that they ever would again, that they were having an affair, for the love of Pete, or that they might consider tying the knot.

As he threw on his clothes, his mind was running in wild, perilous circles. Just as it had all night. Throughout the long, dark hours, he'd been haunted by the image of Bliss's perfect face, the fragrance of her skin, the sound of her laughter. There had also been worries about Dee Dee and thoughts of another sort—memories of the years he'd struggled to prove to himself and the rest of the world that he was as good as anyone else, that the poor boy from the wrong side of the tracks could make good.

Except that he'd screwed up a few times. Seriously screwed up. There was the marriage that hadn't worked, a sister he'd promised to protect but who was constantly in trouble, a few bad deals and his daughter. His heart twisted at the thought of Dee Dee. So beautiful. So bright. So neglected. But no more. Dee Dee deserved security and a home. Here, with him. She couldn't be forever uprooted as Terri chased after this man or that dream. Nope. That part of his life he intended to settle today.

As for Patty, he hadn't yet spoken to her but Jarrod had assured him that she'd been located in Mexico and was flying home. If she knew anything about Isaac Wells's disappearance, she hadn't admitted to it. Mason would find out. One way or another. He'd promised his mother he'd take care of Patty and he'd do just that, though Patty would probably have none of it.

But Bliss Cawthorne was another matter altogether. What in the world was he going to do with her?

Bliss. The image of her face teased him again as he pocketed his keys and wallet. He should never have made love to her, never have taken that darkly seductive step, but he had, and in doing so he had expected that he might regret his desire but he didn't anticipate that he wouldn't get enough of her.

She was a virgin. Had never given herself to a man before.

Who would have guessed?

So what're you going to do about it?

There was, as he'd learned so often before, no going back. But he did have the ability to change a few things in his life.

He slipped into his shoes and flew down the stairs with more purpose than he'd felt ever since returning to Bittersweet. He had a few matters to take care of at the office, then he planned to have it out with Terri. Dee Dee wasn't going to the San Juan Islands or anywhere away from him. If he had to go back to court, he would. But Terri would probably be just as happy with a little cash instead. She'd always had a mercenary streak, even when it came to her daughter.

"I don't know," Terri said, rubbing her forehead as she sat at the kitchen table, which was covered with scraps of cloth as she pieced together a quilt. From her position at the table she could watch the television in the living room where a soap opera was in progress. Dee Dee was outside, lying on a chaise longue near the small pool of the apartment complex.

Leaning against the sink, Mason stared out the window and watched his daughter, sunglasses covering her eyes, reading another book.

Terri said, "I think I'd miss her too much."

"You'd see her at Christmas, in the summer and whenever else you wanted to. The way I see it, Dee Dee needs a home and some security," he said.

"Oh, like she'd get that from you?" Terri laughed and

rolled her eyes. "Don't forget you're a workaholic, Mason, and you're always zipping from one place to another. If there's a problem with the ranch, you're back in Montana, or the spread in Wyoming. Now you think you'll settle down here."

"I will."

"Why?"

"Because it's time."

She skewered him with her wide eyes and shook her head. She still looked young; that pixie quality had never left her despite the lines fanning from her eyes and creasing her forehead. "It's because of Bliss, isn't it?" she said, sadness heavy in her voice.

He didn't answer.

"I knew it. You never forgave me for lying to you about the baby, and you never got over her." She shook her head and sighed. "Oh, Mason, we were such fools." Opening a cupboard drawer, she withdrew a pack of cigarettes.

"I thought you quit."

"I did. Again. But every time I'm around you, I need a cigarette to relax." She lit up and blew a stream of smoke toward the ceiling. "I did love you, you know. A long time ago."

"You had a funny way of showing it."

"Yeah, well…" Sniffing loudly, she glanced into the living room. "We both made mistakes. I suppose you're getting married, right?"

"Don't know yet."

"Then how can you talk about security? For God's sake, who's gonna take care of Dee Dee when you're off on business?"

"She'll go with me or I'll have a live-in nanny."

"Or you'll marry Bliss Cawthorne."

"We haven't discussed it yet."

"You'd better talk it over with her old man, you know," Terri said. "And then you'd better come clean with Bliss. There are things she still doesn't know about that whole mess ten years ago. Oh, hell—" she jabbed out her cigarette "—what do I care? Bob wants to get married and move up north, you know that, and, well, he's not crazy about kids."

"Sounds like a great guy."

"At least he loves me, Mason. That's more than you ever did. If you want to keep Dee Dee, okay, we'll try it out and—"

"No. We're not going to try it out. We're going to do it. No one changes his or her mind. I've already talked to my attorney and we'll make it legal. As I said, you'll see her whenever you like, but I'll have custody. And instead of the child support I've been paying you, you'll get a sizable lump sum."

She lifted a curious eyebrow. "How sizable?"

He had her and he knew it. Good. He reached for his checkbook. "Name your price, Terri. What's it worth to you?"

Bliss scooted back the chair at her desk. So she and Mason had finally made love. She chewed on the edge of her lip and thought, as she had since returning from the ridge, about the only man she'd ever cared for—ever loved. "Oh, you're the worst kind of fool," she told herself as she tossed down her pencil and ignored the plans for a remodel of a warehouse on the Seattle waterfront that had been sent to her and lay open on the desk in her father's den. Work, which usually interested her, held no appeal— not this morning when the sunlight was streaming off the mountains and sparkling in the dewy grass.

Last night she'd watched as Mason had returned, unsaddled and unbridled Lucifer. He hadn't so much as glanced at the house where she'd stood at a window. Instead he'd climbed into his truck and driven away, leaving her alone with her thoughts.

She didn't believe that he'd used her, wouldn't even consider her father's protests that Mason was only getting close to her to get back at him. No, the attraction that she and Mason felt for each other was deep enough to cross time barriers, strong enough to dim the past with all its pain.

So here she was, contemplating loving a man she'd sworn to avoid.

Every time the phone had rung she'd nearly jumped out of her skin, hoping that Mason had decided to call. Each time, she'd been disappointed. She hadn't heard a word from him all day, but then, she supposed, it was her turn to make a move in his direction. If that was what she wanted.

She heard a car in the drive and her heart did a quick little leap. Pulling the old curtains aside, she saw Katie's convertible approaching the house. Her hair was wild and free, her smile wide as she parked, and though Bliss was still thinking about Mason, she was glad for the distraction that her half sister was sure to bring.

A few seconds later, Katie was ringing the bell on the front porch and Bliss threw open the door. A wave of heat rolled inside. "Come in," she said, before the younger woman had a chance to say a word.

"I just stopped by to let you know that John's being released, but Mom's insisting he stay with her in town. She wants him where she can keep her eye on him, and, really, I don't blame her."

"Neither do I," Bliss replied, still unsure exactly how she felt about this dynamo of a half sister but willing to give her benefit of the doubt. "Would you like something to drink or eat?"

"Yeah, a glass of water would be good, then I've got to look under the hood. My car acts like it's about to give up the ghost and it hasn't even reached two hundred thousand miles yet."

"Imagine that," Bliss said dryly.

She poured them each cups of water with ice, handed one to Katie, then followed the redhead outside where her bug-splattered car was resting in the shade of a spruce tree. Above their heads fragrant needles rustled in the hot breeze, and from the safety of a high branch a squirrel scolded Oscar, who whined and barked and ran in circles at the base of the tree.

Katie popped the hood and while she bent over the engine, she talked. "Hold this a sec, would you?" She took a long swallow of water, then handed the cup back to Bliss. "You know, those brothers of mine would know exactly what's wrong, but where are they when you need them, huh? Around? No way. Probably somewhere raising hell. Oh." She lifted her head and offered Bliss a knowing glance. "They're really not as much trouble as all that. Even the twins with their reputations aren't bad guys—just, well, *irreverent* would be a good word to describe them." She turned back to the cooling engine, touched it delicately as the radiator gave out a warning hiss. "Too hot to do anything with right now," she said, blowing her bangs out of her eyes and accepting her glass of water again.

"I decided to drop by and fill you in because I have a few minutes while Mom and Josh pick up John." She scratched her head and frowned, her forehead puckering thoughtfully. "You know, I'd like to pretend that all this is okay and we could be one big happy family, that I was big enough to make nice-nice for Mom's sake, but the truth of the matter is, I'm not cool with everything that went on between them and though I want them both to be happy, I don't think I'll ever be able to call John 'Dad.'"

"I don't blame you." Bliss lifted a shoulder, as if she didn't care, but she was glad that Katie was having the same kind of mental dilemma that she did. The situation was beyond complicated.

"Mom wanted me to tell you that while John's recuperating at her house, you can come over any time."

Bliss wasn't sure about that. She still had more than her share of reservations where her father and Brynnie were concerned. "How long will he be there?"

"Well, that's the problem, isn't it?" Katie said nervously, and Bliss suspected they were finally getting down to brass tacks—the real reason for her half sister's visit. "You know that Mom sold her portion of this place to Mason, though no money changed hands—the deal hasn't closed yet. Now Mason's willing to sell it back to her or John or whoever, which is good, I guess. But the thing is that she did it in the first place behind John's back. Mom should have talked it over with your dad first, I think. I mean, they're getting married and all, so why the secrets? If you ask me, when two people decide to tie the knot they should be able to trust each other implicitly, be able to talk over everything. I mean *every* thing." She picked at a sliver in the fence rail while Bliss felt sweat collect between her shoulder blades. "Call me a dreamer, but that's what marriage means to me."

"I guess it means something different to everyone," Bliss said, remembering her parents' union and knowing now that it was based on lies and deception. She took a long swallow from her glass. "Sometimes I wonder if this wedding is ever going to come off." Her father and Brynnie's relationship seemed more tenuous as the days passed.

Oh, yeah? And what about your relationship, if that's what you'd call it, with Mason?

Katie took a final swallow of water, tossed the melting cubes onto the grass and handed her glass to Bliss. "Look, I've got to run soon. Josh'll be home in half an hour." Her eyes darkened with a personal pain Bliss could only attribute to her son.

"You're worried about him."

"Him and a lot of things. But, yeah, he's at the top of the list. Raising a kid—especially a boy his age—alone isn't exactly a piece of cake."

"What about his father?"

Katie frowned. "Took off when I got pregnant. Haven't heard from him since. I decided I could raise my baby alone and I haven't really had to. Mom's always helped out." She studied the horizon, but Bliss suspected she wasn't observing the mountains or lowering sun, instead she was looking inward, to a private place only she could see. "I don't talk much about Josh's father. It's easier that way, although my curious son has been asking a lot of questions lately." She lifted a shoulder. "What about you? No kids, I know, but why haven't you ever married? And don't tell me you never met the right kind of guy, 'cause I won't believe it. With your looks, money and connections, my guess is that men—most of them potential 'right guys'— were flocking all over you."

"Maybe the right guy turned out to be the wrong one." Bliss eyed the cattle lumbering in the fields of the lower hills and tried not to let her thoughts turn toward Mason again. "Mom and Dad's marriage wasn't exactly picture perfect, but then you know that. Mom always wanted me to date—and I quote—'a strong, moral man with social standing, not some riffraff or rough-and-tumble cowboy like I did.'"

"Oh."

Bliss plucked a piece of dry grass from a clump near the fence post. "According to my mother, no one was good enough for me and I really wasn't interested."

"Because of Mason," Katie guessed shrewdly.

"What?"

"Hey, I've lived here all my life, heard the gossip, and it doesn't take a genius to put two and two together. You got involved with Mason and John gave him the old heave-ho about the time of your riding accident up on the ridge. Your dad blamed Mason for what happened." She glanced at Bliss, then continued. "Terri was pregnant, Mason married her, and you've never given your heart to another man, right?" Her green eyes were dark with unasked questions and Bliss found it increasingly impossible not to like Katie Kinkaid.

Pride inched Bliss's chin up a notch or two. She wanted to argue, but thought better of it. Wasn't Katie reaching out, talking to her, being the sister she'd never had? "Something like that," she admitted. There was more, a lot more, but some things were private and couldn't be shared, especially with a stranger who just happened to have turned out to be a half sister.

"Well, good."

"Good?" Bliss couldn't believe her ears. For years, Margaret had paraded eligible suitors in front of her face, begging her to find someone to share her life with and get over whatever it was that had been eating at her—especially if it had to do with a certain cowboy John had told her about.

"Yeah. Good." Katie tossed her hair away from her face. "Now you and Mason can get together. He's divorced, you've never married and the rest can become, as they say, history."

"I think that's a little premature."

"Ten years is a long time."

Bliss bristled. "Listen, if anyone needs a man, it's you."

Katie's small jaw became granite. "Believe me, Bliss, no one ever *needs* a man, but sometimes it's nice to have one around. I'm doing just fine on my own."

"So am I."

"Well, I wouldn't pass Mason up, if I were you. He loves his kid and is a good man. Last night we had Dee Dee over, you know." She thought for a minute. "She's a good kid—a little on the quiet side—but then I'm used to Josh, who's more than outgoing. But I'd only been around Dee Dee a couple of times before, but I liked her. She made sense. It's too bad her folks don't see eye-to-eye."

"Mason's crazy about her."

Katie's smile was wistful. "I know, and Terri doesn't realize what a godsend that is. There are so many fathers who are deadbeats or more interested in themselves than their kids." She sighed, then shook off the wistfulness that had come over her. "Anyway, as I said, Mason's a catch, Bliss, and now that you're my sister I guess I have the right to give you some advice. Don't make the same mistake twice."

"I'll try not to," Bliss replied, a little unnerved at Katie's boldness. Sure, they were related by blood, but that didn't give her half sister the right to try and run her life.

Katie dusted her palms together. "Time to tackle the car again." She walked back to the worn-out convertible and stuck her head under the still-open hood. Perplexed, she wiggled a few wires, then unscrewed the caps on the battery. "What I wouldn't give to have taken auto mechanics in high school. Damn." She replaced the caps and wiped her fingers on her jeans. With a sidelong glance at her half sister, she said, "So you're out here all alone for the next few nights."

"I've got Oscar." At the sound of his name, the dog gave out a yip and wagged his tail, but his head was still craned upward as he focused on the squirrel.

"And Mason, if you want him."

Bliss stiffened. "Give me a break."

"Don't tell me he's not interested." Katie closed the hood with a loud clunk. "I may not have ever been married, but Mom's walked down the aisle enough for the two of us. I've seen love and maybe even been there once myself. You, Bliss, have got it bad, and so does Mason."

"You don't know—"

"Sure, I do. I've known Mason a long time. So have my brothers. He's in love with you, Bliss, whether you want to know it or not. Well, speak of the devil." A satisfied smile stole over her face.

Oscar gave a quick little bark as Mason's truck rolled into the drive.

Katie laughed as she walked toward the driver's side of her car and Bliss's pulse, though she was loath to admit it, skyrocketed. "Someone just proved my point."

Mason waved to Katie as she climbed into her rattletrap of a convertible and twisted on the ignition. The engine coughed twice before catching. Then Katie gunned it, and in a plume of blue smoke, the old car lumbered down the drive.

Bliss stood her ground and wished she knew what to say to this man who could turn her world upside down with one long, slow, life-altering kiss.

Mason felt a tightening in his gut at the sight of her. Dear Lord, Bliss Cawthorne was beautiful and seductive and sexy without even trying to be. As he braked, she smiled slightly, the wind catching in her sun-streaked hair. His heart stopped for a second that was destined to change his life forever. He didn't have a reason to be here, but all day long he'd thought of last evening and making love to her. The image of her blue eyes, dusky with desire, her lush lips and rosy-tipped white breasts had filtered through his mind time and time again.

"Well, Mr. Lafferty. I didn't expect to see you so soon."

"No?" Was she kidding? "I thought we needed to talk."

"I suppose," she agreed, though her eyes were bright with suspicions. She rolled one palm toward the heavens. "What do you want?"

"What do I want?" he repeated as he stared at her. *You. I want you, Bliss Cawthorne, and I always have. I wish things were different between us, and God, I wish I never had hurt you.* He crossed the span of the driveway and stood so close to her he saw the slight trembling of her lip and caught the light scent of her perfume. "There are lots of things, Bliss."

"Such as?"

"I wanted to see you again." He searched her eyes.

She swallowed hard and some of her false bravado slipped away. "Look, just because we made love doesn't mean you have some kind of responsibility, a duty to—"

"Is that what you think?"

"To tell you the truth, Mason, I don't know what to think."

He believed her. She'd never looked more confused in her life. Well, he intended to set one thing straight. Before she could back up a step, he gathered her into his arms and lowered his lips to meet hers. Her mouth was soft and supple and yielding, her body warm and inviting. With a groan, he held her fast, hands splaying over her back, his blood pumping through his veins.

Lifting his head he stared into eyes that reflected his own

passion. "Now that we've settled my sense of 'duty,'" he said, running a thumb over her lower lip, "let's talk about us."

He felt her stiffen. "I thought I told you goodbye last night."

"You didn't mean it."

She lifted a teasing eyebrow. "Didn't I?"

It was all he could take. "No way, lady," he said and heard her gasp as he lifted her deftly off her feet and carried her into the house.

"Mason, stop! Let me down!" she cried as he marched determinedly down the short hallway to the bedroom where he'd first carried her bags years ago.

He dropped her onto the old double bed and as she landed, fell onto the sagging mattress with her.

"What do you think you're doing?" she demanded.

"Making love to you."

"What? No—" He cut off her protests with a kiss that started in his lips but touched him so deeply that his groin tightened and his erection, already at half-mast, stiffened in anticipation.

Her arms wound around his neck and she sighed contentedly into his mouth. "Why is it I can never say no to you?" she asked as she opened the buttons of his shirt.

"Because I'm so damned irresistible."

She laughed. "Oh, that's it," she said.

"Why else?" His breath fanned her ear and she couldn't think. His hand caressed her breast and she moaned. From that moment onward, she was lost.

He spent the night and it seemed natural to wake with his arms around her, his face buried in the crook of her neck. How many years had she dreamed of opening her eyes to see the sunlight caress the contours of his face? His beard had grown overnight and his eyelashes brushed the tops of his cheeks. In slumber there were no lines of worry disturbing the skin of his forehead, no creases of suspicion pulling at the corners of his mouth.

I love you, she thought, but didn't dare utter the words. This was an affair, nothing more; the culmination of years of old dreams. They weren't kids any longer, but adults with their own sets of problems; their own lives. He ran several ranches and a corporation or two, she was working on becoming a partner in the firm where she worked in Seattle. He had an ex-wife and a daughter; she had Oscar, who, by the sounds of the whining at the bedroom door, needed to go outside.

She threw on a robe, padded down the hallway and let Oscar out the front door. Delores, the cook and housemaid, had the week off, but a few of the ranch hands had already parked their trucks near the barn.

Out of habit she started the coffee and was unloading the dishwasher when she heard the shuffle of bare feet on the floor. She turned and found Mason, dressed only in his worn jeans, rubbing his jaw and glancing out the window. His hair, mussed and falling over his forehead, made him seem younger than his years and his broad shoulders were tanned. But she couldn't ignore the scar that ran around his upper arm, a reminder that his arm had nearly been torn from its socket as he'd tried to save her all those years ago.

"Good morning," she said as the coffeepot gurgled to life.

"It is, isn't it?" One side of his mouth lifted in a playful smile that she found absolutely endearing. She'd miss that smile as well as his lips upon her skin when she returned to Seattle.

"The best. Coffee'll be done in a second."

"Good."

"How about breakfast?"

"You get dressed and I'll buy."

"No reason," she countered. "I can cook."

"What d'ya know? Three languages, ballet, a B.A. in architecture *and* she can cook."

"That's a Masters in architecture," she reminded him as he walked up behind her, wrapped his arms around her waist and kissed the back of her neck.

"My kind of woman."

She laughed and felt him fiddle with the belt of her robe. "Hey, wait a minute—"

"Breakfast can wait," he growled against her ear as the robe parted and he lifted her from her feet.

As it was, breakfast was forgotten.

The fax machine whirred to life and Bliss waited, pushing aside the drawing she'd been working on. It had been four days since her father had been released from the hospital, and each night she'd spent with Mason. They'd talked of everything and nothing, but never once broached the subject that seemed forbidden to them. The future was off-limits. He was worried about his sister and his daughter; she was concerned about her father and the marriage that was once again "on." By the end of next week, Brynnie would officially be her stepmother.

And then what? Pack up Oscar and return to her life in Seattle?

Twiddling her pencil, she walked to the fax machine and read the memo from the office—another bid and a friendly note from one of the partners asking her when she planned to return.

"Never," she thought aloud, then caught herself. Because she wanted to stay here in this tiny town to be near her father? Or Mason? Or both?

Disgusted by the turn of her thoughts, she decided to drive over to Brynnie's to see John, but she'd barely made it out the front door when a brown station wagon pulled into the drive and parked between two of the pickups used by the hired hands.

Tiffany Santini climbed out of the car, glanced at a couple of the workers who were unloading hay into the barn and hurried to the front porch.

"Oh—did I come at a bad time?" she asked, seeing the car keys swinging from Bliss's fingers.

"No, come on in. I was going to visit Dad, but it can wait."

"He's not here? I thought he was released from the hospital."

"He was, but he's staying at Brynnie's for a little while. Come in." Bliss was glad for the distraction and the truth of the matter was that she was intrigued by her slightly uptight older half-sister. She didn't expect they'd become friends overnight, but at least they could get to know each other.

On the front porch, Tiffany said, "Look, I want to be honest with you. I heard that he was rushed to the hospital, that they thought it was his heart but it turned out that he'd gotten too much sun or something—and I didn't know what to do."

"It's hard."

"I thought the decent thing to do was to stop and see him and yet I didn't think he'd ever really done the decent thing by me or Mom, so...I waited. Anyway, here I am and I'm wondering what in the world I should say to you or to him." She rolled her large eyes.

"Well, come on in." Bliss held open the screen door. "I've got coffee or iced tea or—"

"This really isn't a social call," Tiffany snapped, then

caught herself. A small line formed between her eyebrows. "I—I don't know what it is."

"Neither do I, but if we don't talk, we'll never find out, will we?" Bliss was wary of this woman and yet she was curious. There was, after all, the same Cawthorne blood running through their veins.

Tiffany hesitated for a second, then must have decided that leaving would look cowardly because she nodded stiffly and followed Bliss inside. Her dark brows rose as she entered the ranch house for the first time, Bliss guessed. "It's not as if he was—or is—a big part of my life."

Bliss let that little jab slide by as they walked into the living room and, for the first time, Tiffany's eyes took in the watercolors of Indians and cowboys, the river-rock fireplace, the scatter rugs and marred wooden floor.

"So, now that you've been in town a few of weeks and met your stepmother-to-be, how do you feel about John's marriage to Brynnie Perez?" Tiffany asked suddenly.

Dropping her keys into her purse, Bliss stopped at the fireplace and decided to tell the truth. No reason to pussyfoot. She and these newfound sisters had a lot of ground to cover if they were to ever get along. That, she decided, staring into Tiffany's eyes, was a mighty big if. "Of course, I resented Brynnie when I first found out about her. How could my father—my *father*—have carried on an affair for so many years? I knew he was no knight in shining armor—"

Tiffany snorted her agreement.

"But I thought he had more morals than a tomcat." She shoved a shank of hair around her ear. "I was all set to hate Brynnie on sight. This was the woman who had defiled my mother's reputation, had been the 'love of my father's life,' who had been married a zillion times and had let another man claim Katie as his when she was really Dad's.

It was crazy. Like I'd just walked 'Through the Looking Glass' or entered the 'Twilight Zone.'"

"But you accept it?"

"I don't have much of a choice, do I? I mean, I can't tell my father what to do and anyway, as far as I was concerned, the damage was already done."

"To your mother."

"Yes, and to my idea of what my family was." Bliss sighed. "So I fought it for a while, decided I couldn't do anything and then, of course, I met Brynnie."

Tiffany walked to the window and stared through the panes to the front porch. "And let me guess how this little fairy tale ends—you fell in love with her, too, and now we're supposed to all be one big happy family."

"Wrong. I thought I'd hate my father's mistress on sight. And I decided I could live with that. You know, be outwardly civil while inwardly cold. But—and I wouldn't want my mother, if she were alive, to hear this—Brynnie's a hard person to hate."

Tiffany didn't respond, just ran a finger along the windowpane as she stared outside.

"So-o-o, I'm trying to put all my prejudices away if I can. I'm trying to convince myself that it's time to look forward, not backward. But if you want to know the truth, I'm having a rough time with all of it, okay? It's not easy, but there it is." She lifted a palm.

"There are always choices," Tiffany argued, though she didn't elaborate and Bliss guessed that she was talking about her own private problems.

"Dad didn't give you many."

Tiffany paled, then said, "No, he didn't. And you probably want to know how I felt about it. Well, I felt rotten. Once Mom came clean and told me the truth, I was sick to think that he didn't love me enough to claim me."

Bliss was horrified. "That's not what it was like. Tiffany, you've got to understand that—"

"What?" Tiffany said hotly, then appeared to bite back another sarcastic remark and sighed audibly. "Look, it's not your fault, but I blamed you. When I finally wanted to know more about my 'dad'—if that's what you could call him—I asked around about John. It turns out my grandmother had a wealth of information and was more than happy to let me know every intimate detail of my father's life. That's when I found out about you and discovered that you had this privileged life up in Seattle—that you had Dad—so I made the mistake of calling you 'the princess' in front of my son."

Her cheeks colored as she explained. "You seemed to have everything—anything a daughter could ever want. You and your mom had my father's name and his money and everything while my mother struggled, never married, and worked two jobs just to raise me. Even though my grandmother was and still is supportive, it was hard. Real hard." Tiffany turned back from the window and offered an unhappy smile. "Obviously, coming here was a mistake. I'm not going to your dad's wedding and I'm not going to act like the past didn't happen, okay? I can't."

She turned and Bliss caught hold of her arm. "I understand your frustration."

"I doubt it."

"Okay, so maybe I can't. But I think we should try to get to know each other."

Tiffany silently appraised her. "I was wrong. I shouldn't have called you 'princess.' Pollyanna would have been more appropriate."

"Maybe so, but no matter what happens," Bliss said, unable to hold her tongue, "I'm not going to be bitter about it or carry a huge chip on my shoulder."

Tiffany shook her head. "Good for you, Bliss."

"Would it be so terrible to get to know each other?" Bliss asked, and wondered why it was suddenly so important. So what if Tiffany didn't want to have anything to do with her? She'd lived all her life not knowing she had a half sister, so why push it?

Tiffany's eyes were cold as ice. "I just don't know if there's any reason to pursue this. I'm not going to make any bones about not liking your father. And trust me, I'll never think of him as mine, so, as for you, all that I feel toward you right now is idle curiosity."

"But you came over here."

She shook her head. "I guess I was feeling guilty, but I can't for the life of me figure out why. The thing is that even though I don't care about John Cawthorne, I wouldn't want him to suffer, so I'm glad to hear that he's recovering. Other than that, I don't have much to say."

Bliss dropped her hand and Tiffany left.

Why Bliss felt a sense of loss, she didn't understand. As far as she was concerned, Tiffany Santini had never been her sister and never would be. Tiffany had decided.

Brynnie's house was situated two blocks from the park and painted a faded shade of salmon. It had once been a small cottage but had been expanded over the years to accommodate various husbands and additional children. A wing from the kitchen shot into the backyard, the attic had been turned into a bedroom/loft and the garage had been converted into an apartment attached to the house by an open breezeway. A few petunias splashed color from barrels placed by the front door, where the torn mesh of the screen needed replacing. Three cats lazed on a cracked driveway.

As Bliss knocked on the door, she heard her father's

voice through the screen. "I told you, this isn't happening—"

"Come in, the door's open," Brynnie yelled over John's deeper, angry voice.

"I don't care what any damned doctor says, I'm not lyin' around here twiddlin' my fingers and toes." John Cawthorne was seated on a plaid couch and pulling on a boot. His face was red, his jaw set and Bliss knew from experience that he wasn't going to change his mind. "Hi, kiddo," he said as Bliss entered, then went right on ranting at Brynnie.

"I have to check with the accountant about my insurance payments and the foreman of the ranch about how much feed we'll need this winter. Bill Crosswhite's got a bull I might want to buy or use, and I'd like to see the animal myself. Then there's the properties up in Seattle—the house is up for sale and the boat. I've got two empty warehouses that someone wants to convert to apartments and..." His voice trailed off as he realized both women were staring at him as if he'd lost his mind.

"And what about the wedding?" Brynnie asked. "Are you gonna be able to squeeze that in?"

"Of course, but—"

"We're supposed to talk to the preacher this afternoon."

"The preacher. Right." John rubbed the side of his face and scratched at the silver stubble on his jaw. Rather than address the subject, he asked Bliss, "How're you doing out at the ranch all alone?"

"I'm not really alone, Dad. You've got workers."

He snorted. "Such as they are."

"Well, they're keeping things in line and Mason has been by a couple of times."

"Great," her father grumbled. "He's probably gonna change his mind again and find a way to finagle me and keep the damned place.'' He shot Brynnie a damning glance. ''Or has he been hanging around because of you?'' He eyed his daughter and reached for his other boot.

''I don't think all of Mason's motives are evil,'' she said with a smile.

''Is that so? Listen, Blissie, don't defend that bastard to me. He's even gone so far to work a deal with Brynnie behind my back. Helluva guy, that Lafferty.''

Brynnie, who had been reading her horoscope in the newspaper, said, ''That was my fault, John Cawthorne, and you know it. Now Mason's trying to make amends and the least you could do is be big enough to see it.'' Obviously irritated, she snapped the paper, then dropped it onto a coffee table already laden with empty glasses, ashtrays, magazines and books of matches.

John was having none of it. ''That bastard hurt my baby.''

And so have you, Dad, she thought silently. *With all of your lies.*

''Come on, let's not fight,'' Brynnie said to John. ''I don't know why you're so darned ornery today. You know you're not supposed to be getting all riled up. Just lie back down, switch on the television and wait for Reverend Jones.''

''I just can't stand lyin' around doin' nothin'.''

''The doctor said that if you take it easy, you can move back to the ranch soon—''

''The doctor can shove it, for all I care. Blast it all, anyway.'' He yanked on his boot, rolled to his feet and stood without so much as swaying. If nothing else, John Cawthorne was blessed with more than his share of grit and willpower.

Bliss cleared her throat. ''I thought you should know that Tiffany stopped by. She was looking for you, but when I told her you were here, she decided she didn't want to come looking for you."

John's face softened. "Well, I'll be."

"Don't get your hopes up, Dad. She wasn't all that friendly."

"But she tried."

"Yeah." Bliss nodded and didn't bring up the fact that she and her elder half-sister had nearly had a shouting match. She'd said enough. Whatever happened next was between Tiffany and John.

"See there?" Brynnie sniffed. "I've always told you there is a God and He's watching over you."

So who was watching over Mom? Bliss wondered, when Margaret Cawthorne lay dying and her husband, though seemingly concerned, was involved with another woman. She gave herself a quick mental shake. She had to quit thinking in those terms. Her mother, rest her soul, was gone. Yes, her father had been unfaithful, less than true, and a liar, but that was all in the past. Now he was marrying a woman whom Bliss couldn't find it in her heart to hate. As she'd told Tiffany, she couldn't dwell on the sins of years gone by but had to focus ahead, on the future. With her father.

And with Mason.

She pushed that wayward thought aside. Mason and she were having an affair—that much was true. And she knew that she loved him, but never had he said he loved her; never had she felt that he cared for her as she did for him.

Once again, she'd let him play her for a fool.

But not for long.

As soon as John and Brynnie were married, she was moving back to Seattle.

What was the old saying, something like it was better to have loved and lost than never to have loved at all?

Bliss wasn't convinced.

Chapter Fourteen

"This time, Mason, you've really flipped!" Patty Lafferty hoisted one of her bags into the back of his truck. Overhead, a jet taking off from the airport roared upward into the cloudy heavens. "Do you really think I was somehow involved with Uncle—if that's what you'd call him—Isaac's disappearance?"

"You took off around the same time."

"Give me a break." Eyes as gold as his own sparked angrily. "So what?" She glared at her brother as they stood toe-to-toe in the airport parking lot. "You don't believe me."

"You've lied before."

"Not about something like this! Oh, Mason, come *on!*"

He frowned at her and wished he could believe her, but she'd been in more scrapes than he cared to count.

"Swear to God!" She licked two fingers and held them

up beside her head as proof of her integrity and innocence. "Scout's honor."

He snorted.

"Oh, for the love of God, Mason, think about it. Why would I help Isaac disappear?"

"You tell me."

Another jet screamed down the runway.

"I can't!" She threw her hands up in the air. The wind caught the long red-blond strands of her hair, tossing them in front of her face. "Why won't you trust me?"

"Past history."

"I just went to Mexico for a while." She climbed into the cab of the truck and played with the frayed hole in the knee of a disreputable pair of jeans.

"Maybe you'd like to tell me why?"

"Maybe not. It's none of your business." Her jaw was set and she slid a pair of sunglasses onto the bridge of her nose.

"Why won't you tell me?"

"I didn't do anything illegal, okay? I just needed to get away for a while. Fun and sun, that's all."

"And you couldn't call?"

"I didn't want to. Whether you know it or not, Mason, you're not my keeper." She fished into her purse, pulled out a tube of pale pink lipstick and applied it without benefit of a mirror. "And don't give me any guff about a promise to Mom, okay? It doesn't wash anymore. I'm way too grown-up to have an older brother breathing down my neck." She slipped the cap onto her lipstick tube and tossed it back into the messy interior of her bag.

Mason, starting the engine, was still suspicious.

"You know, Mason, you should lighten up." She found a decorative elastic band, scraped back her hair and snapped the band into place. "You're starting to imagine things."

He jammed the truck into gear and drove through the parked cars. Sunlight glinted off windshields and fenders, while people with bags of every sort and size clustered in knots at stations for the shuttle. Was he imagining things? He didn't think so. He cared about his sister even though she'd given him nothing but grief ever since he could remember.

"You know, Patty," he said as he slowed to pay for his short stay in the parking lot. He handed the attendant in the booth a ten-dollar bill and waited for change. "It wouldn't hurt you to settle down."

She laughed as the gate opened and he drove through. "Oh, yeah, what's this? You know the old saying, the pot calling the kettle black or some such hogwash. You could take some of that advice yourself."

He slid his sister a knowing glance. "How did Jarrod find you?"

At the mention of Jarrod Smith's name, Patty's expression changed. She avoided Mason's eyes. "You know your old friend. He could find a black cat in a dark room on a moonless night."

"I'm surprised he didn't come back with you."

Patty lifted a shoulder. "I didn't invite him," she said and reached into her bag for a pack of gum. She made a big show of unwrapping a stick before plopping it into her mouth. "I think he said he'd be back in a few days, in time for his mother's wedding. I didn't really pay a lot of attention. He made sure I got on the flight and I took off."

She seemed to take sudden interest in the other cars on the freeway as Mason melded his truck into the flow of traffic, then slid lower in the seat, as if she intended to get a little shut-eye. "Jarrod did tell me that you were seeing Bliss Cawthorne again," she said.

"She's back in town."

"Is that good news or bad?"

Definitely good, he thought, but kept his feelings to himself. He knew Patty was just trying to distract him and, damn it, her ploy worked. Now that his sister was safe and, for the moment, out of trouble, he could concentrate on other things. Terri was coming around about Dee Dee, and that left Bliss.

Bliss.

What in the world was he going to do with her?

Ask her to marry you, that's what. You can't take a chance on losing her again.

His jaw slid to one side and he adjusted the air conditioner to lower the temperature in the cab. He'd struggled with his feelings for over a week. She was the one woman he'd sworn to avoid and now he couldn't get enough of her. Making love to her was pure heaven. Holding her close at night was something he wanted to do for the rest of his life. And she'd be leaving soon. John and Brynnie's wedding was scheduled for the end of next week. Then Bliss was planning to return to Seattle.

That thought settled on him like lead. It was time to come clean. As soon as he'd deposited Patty at her apartment, he'd have it out with old man Cawthorne.

Bliss gave Fire Cracker her head and felt the hot summer air stream through her hair as the game little mare raced over the dry stubble of the field. The sky was on fire, deep shades of magenta and gold blazing over the western hills, as the sun set in a splash of brilliance.

It was a glorious evening and Bliss felt a rush of adrenaline as Fire Cracker's hooves thundered over the dry acres.

Cattle and horses dotted the hillsides, and shadows grew long at the base of trees. How could she ever leave? In the past few weeks she'd grown to love this ranch, just as her father did. And despite all her talk to the contrary, she'd fallen in love with Mason.

Not that he loved her.

She kneed Fire Cracker and the mare leaped over a dry streambed, sailing through the air and landing with a bone-jarring thud on the other side. A field mouse scurried for cover. Birds flew and scattered.

Bliss would be returning to Seattle in a few days, as soon as her father was married and off on his honeymoon. At that thought her heart twisted. She would miss this place; miss the freedom, the quiet nights, the smell of leather and horses, her father's grumblings and the prospect of getting to know her half sisters. But most of all, she'd miss Mason.

"Idiot," she muttered as the barn, stables and outbuildings came into sight.

She pulled up on the reins and caught her breath as the mare slowed to a walk at the paddock near the stables. Dirty but exhilarated, Bliss climbed down from the saddle and walked Fire Cracker into the darkened interior.

She spent the next forty-five minutes cooling the horse down, then brushing her sleek hide before offering a measure of oats and bucket of water. "You know," she admitted, scratching the mare between her ears and avoiding being swatted by the sorrel's tail, "I'm going to miss you, too."

She'd considered moving down here. Lord knew, her father was doing his best to promote it. Now that he'd moved back to the ranch and was feeling better, he'd thought of every bribe imaginable to keep her in Bittersweet. Not only had he given her the horse, he'd promised her land, offered her a job, suggested her sisters needed her; but she'd been undeterred. Her job, her friends, her entire life was in Seattle.

But Mason was here. Her soul darkened a bit. She loved him. More than she ever had. And that was a problem. Once before, she'd been involved with him and the love affair had been one-sided; now, since they were older, the only difference was that they were physically intimate. Just because they'd made love was no reason to think that they had a future together.

He had his corporations, his ranches, his own life and a daughter.

"Oh, stop it," she told herself as she finally let Fire Cracker out of her stall. Bucking and snorting, the horse romped to the middle of the corral and immediately dropped to the ground where she rolled back and forth, her legs kicking wildly in the air, a cloud of dust billowing from beneath her. "Great. All that brushing for nothing." Bliss chuckled as she walked toward the back door of the house.

Lights were already glowing from the windows as the sky darkened and night crept over the landscape. Oscar, lying on the front porch, let out a quiet "Woof" and thumped his tail, but Bliss barely heard him. Through the screen door she heard the sound of voices. Loud voices.

"Look, Lafferty, I don't like the game you're playin' with Bliss." John Cawthorne's voice brooked no argument.

Bliss stopped dead in her tracks. Mason was here?

"I'm not playing any games." Mason's voice, clear, calm and cold.

"She's falling for you again. Just like before."

"This time it's different, Cawthorne."

Different? What was he talking about? Bliss's heart was like a drum, pounding out a wild, erratic cadence.

"Trust me." Mason's voice was stern. Determined. Oh,

God, how she loved him. She was about to walk inside, but held back. The air was charged and she knew, deep in her heart, that she should just walk back to the stables and forget every word that was being said. Or she should announce herself and barge into the kitchen. But still she hung back, her throat as dry as a desert wind, her heart pumping madly.

"The day I trust you is the day I give up the ghost, Lafferty. I wanted you as far away from my daughter as possible. I thought I made that clear a few years ago. Seems to me we had an agreement."

"It's off."

"I paid you good money."

Bliss bit her lip. She knew about the cash. So what was the big deal? She reached for the handle of the door.

"Just like the money you paid Terri to pretend she was pregnant?" Mason demanded.

What? Bliss's heart stopped. Surely she'd heard wrong.

"Don't know what you're talkin' about, son."

"Sure you do, Cawthorne. Paying me to stay out of Bliss's life wasn't enough, was it? You bought yourself some insurance by sweetening the deal with Terri. Fortunately for you, she was only too willing to go along with the scam."

No!

"You're just blowin' smoke, Lafferty."

"Am I?" Mason snorted. "I only wish I'd been smart enough to demand the results of a pregnancy test before I married her."

Oh, God, please, no! Bliss's knees nearly gave out. With one hand she balanced herself against the post supporting the roof. Was she hearing correctly? Had her father actually talked Terri into lying? Paid her off? *What?*

"If I live to be a hundred," Mason said, "I'll never believe another woman."

"Even Bliss?"

"I think we should leave her out of this."

"She's the reason you and I are at odds, boy."

A few passing seconds seemed like an eternity. "Bliss wouldn't set me up and try to trap me into marriage with a baby—even a nonexistent one like Terri did."

Bliss's insides were shaking.

"And besides, Terri was coached, wasn't she? By you."

No!

John clucked his tongue, then sighed audibly. "So Terri blamed me? Always knew she couldn't be trusted."

"I saw the records, Cawthorne. When I got suspicious I paid a kid who worked in the lab for a copy of all of Terri's reports. When I confronted her, she told me the whole sick story.

"Of course by the time I got the news, it was too late." Bliss heard the scrape of boots. "I was already married and guess what? By that time Terri really was pregnant."

"And you ended up with a daughter."

"The only bright spot in this whole sordid deal. In fact, Dee Dee was worth all of this. But now, it's time to come clean."

"You want me to tell Bliss."

"I think it would be a good idea."

"It'll never happen, Lafferty," her father said, but his tone was less firm than before. "Because, unless I miss my guess, Bliss will never believe you."

Dear God. Was her father really so controlling that he would interfere in her life to the point of all this lying and deceit? Fury pumped through her blood and her fingers curled into fists of rage. To think that—

"It was Margaret's idea."

"What?" Bliss couldn't stop the word and suddenly there was silence—hollow, soul-numbing silence. Steeling herself, she yanked hard on the door handle and marched, ready to do bodily harm if necessary, into the house. Oscar gave out an excited yip and followed her inside, but she ignored the dog and glared at her father. "Why are you lying?" Bliss asked her father.

"So that's the way it was. I wondered," Mason said. His face was set and hard, his eyes slits as he stood, his hips balanced against the kitchen counter, his arms folded over his broad chest.

The odors of day-old coffee and floor wax drifted to her nostrils. The only noise for a few long seconds was the hum of the refrigerator and the ticking of the clock.

"I didn't know you were listening," her father said.

"I didn't mean to, but I think you'd better explain."

Sighing loudly, John reached into his breast pocket for a nonexistent pack of cigarettes and avoided the accusation in Bliss's gaze. He found a plug of tobacco in his back pocket.

"It's the truth," he admitted with a lift of one thin shoulder. "Margaret was undone when I let it slip that you were getting involved with one of the ranch hands. She was certain you were going to make the same mistake she did, and since she knew all about Brynnie... Well, she threatened to expose Brynnie as my mistress, divorce me and take me to the cleaners. In addition to all that, she was determined to make sure that you never spoke to me again."

Trembling with rage, Bliss leaned over the table and stared at her father—so old, so tired, so forlorn. "I don't believe a word of this."

He blinked before looking at her again. "It's true, Blissie, and you meant so much to me that I caved in and bribed Terri to claim she was pregnant. Then, after the accident, when you were so hurt, I worked a deal with Mason." He wiped a hand over his brow and closed his eyes for a second.

"Oh, Dad, how could you?" Bliss suddenly felt cold to the marrow of her bones. She didn't want to believe that either of her parents would be so manipulative.

"It was for your best interests," her father said.

"*My* best interests? Didn't I have a say in them?" Stunned and reeling, she nearly fell into one of the chairs at the table and fixed her gaze on the man who had sired her.

"You were seventeen. Didn't know up from sideways."

"But it was my life. Mine!" She thumped her fingers against her chest. "You had no right—"

"I saw you with Lafferty and knew it would only be a matter of time before you got yourself into big trouble, so I went along with your mother."

"I can't believe it." Bliss cradled her head in her hands. All these years. All the lies. "You...you could have ruined so many lives. Mine. Mason's. Terri's."

"No one was really hurt," John argued.

"Untrue. We were all hurt." She felt the sting of tears behind her eyes at the thought of her parents' betrayal. Whatever were their reasons, there was no excuse, no explanation good enough to justify their actions. "Just because I wasn't 'of age' or whatever you want to call it, didn't mean I didn't have feelings, that I shouldn't have some say in my life!"

Her father's jaw was rock hard. "I did what I thought best."

"Because you were coerced into it by Mother."

"She loved you more than life itself, Blissie. You know that." He blinked, as if the thought of his wife and how he'd treated her brought tears to his eyes. "We were the best parents we knew how to be."

"I can't believe this," she whispered.

"Believe it." Mason's voice was hard and the wrath in his gold eyes reflected his years of pain. "We were both deceived, Bliss."

"And what about you?" she demanded, hurting and raw, as she stared at Mason. "Taking money from Dad, staying away from me and never looking back." Mason, too, had used her.

"I'm sorry," Mason said. "I should have come to you in the hospital and explained—"

"Explain what? That twenty-five thousand dollars meant more to you than I did? That...that you were willing to marry another woman rather than face me again? I never thought I'd say this," she whispered, anger burning through her, "but you're a coward, Mason Lafferty, and I thought I loved you. For years I believed..." Hot tears stung against her eyelids. "I—I mean— Oh, just forget it." She couldn't stand to remain another second in the house, turned and hurried out the door.

"Bliss, wait!" Mason yelled. "Oh, before I forget why I came here, Cawthorne, this is yours." There was a slap of paper on a hard surface. "The deed to this place, signed back to Brynnie. Now it's official. I don't want your spread anymore, Cawthorne. I don't want anything of yours."

"Includin' my daughter?"

Bliss didn't wait for Mason's answer. She ran down the steps, across the yard to the paddock where Fire Cracker was grazing. *Run. Get away now. You've already lost your heart to Mason, but you can't let him know.* Tears streamed from her eyes. Dear God, she'd fallen in love with him all over again. The one man she didn't dare trust with her heart seemed to have it in a crushing grip that she couldn't pry open. How many nights had she dreamed of lying naked in his arms, oblivious to anything but the feel of his breath against her bare skin? How many hours had she spent thinking of him, wondering if there was any way they could have a future together?

"Wait a second!" Mason's voice and the sound of his boots crunching on gravel caught up with her.

She headed straight for the mare. Hearing the commotion, the horse snorted and pricked her ears forward. Overhead, swallows disturbed from their nests, dipped and fluttered near the eaves of the stables.

"I said, 'Wait,'" Mason nearly yelled as he caught up with her.

She whirled and almost ran into him in the darkness. "Why?"

"Because we should talk this out."

"We could have. When you found out the truth—which, it sounds like, was years ago. But no, you kept it a secret. Were you ever going to tell me?" she demanded, angling her furious face upward and feeling heat pulsing in her cheeks. Curse the man! He was just too damned sexy with his thin lips, thick-lashed eyes and taut, tanned skin over high, angry cheekbones. Just staring into his lying eyes caused a rolling, needy sensation deep inside her. A sensation she suddenly hated.

"If and when I thought it was necessary."

"If *you* thought it was necessary. What about me? This was my life, too, you know." Brushing the condemning tears from her cheeks, she added, "I don't need any man— not my father and certainly not you—trying to protect me or keep secrets from me, or do whatever it is you thought you were doing. Okay?"

"I did what I thought was best."

"Yeah. Just like Dad. Next time, ask me. Better yet, don't. There won't be a next time."

She strode into the stables and grabbed a bridle. Mason followed and took hold of her arm. "Slow down, Bliss. We need to talk."

She whistled to the mare—the way she'd learned from Mason so many years before.

"You should have thought of that before," she said as the mare clomped up to her. Deftly, she snapped the bridle over Fire Cracker's lowered head. "Goodbye, Mason," she said, untying Fire Cracker's reins.

"Maybe you should listen to my side of the story."

"And maybe you should go straight to hell." She swung onto the mare's dusty back.

His eyes were dark with old, hidden demons. "I've already been there and back." He stepped forward as she jerked on the reins and dug her heels into the mare's sides. "Bliss—"

"Hi-ya!"

Fire Cracker took off in a thunder of hooves and over the noise Bliss thought she heard Mason call after her. *Damn it, woman, I love you.* The words toyed with her mind, but she shoved them aside and told herself she hadn't heard anything but the voice of the wind.

Mason experienced a sense of déjà vu as he watched her race away. The mare galloped through the twilight-dark fields and he felt every muscle in his body grow tense. Though it was a hot, sticky night, with only a few clouds drifting over the glittering stars, he was reminded of another time, in this very spot, when heavy raindrops had veiled his vision and Bliss had ridden, hell-bent for leather, into the heart of a lightning storm.

This time was different.

Or was it?

A deep, frightening dread inched up his spine and though he told himself he was every kind of fool, that he didn't believe in fate, or premonitions, or anything remotely touching predestination, he couldn't shake the feeling.

He'd come here to give the old man his deed back, and that accomplished, he should just leave, but instead of his footsteps taking him to his truck, he half ran to the tack room, snagged a saddle, blanket and bridle and found Lucifer grazing in a nearby field. With a sharp whistle, he gained the stallion's attention and within minutes he was astride the blue-eyed pinto, chasing after Bliss and feeling his fear mount with each of the animal's swift strides.

"Come on, come on," he urged Lucifer as he silently cursed himself for not watching which of the old cattle trails that webbed over the base of the hills she'd taken. He rode by instinct, sweating beneath his shirt, his eyes narrowed on the terrain ahead.

At the base of the hills, he guided Lucifer upward, heading along one of the dusty paths, hoping to catch a glimpse of Bliss or her dogged little horse. He stopped twice, listening for the sound of hoofbeats and hearing nothing but a train rumbling on distant tracks.

"She'll be all right," he told himself. "She's got to be. Come on, you miserable piece of horseflesh. Run!"

Beneath branches, through swarms of insects, around stumps and boulders the game horse ran. Across patches of moonlight and past a creek with a tumbling waterfall that sprayed a soft mist, he rode until at last the trees gave way to the ridge.

His heart stopped. He saw her silhouette, darker than the surrounding hills, astride Fire Cracker and riding wildly past the very tree struck by lightning ten years before. The old trunk was leafless and dead, the core burned black by the decade-old bolt from the sky.

"Slow down!" Mason yelled. "Bliss!"

She twisted in the saddle, her hair fanning around her.

"I love you!"

She froze, but the horse kept moving.

"Bliss—"

She gathered the reins back, slowing the mare while rocking.

"Move," he yelled at his mount. "Come on!" He remembered the last time, how she'd nearly died. Because of him. Again! "Oh, sweet Jesus!" He kicked his horse forward. Bliss toppled. She screamed. Thud! She hit the ground with bone-cracking certainty.

Mason vaulted off his horse. "No, oh, God, no!" He reached her in an instant, dragged her crumpled body to his. "Bliss, Bliss, oh, love," he whispered, holding her and praying to a God he'd had no words with in years that she was all right. He couldn't have hurt her again, couldn't have been the cause of any more pain. But a bruise and scrape marred the perfect skin near her temple and she sagged limply, as if there were no life left in her.

"I love you," he said and felt tears clog his throat. "Please, sweetheart, don't…" He couldn't lose her. Wouldn't! She was breathing shallowly, but her eyes fluttered open for an instant and a faint smile touched her lips.

"Mason," she mouthed.

"Hang in there, baby, I'll take care of you."

"I…I know…" Then she drifted off again and he felt the cold mind-numbing fear that she might be lost to him forever. He whistled to his horse, rose to his feet and carried her gently. She wasn't going to die on him, nor was she going to leave him.

It had been ten years and he wasn't going to wait any longer. This woman was the only woman he'd ever loved, the only one who could touch his heart. Somehow, someway, he was going to save her.

Bliss felt as if she were drowning. The water was warm and calm, a blackness dragging her under.

"Can you hear me? Bliss?"

A voice. Mason's voice. Oh, Lord, how she loved him.

"Blissie. Wake up now."

Her father. And he sounded worried. So worried. About her.

"Don't leave me." Mason again. She would never leave him. Why would he think...? She struggled to open her eyes only to allow a blinding flash of light to pierce her brain. Pain exploded at her temples.

"Did you see that?"

"She's comin' around."

"Mason?" she said, but no sound escaped her and her throat felt as dry as sandpaper.

"I'm here, darlin'," he replied and she felt his hand, big and callused, rubbing the back of hers. Again she tried to force her eyes open and this time, despite the painful brilliance, she managed to blink and stay awake.

"Where—where am I?"

"At the hospital in Medford," Mason said. His face, all harsh planes and angles, was hovering over hers, and she watched as relief washed over his features.

A doctor appeared, nudged Mason aside and shone yet another light into her eyes as she lay on the starched white sheets. "You're going to be all right," he assured her, though she hadn't been worried. "You'll be able to go to your father's wedding."

"Good."

"Just as long as she goes to hers," Mason said.

She blinked again. "Wh-what?"

The doctor moved aside and Mason took her hand, linking his fingers through hers. "Marry me, Bliss."

"Now, wait a minute—" her father protested from somewhere behind Mason.

"Forgive me and marry me." Mason swallowed hard. "I love you. I want you to be my wife, to be Dee Dee's stepmother. To be the mother of my children, our children."

Tears filled her eyes. Her heart melted. *Children. Mason's children.*

Mason kissed her on the temple. "I've always loved you, Bliss Cawthorne, and I swear, I'll love you for the rest of my life."

"And I'll love you for the rest of mine." Her voice was weak and cracked, but her conviction was strong. Managing a smile through her tears of joy, she stared into the golden gaze of the man she'd loved for as long as she could remember. "There's nothing to forgive, Mason, nothing. And of course, I'll marry you."

"Oh, hell," her father said.

"No, Dad, it's heaven," she assured him.

"Whatever makes you happy, Blissie," her father said, his voice filled with emotion.

"Maybe we should plan a double ceremony," Mason teased.

"I don't think so," she said. "I don't want to share our wedding day with anyone but you."

Her father cleared his throat. "Whatever you want. Brynnie will be thrilled and your sisters— Hell, I forgot. Katie's been worried sick about you."

"And Tiffany?"

There was a pause. "She's still not talkin' to me, but she called Katie once and this hospital twice. She's concerned about you, kiddo. Looks like you might have finally won her over.''

Bliss wasn't sure but she smiled inwardly. Sisters…and children…and, of course, a husband. Mason.

"I'll go give Brynnie a call. She'll tell your sisters. Love ya, kid,'' her father said, touching her lightly on the shoulder. "Try and forgive a foolish old man for trying to protect his daughter, would you?''

"Sure, Dad,'' she said, just thankful to be alive. She wasn't happy with what he'd done and there were still some issues they had to resolve, but she'd give him another chance because she truly believed that both of her parents had thought they had her best interests at heart. She heard her father leave the room and vowed to work things out. With him. With her half sisters. With Mason's daughter. Somehow, she would make things work.

"So as soon as I get the doctor to spring you from here,'' Mason said, interrupting her thoughts and staring down at her with his incredible gold eyes, "I'll expect you to start making wedding plans.''

"Will you?''

"Unless you want to elope.'' His smile was positively and deliciously wicked.

"It doesn't matter,'' she said. "Just as long as you promise to be with me forever.''

"No longer?''

She laughed, and he winked at her.

"It's a deal, Bliss Cawthorne. You and me. But only until forever.''

"Should we shake on it?'' she asked, grinning, her heart so filled with happiness she thought it might burst.

"Shake on it? Hmm.'' His eyes twinkled. "We could, but you know, I had something else in mind. Something more…intimate.''

She sighed and rolled her eyes. "You're trouble, Lafferty. Big trouble."

"I am," he agreed. "But only with you, love. Only with you."

*   *   *   *   *

A Note From the Author

Dear Reader,

Welcome to Bittersweet, Oregon. It's a fictitious town set in the southern part of the state, and a beautiful place to visit.

When I first started this project, I envisioned three women, all very independent, all living their lives on their own, until they discover they are half sisters, related because a man whose various affairs and marriages brought them into the world. I wanted these women to not only find the love of their lives in the heroes of the books, but to come to terms with the fact that they have women siblings with whom they can share both joy and pain. I hoped that my heroines would learn to deal with their father, a selfish, perhaps single-sighted man that none of them can really trust, but a man who loves them all.

In *A Family Kind of Guy* you met Mason Lafferty and

Bliss Cawthorne. The next book is *A Family Kind of Gal.* Widowed Tiffany Santini is not only struggling to raise two children alone, she must also deal with her sexy, disapproving brother-in-law, J.D. Santini, a man whom she finds attractive, but doesn't believe.

In *A Family Kind of Wedding* Katie Kinkaid, the third of John Cawthorne's daughters, has to cope with her often-wed mother finally marrying her father, as well as deal with her sisters. On top of that, she's determined to set her career in motion, raise her young son and take the world by storm. Unfortunately, a mysterious cowboy named Luke Gates has other plans. Luke is trouble with a capital *T* but Katie's not one to back down, not even when her heart and maybe even her life are at risk.

I hope you enjoyed your visit to Bittersweet. Come back again.

Best,
Lisa Jackson

Available September 1998
from Silhouette Books...

World's Most
Eligible Bachelors

THE CATCH
OF CONARD COUNTY
by Rachel Lee

Rancher Jeff Cumberland: long, lean, sexy as sin. He's eluded every marriage-minded female in the county. Until a mysterious woman breezes into town and brings her fierce passion to his bed. Will this steamy Conard County courtship take September's hottest bachelor off of the singles market?

Each month, Silhouette Books brings you an irresistible bachelor in these all-new, original stories. Find out how the sexiest, most sought-after men are finally caught...

Available at your favorite retail outlet.

Silhouette®

MEN at WORK

All work and no play?
Not these men!

July 1998
MACKENZIE'S LADY by Dallas Schulze

Undercover agent Mackenzie Donahue's
lazy smile and deep blue eyes were his best
weapons. But after rescuing—and kissing!—
damsel in distress Holly Reynolds, how could
he betray her by spying on her brother?

August 1998
MISS LIZ'S PASSION by Sherryl Woods

Todd Lewis could put up a building with ease,
but quailed at the sight of a classroom! Still,
Liz Gentry, his son's teacher, was no battle-ax,
and soon Todd started planning some
extracurricular activities of his own....

September 1998
A CLASSIC ENCOUNTER
by Emilie Richards

Doctor Chris Matthews was intelligent, sexy
and *very* good with his hands—which made
him all the more dangerous to single mom
Lizette St. Hilaire. So how long could she
resist Chris's special brand of TLC?

Available at your favorite retail outlet!

MEN AT WORK™

 HARLEQUIN®   Silhouette®

Look us up on-line at: http://www.romance.net

PMAW2

International bestselling author

JOAN JOHNSTON

continues her wildly popular Hawk's Way miniseries with an all-new, longer-length novel

THE SUBSTITUTE GROOM

HAWK'S WAY

August 1998

Jennifer Wright's hopes and dreams had rested on her summer wedding—until a single moment changed everything. Including the *groom*. Suddenly Jennifer agreed to marry her fiancé's best friend, a darkly handsome Texan she needed—and desperately wanted—almost against her will. But U.S. Air Force Major Colt Whitelaw had sacrificed too much to settle for a marriage of convenience, and that made hiding her passion all the more difficult. And hiding her biggest secret downright impossible...

"Joan Johnston does contemporary Westerns to perfection." —*Publishers Weekly*

Available in August 1998
wherever Silhouette books are sold.

Silhouette®

Silhouette®

SPECIAL EDITION®

COMING NEXT MONTH

#1195 EVERY COWGIRL'S DREAM—Arlene James
That Special Woman!
Feisty cowgirl Kara Detmeyer could handle just about anything—except
the hard-edged stockman escorting her through a dangerous cattle drive.
Rye Wagner had stubbornly insisted he'd never settle down again, but a
daring Kara had *every* intention of roping in the man of her dreams!

#1196 A HERO FOR SOPHIE JONES—Christine Rimmer
The Jones Gang
Vowing to reclaim his father's lost land, ruthless Sinclair Riker embarked
on the heartless seduction of beguiling Sophie B. Jones. But Sophie's
sweet, intoxicating kisses had cast a magical spell over him—and he
ached to do right by her. Could love transform Sin into Sophie's saint?

#1197 THE MAIL-ORDER MIX-UP—Pamela Toth
Winchester Brides
Travis Winchester fought an irresistible attraction to his missing brother's
mail-order bride. Even though he didn't trust Rory Mancini one bit, he
married the jilted city gal after taking her under his wing—and into his
bed. But he couldn't stop wonderin' if Rory truly loved her *unintended*
groom....

#1198 THE COWBOY TAKES A WIFE—Lois Faye Dyer
Sassy CeCe Hawkins was forever bound to her late husband's half
brother, Zach Colby. Not only was her unborn baby heir to the Montana
ranch Zach desperately coveted—and half-owned—but a forbidden
passion for this lonesome, tight-lipped cowboy left her longing for a
lifetime of lovin' in his arms.

#1199 STRANDED ON THE RANCH—Pat Warren
When sheltered Kari Sinclair fled her overprotective father, she found
herself snowbound with oh-so-sexy rancher Dillon Tracy. Playing house
together would be a cinch, right? Wrong! For Kari's fantasies of happily-
ever-after could go up in flames if Dillon learned her true identity!

#1200 OLDER, WISER...PREGNANT—Marilyn Pappano
Once upon a time, tempting teenager Laurel Cameron had brought
Beau Walker to his knees. Then, she'd lit out of town and left Beau one
angry—and bitter—man. Now she was back—pregnant, alone, yearning
for a second chance together. Could Beau forgive the past...and learn to
love another man's child?